WALLS

To Joe –

I hope you enjoy reading this as much as we enjoyed writing it — Thanks for your support

D. C. Winton

All the best - - -
Nancy Rabuck Wilson

WALLS

D. C. Wilson and Nancy Rabuck Wilson

Writers Club Press
San Jose New York Lincoln Shanghai

WALLS

Writers Club Press
an imprint of iUniverse.com, Inc.

For information address:
iUniverse.com, Inc.
5220 S 16th, Ste. 200
Lincoln, NE 68512
www.iuniverse.com

ISBN: 0-595-20210-1

Printed in the United States of America

This book is dedicated to the men and women of the Houston Police Department and especially to those officers on the Hostage Negotiation Team.

Acknowledgements

The authors wish to thank Lieutenant Robert Cain, head of the Hostage Negotiation Team of the Houston Police Department, without whose help the writing of this work would not have been possible. The authors also wish to thank Ms. Cathi Gillette for her kind assistance in proofreading this work.

PROLOGUE

June 14th
FBI Office, Houston, Texas

The two men, Assistant FBI Director James Vernon and his aide, Special Agent Philip Kimble, sat impassively in the straight-backed office chairs. A video camera had been set on a tripod between them; the windowless room was virtually devoid of other furnishings. Both men wore the typical federal agent uniform—ill-fitting, gray, business suits with thin, black ties. Their hair was cropped close to their heads, in military style.

Kimble, a stocky man with a pudgy face and slightly protruding eyes, seemed the antithesis of his superior, who towered over him. Vernon's lean, swarthy look silently commanded respect. The blinking red light on the camera indicated that it was in the process of recording. Opposite the two men, a slightly-built, dark-haired inmate, dressed in an orange smock with the words "Harris County Jail" stenciled across the back, and in his mid-thirties, tried to come to an agreement with the government officials.

"I ain't gonna be spendin' the next fifty years in jail. I can't and you guys can fix it."

Shaking his head, Vernon spoke authoritatively, "Vizziani, I don't know what the hell we're even doing here talking to you. You murdered a city councilman, you're guilty as hell, and unless you give up who ordered it, we have nothing left to talk about."

"It was only business. You understand *that*. Besides, the guy was takin' bribes. He screwed us. That's all I'm sayin'."

Vernon's voice was now tinged with irritation. "Who gave the orders?"

"I'm not sayin'. I can't."

"In that case, this conversation is over."

As Vernon rose to leave, he bellowed toward the door, "Guard!" And almost as quickly, the prisoner scrambled to his feet. "Wait, I can give you somethin' else."

"We're done here, Vizziani. You're going back to prison; we're going back to Washington."

"No. Listen. I know about a plan to whack a guy. And it's high profile—a national figure."

The agents looked at one another and then at the murderer. Their interest was visible. Vernon commanded tersely, "Tell me."

"There's this guy, a senator, see. He's gonna get killed, and real soon. So do we have a deal?"

"Give me more."

Sal Vizziani spilled his guts. He outlined the plot in great detail, providing dates, times, and even the way the assassination would be carried out.

"How do you know this?"

"I ain't tellin'. I can't tell you."

At that point, Vernon snorted. He looked at Kimble, then back at the prisoner, and shook his head. His raised voice revealed his irritation. "You know, asshole, you're full of shit. What do you think we are, a couple of idiots? At least if you're gonna blow smoke out your ass, have the smarts to come up with something believable."

"I swear it's all true."

"No! What *is* true is that this conversation is over."

Vernon again rose to signal the guard to escort Vizziani back to his cell. The mobster leaned forward and hissed in Kimble's face, "You fuckers are on the Family's payroll. You get me outta here!" Then he kicked his chair back and angrily skulked out of the interrogation room.

*   *   *   *   *   *   *   *   *

On the morning of July 5th, the front page of The Washington Chronicle featured a bold-type headline with the following story:

SEN. KEITH, WIFE KILLED IN EXPLOSION

Fort Worth, Texas. UPI. Presidential aspirant, Senator Terence Keith, and his wife were killed Friday when the pleasure boat on which they were sailing exploded into a ball of flames on Lake Grapevine, a few miles north of the Dallas-Fort Worth metroplex. The bodies of Senator Keith and his wife were recovered and released to the Tarrant County Coroner's Office. When the accident occurred, the Keiths were on their annual Fourth of July vacation.

Associates for the Senator expressed shock and dismay. Senator Keith was the Chairman of the powerful Senate Rules Committee, the head of the Subcommittee on Organized Crime, and a staunch opponent of legislation designed to repeal controls on handguns and assault weapons. The couple had planned a campaign swing through the

Midwest, hoping to further shore up support for Keith's bid for next year's Democratic presidential nomination. At the time of his death, Senator Keith was considered to be the party's frontrunner in the upcoming primaries.

In a news conference yesterday, James Vernon, Assistant Director of the Federal Bureau of Investigation, announced that he would personally handle the investigation of the case. Early this morning, Mr. Vernon stated that there were indications that the explosion was due to a faulty gasoline valve on the craft's engine and denied suspicions of possible foul play in the Senator's death. *(See related stories on 2A, 3A, and 6A).*

*   *   *   *   *   *   *   *   *   *

The following afternoon, Special Agent Philip Kimble was summoned to a meeting. The fine accouterments of the office he entered were impressive—neat bookshelves lining one wall, a personally autographed picture of the President just to the right of the American flag, and a large, cherry desk in the center of the room. The man seated behind that desk, James Vernon, looked up and motioned for the agent to sit. The Assistant Director leaned forward gravely. "We have a very serious problem."

"Yes, Sir."

"Who knows about that conversation we had in Texas in June?"

"The boys at the field office know we questioned the suspect but they were never privy to anything that was said."

"Is there anyone other than you, me, and Vizziani who might even remotely be aware of the content of that conversation?"

"Nobody."

"You're sure."

"Absolutely."

Vernon looked down, slowly shook his head, then quietly stated, "If certain information from that meeting ever were to be made public, it would be very damaging. I think to save the Bureau from the possibility of embarrassment. We should act in the best interests of all and ensure that there will never be any leaks. Do you understand what I'm saying?"

"I, I believe so."

"Well, let me be perfectly clear. You are to take whatever measures are necessary to make sure that information of a sensitive nature with respect to this case will *never* surface."

"I understand. We could have someone handle the problem from inside. Just dust the fucker."

Vernon's fist hit his desk and his reply was swift and emphatic. "No! There are too many of Garubba's thugs in that prison. He'll find out and we'll have even bigger headaches than we do now."

"Look, sir, we can get someone just to off him. It's not that big a problem."

The Director's voice came in a sneer. "You heard me, Kimble. Word will get out and all those perks we got from dealing with Garubba will be down the drain…along with our careers. It must, and I repeat, must, look like we had nothing to do with it. Make it look like it was his own fault, that he did it to himself."

Kimble pondered this for a second and offered, "Let me make some contacts and see what I can do."

"Good, but do it in a hurry. We'll speak, say, in two days. By then, I want a plan on my desk."

✳   ✳   ✳   ✳   ✳   ✳   ✳   ✳   ✳   ✳

At the appointed time, Philip Kimble sat down in a chair facing his boss, satisfied that he had developed a plan that would solve their dilemma.

"I spoke with Garubba's man in Houston. Told him that their boy was getting ready to speak with some of our agents down there and that he could finger all of them."

"And?"

"They're going to come up with a plan to spring Vizziani. Get 'im out of there."

"Do we know exactly when and how this is going to happen?"

"It'll be soon. As to how, I'll find that out in a day or so."

"Then keep me apprised. We can't let this one slip by us."

Without waiting for a response, Vernon waved his hand dismissively.

✳   ✳   ✳   ✳   ✳   ✳   ✳   ✳   ✳   ✳

The penthouse, Transco Tower, Houston, Texas

Don Garubba was a tall, imposing man. His weathered and tanned face was the physical manifestation of a life that had toughened him. His steely eyes shot across his expansive mahogany desk and settled on the man whose demeanor showed obvious deference. His gaze weighed heavily on his subordinate, and after long moments, he spoke, "Louis, we want Sal out as quickly as possible. Tell me what you've come up with."

"Yessir. I contacted a guard who owes us a favor. We got him outta some gambling debts last year and he's agreed to set it up from the inside."

Impatiently, the older gentleman demanded, "And?"

"He's got a few inmates he can persuade to work for us. The plan is that they hold a coupla guards hostage in the laundry or wherever. Sal goes in and switches clothes with one of 'em. They hold out for a while then walk out and give up. Sal pretends to be a guard and just walks away. It's real simple. And there's no connection with us whatsoever."

An unmistakable sneer crossed the patriarch's face. "Why not get him a guard's uniform and let him just walk out now?" Garubba removed a Cuban cigar from his desktop humidor and rolled it appreciatively between manicured fingers.

"He'll never make it. They check the IDs too close."

"And you think they won't check 'em after some sort of hostage deal?"

"Not this time, they'll be too busy. Too much'll be goin' on."

"Like what?"

"Diversions. I have no doubt they won't even know what's happening."

"You're sure?"

"Absolutely."

After a slight pause, Garubba asked, "What's in it for these prisoners?"

"They'll be promised two-hundred-fifty grand each, to be deposited into special accounts."

"That's pretty expensive." The Don bit off the end of his cigar and lit it.

Louis shrugged. "It's only a promise."

Garubba's voice took on a sardonic tone. "So you think the whole thing'll work?"

"Yep. We even have some help from the outside."

"Who?"

"Mr. Kimble and Mr. Vernon."

A wry smile crept across Garubba's face. "It'll work."

*   *   *   *   *   *   *   *   *   *

Washington, D.C.

After having been briefed on the specifics of Garubba's plan, James Vernon looked up at Kimble and stated matter-of-factly, "So, we know how they're going to do it."

"Yes."

"And?"

"We can feed them information. Make sure they pull it off."

The incredulity in Vernon's voice was not disguised. "And Vizziani walks on out, heads right for the newspapers, and we're dead?"

Kimble stared into his boss's eyes, and without blinking, replied, "Not exactly. We augment their plan just a bit."

A look of understanding passed between the two men.

"It can be done with no connection to this office?"

"None."

"Make sure of it."

                    ✳   ✳   ✳   ✳   ✳   ✳   ✳   ✳   ✳   ✳

That evening, Philip Kimble packed his briefcase and drove to his house in the wooded hills of Virginia, west of D.C. In the basement of the split-level home, he removed a footlocker from a locked closet, opened it, and carefully inspected the contents. He then sealed the trunk and put it into the back of his Chevy van, for delivery to the Greyhound Bus Terminal in Alexandria and eventual transport to Texas.

CHAPTER 1

Monday, August 20th
Hermann Hospital, Houston, Texas

It was 3:15 p.m. and all that Thom could hear was a faint but persistent squeak that was coming from somewhere near his left foot. He had the strange thought that it was a supermarket cart with one bad wheel. Thom wasn't cruising any of the aisles at the local Kroger, though. Barely conscious, he noticed the eerily pulsating lights; in a split second, the lights brightened, then diminished, then brightened, diminished, brightened.... *God, I'm cold.*

He heard a man's urgent voice that seemed to come from far away, "Get this guy in, stat. We're *not* going to lose him."

A woman's muffled voice responded, "He's lost a lot of blood."

"Did you order the new I.V.? Everything set?"

"Yes, Doctor."

"Let's go."

* * * * * * * * * *

Thom Christopher didn't know where he was, but he did know he was lying on his back, unable to move. His jaw ached, a burning sensation traveled up his arm, and he was aware of a slight tugging on the top of his right hand. Drugs, dripping from a suspended bag, dulled the pain from what, an hour earlier, had been a gaping hole in his side. He willed himself to lift his arm…. Nothing.

As he lay there, he tried to remember what had happened, to sort it all out. His temples pounded. *What's happened?* Thom attempted to organize his thoughts. The day had started as usual; he had gone to work and then, in the late afternoon, had headed for his second job. The events replayed themselves in slow motion through hazed consciousness. Still, the pressure on his hand continued, just as if someone were trying to pull him out of an endless abyss. Another dazzling white light obliterated all mental images….

"Doctor! We're losing him…."

CHAPTER 2

Thursday, August 16th

It was 4:55 p.m., and the speedometer told him he was already doing between 80 and 85 but, *what the hell,* Thom thought, *this is Texas.* He had left his office at Texas State University-Conroe with barely enough time to make it to the Wynne Unit in Huntsville, one of Texas' seedier prisons, where he was occasionally scheduled to teach. He now had to race just to make sure he wasn't late.

Driving up I-45, he could feel the mid-August sun, still searingly hot, as it burned the back of his neck. He pointlessly wondered how he could be too lazy to put the Miata's top up and switch on the air conditioning. The weather, 98 degrees with 95% humidity, and the fact that he knew what awaited him, irritated him to no end. Even so, he didn't have much choice but to go.

Five years ago, when he had accepted a job with the Texas State University System, he knew he'd have to supplement his income somehow and teaching an extra course for the prison system was obviously the easiest way to achieve this. The problem was, each new semester at one of the prison units translated into all new, unfamiliar students, and Thom was never quite sure what to expect. The fresh crop of inmates might not react favorably to his jocular teaching style.

Although being the only "civilian" in a classroom filled with convicts bothered him more than a little, Thom knew that tonight would be just another mundane, predictable evening, just the same old routine he had lived through countless times before. It always worked out.

*   *   *   *   *   *   *   *   *   *

At thirty-six years old, Thom prided himself on the fact that he still weighed 156 pounds and had managed, by running six miles four or five days each week, to avoid two of the curses of middle age, a beer gut and those dreaded love handles. When his close-cropped brown hair started to turn "salt and pepper," his wife had told him it just made him look more sophisticated. He liked that. Years before, he had promised his now-departed mother that when his beard turned white, he would shave it off; it would only make him look old. He had kept that promise the spring before, but decided that he would keep his graying mustache forever.

Thom Christopher was a psychobiologist who taught courses in experimental psychology, physiological psychology, and statistics. Students usually entered these classes with a good deal of anxiety, but after a few weeks, seemed to enjoy the classes, in spite of the cut-and-dried information.

In the prison, his students were of two types: those who would do very well and those who would not bother to exert themselves. Inmates of the first type were fairly good students, often outscoring the students in his on-campus classes. They came to class all gung-ho, well-prepared and ready to do battle with the material. He guessed they had figured out that doing well in college courses might help with the parole board.

The latter type, the ones Thom hated having in class, sat in the back of the room either slumped over their desks or with their feet stretched out a yard in front of them. They had a particular look about them that generally affected boredom. This was often combined with undisguised, smirking contempt. These convicts arrived in class ready to wage a different kind of battle. Regardless, in four and one-half years of teaching at the units, he had never been confronted by any serious problem that involved inmates.

*   *   *   *   *   *   *   *   *

As Thom Christopher began his trek up Interstate 45, Philip Kimble sat unnoticed in the employee parking lot of the Texas Department of Criminal Justice's Wynne Unit. The window of his rented Ford Taurus was rolled down, and he was drawing on a legal pad. On this, his fourth visit to the unit in as many days, he continued to make detailed diagrams of the yard, the main cell areas, and the outbuildings. He was certain that he would succeed in his mission. It was imperative.

CHAPTER 3

The Wynne Prison Unit

At 4:58 p.m., prior to the first class of the new semester, Inmate 602131, Arnie Cox, sat alone, leafing through a dog-eared textbook in a corner of the dining room, while eating his dinner of chicken-fried steak, cold mashed potatoes, and pinto beans. A corpulent black convict walked up to the table and stuck his finger into Arnie's chest. "Hey, asshole, I hear you called me a nigger."

Arnie made no attempt to hide his annoyance. "I don't know what yer talkin' bout. Who told you dat shit, anyway?"

"A buddy of mine tol' me, an' you ain't fuckin' gettin' away with it." He leaned threateningly into Arnie's suddenly ashen face.

He was not going to be intimidated. "Look, man. I never said nothin' 'bout you. Just leave me the fuck alone."

In an even more menacing tone, the other man added, before he turned and lumbered out of the dining area, "Yeah? Well you just watch your back, asshole."

* * * * * * * * * *

In another part of the prison, Raoul Sanchez made his way toward the community toilet. Without warning, a lone thug grabbed Sanchez by the back of the neck, hustled him into a stall, and viciously kneed him in the groin. Sanchez doubled over in pain while his assailant repeatedly rammed his face into the filthy toilet. He didn't know why this was happening; he couldn't remember ever seeing this guy before, but as he heard the crunching of the cartilage in his nose and the shattering of several teeth, Sanchez knew that he would be lucky to survive.

*   *   *   *   *   *   *   *   *   *

Outside the Wynne Unit's main building, Inmate 409232, Mark Sumner, whiled away some time with a game of pick-up basketball. He went in for a clean lay-up. He winced when the inmate guarding him checked him with a forceful body slam. The next time Mark had the ball, the same inmate checked him again, and this time, Sumner swore his jaw was dislocated. He fired the ball at the other convict who, in turn, grabbed Mark's throat in his enormous hand, punched his face, and pushed his head into the concrete wall at the end of the court. Inmate 409232 lost consciousness as the other players calmly and coolly walked away.

*   *   *   *   *   *   *   *   *   *

Passing through a crowd of inmates who were standing in front of the doors of the Education Section, Arnie Cox walked into the foyer that led to the stairs he eventually would descend to go to his classroom. The greasy chicken-fried steak had given him indigestion, and he belched. Two inmates, involved in a rather physical discussion, jostled into Cox, pushing him up against a railing. He pushed back to free himself from the melee, and realized too late that one was the black man who, not an hour before, had harangued him in the cafeteria. In a second, Cox became the target of the others' aggression. Punched, kicked,

and then tossed like a limp rag down the flight of stairs, he lay unconscious on the floor, in a bloodied heap.

✻   ✻   ✻   ✻   ✻   ✻   ✻   ✻   ✻   ✻

The convicts who had carried out the attacks on Sanchez, Sumner,
and Cox quietly and calmly returned to their respective cells, and made
sure that the cartons of contraband cigarettes they had received for
their actions were still carefully hidden.

✻   ✻   ✻   ✻   ✻   ✻   ✻   ✻   ✻   ✻

At exactly 5:00 p.m., a cellular phone rang in a blue Taurus in the
parking lot of the prison.
"Kimble here."
"Tell me what's happening."
"Everything's going according to plan."
"Good. Has the envelope been delivered?"
"This morning."
"Anything else that needs to be done?"
"No, Sir."
"No problems then?"
"Everything is under control."
"It better be. Call me on my direct line when you've successfully dealt
with the problem."
"I will, Sir."
And with that, the receiver went dead in Philip Kimble's hand.

✻   ✻   ✻   ✻   ✻   ✻   ✻   ✻   ✻   ✻

At 5:28 p.m., a guard in Cell Block C reported three inmates missing.
A cursory search of the immediate area resulted in their being located,
and given their physical conditions, Sanchez, Sumner, and Cox were
immediately transferred to the unit's infirmary. As individual reports

on the inmates were written up and sent through the chain of command, the appropriate authorities responded and a memo was sent down to Education with the message that three students would be absent from Thom Christopher's evening class.

CHAPTER 4

The Wynne Unit

Roy Palmer arrived at his desk in the Education Section a few minutes later than he normally would have. He dropped into his swivel chair, and automatically checked his "in" box for messages. Seeing nothing unusual, he pulled out the evening's rosters and two reams of paper from beneath the desk. Then, he took a cellular phone from his briefcase and shoved it into a desk drawer. He punched in a number on the desktop phone and asked his sergeant to let the convicts come down.

Everybody knew the routine: show your identification card, get the classroom number—tonight it was Room 9—down the nearest hallway, and then proceed to the class.

The inmates filed in, all doing what was expected, and dutifully went to sit and wait. Three convicts at the end of the line approached Officer Palmer, and without producing identification cards, were immediately waved through. Roy Palmer, not even glancing up, checked off the names: Cox, Sanchez, and Sumner.

A few minutes later, one remaining inmate walked up to the guard's desk and was told to go to Room 6 in the far corridor.

＊　＊　＊　＊　＊　＊　＊　＊　＊　＊

Interstate 45

At 5:47 p.m., the 60-foot-high statue of Sam Houston came into view as Thom neared Huntsville. Now the mile markers began to whiz by…110, 111, 112. The Goree Unit came into view on his right. On the left was the entrance to Elkins Lake Estates. *Thank God, only three more exits.* When he saw the Holliday Unit, Thom knew he had beaten the clock. Just off Exit 118, around the DPS office, and up Hwy 75N for less than a mile, Thom made it with all of three minutes to spare.

His last thought as he turned off the highway was that he hoped his wife, Ellen, had gotten the message that he would be home late tonight.

CHAPTER 5

The Woodlands, Texas

Ellen Christopher, thirty-four years old, looked youthful for her age. She had managed to keep her weight at a slender one-hundred-ten pounds since her college days. A straight aquiline nose, prominent cheekbones, and highlighted ash-blonde hair added to her good looks. She was a woman who would make men stop and stare.

It was just shy of six o'clock when Ellen gratefully pulled into her own driveway. The first week back to school after summer vacation was always a killer and she longed for the good old days when the academic year didn't intrude upon leisure until after Labor Day. *What moron came up with the idea to send us back to the classroom in August, anyway?*

The first thing Ellen did when she got into her air-conditioned house was to kick off her pumps. They were murder after schlepping around for a couple of months in sandals.

Her throat was sore from talking all day and a dull ache surrounded her forehead. She went directly to the cooler, filled a glass with ice water, and then went to the bedroom, where she found the ibuprofen. Tossing two caplets into her throat, she noticed the message in soap on the bathroom mirror—I adore you and miss you! Ellen smiled.

After changing into shorts and a tee shirt, Ellen poured herself a tall glass of iced tea and went out onto the patio. The gardens did not look good. It had not rained in several weeks and most of the flowers had a droopy, woebegone appearance. She hated walking around with the hose at the end of a long day, but she hated dead flowers even more, so she turned on the faucet and absentmindedly began the task of giving the impatiens and geraniums a much-needed drink.

At least she wouldn't have to make dinner; it was Thom's night to teach his overload, so he'd be in Huntsville until at least ten o'clock. She and Amy would probably have salad bar and cheese sticks at the Pizza Hut, unless her daughter was more in the mood for Mexican food. Then, Ellen could watch a little TV and do some toning exercises before hitting the sack. She could already imagine how soothing the cool cotton pillow would feel and she hoped Thom would come straight home from the prison and not stop off to have a drink with Richard after class. Ellen was tired and she wanted to be able to get to sleep at a decent hour. No matter how exhausted she might be, she knew she wouldn't be able to fall asleep until he was there, lying next to her on his side of the bed.

Coming back into the house through the sliding doors, she noticed the blinking light on the answering machine and pushed the message button. "Hon, I won't be home until late. After class I'm gonna meet Richard for a couple drinks." *Damn. Well, at least he called.*

CHAPTER 6

As he crossed the entrance to the Wynne Unit, Thom passed brick gates on both sides and a succession of signs. Raised silver metal letters, four inches high, provided the first announcement:

WYNNE UNIT
TEXAS DEPARTMENT OF
CORRECTIONS

And then a much smaller white metal sign with large black lettering:

THINK SAFETY!

After that came the myriad of even smaller signs warning that any intruders that they, and their vehicles, were now subject to search, that it was considered a felony to bring controlled substances into the prison, and that all firearms were to be checked at the front picket. The only warning that Thom had ever really taken notice of and thought about, though, was the one on the gate, just at the entrance to the inner yard. It stated rather unequivocally:

NO HOSTAGES EXIT THESE GATES

*   *   *   *   *   *   *   *   *   *

Making a left into the parking lot, Thom cut the corner a little too closely and almost sideswiped the blue Taurus that was sitting in a corner slot. A momentary wave of panic hit him, but the other driver seemed completely oblivious, did not even look up. After parking the car, Thom carefully avoided the Taurus and walked up to the guard tower, or picket. He looked up and called out his name. The girl in the tower shouted back that she needed to see some ID., then lowered down her white plastic bucket that was attached to a thick, white rope. Thom dropped his faculty card into the bucket and watched as it started its ascent to the top of the guard tower. Five seconds later, the guard yelled down that she had to call into the Unit to make sure he was supposed to be there. Although it was 6:00 p.m. and he really didn't want to go in, Thom didn't appreciate this extended wait in the still-hot, East Texas sun.

Minutes passed before she yelled down, "OK, you're all right." The bucket descended and Thom retrieved his ID.

"Thanks a lot," he muttered.

It was now 6:06 p.m. He approached the first gate, a typical cyclone fence topped off with coils of razor wire, and he waited. No problem with being late now, the guard in the picket had caused the delay, and besides, he had arrived on prison property prior to six o'clock. Thirty seconds went by, then Thom heard a loud click and the hum of electricity. He pushed the metal handle, entered a six-foot by four-foot fenced-in area, and waited for the second cyclone gate to click.

As he stood in the tiny "holding area," he looked to the left and then to the right. Stretching ahead of him was the long, grassy corridor that was formed by two twelve-foot tall cyclone-fenced walls. *No, not much chance of anybody escaping this way.* Surprisingly, a good portion of the prison was surrounded only by a small wire fence—no razor wire, no electricity—just a single strand of metal wire. This cordoned-off the area where "trustees" exercised and this was what the public could see from FM 2821, which bordered the prison. Occasionally, an inmate would just walk away or get picked up by a waiting car, but this was very rare. An escape attempt could cost a convict an additional fifteen years, with several weeks in the "hole." The ones who *were* dumb enough to try it usually hadn't attained trustee status, and if they had, they would typically be retrieved within a few hours by law officers at a girl friend's house or at their mother's, not knowing where else to go once in the "free" world.

Thom had heard about a convict who had taken off just because he wanted to have sex with his girlfriend. He was picked up the next morning and didn't see the yard for another three years. A hefty price to pay for a single night of copulatory bliss!

✳ ✳ ✳ ✳ ✳ ✳ ✳ ✳ ✳ ✳

Ten more seconds elapsed while Thom waited for that ominous click and then the hum of electricity. Now he stood within the yard leading to the main building. As he walked toward the front door, he noted that the bushes were still impeccably trimmed, all in neat round balls, each coming to a height of exactly eighteen inches. He noticed that, again, the flowers were in full bloom—they were always in bloom because the convicts were constantly planting different flowers, appropriate to each season in East Texas. The grass was also immaculately groomed. *Hmmm, cheap labor.*

Thom walked up the short ramp and entered the building. At once, the strong prison stench nearly bowled him over. *Yep, I'm here.* Through the foyer, he made a right, then a quick left down the hall to a set of paint-chipped, barred doors. Six feet beyond was a guard in a small cage. Thom showed his ID. once again, heard another click and yet another hum of electricity. He entered and automatically opened his briefcase, so the guard in the cage could inspect the contents. She scanned the stack of now-disheveled lecture notes.

"Where are you going?"

"Education."

She motioned to the briefcase. "Is that all you have with you?"

"Yep."

Thom had long ago decided that if he were ever subjected to a body search, he would quit just before it happened and never come back. Fortunately, it had never happened.

"OK, go ahead."

As all this was going on, he shook his head in resignation because of the hoops he was forced to jump through just to make an extra buck. With great annoyance, he pushed through one more set of barred doors and entered the "bull pen," a circular room about forty feet in diameter, with several hallways radiating from it. One hallway went to the inmates' barbershop, one to the mailroom, one to a visitor's room, and the others apparently to storage areas. Looking up, he could see four circular tiers, each stacked above the other, and each with several white-clad convicts just leaning against the railing looking down over the edge.

Something seemed to be not quite right. *Are they looking at me? No, that's stupid. I must be getting paranoid.* It was just the aggravation, the stifling heat, and his overactive imagination. *Let's just get this over with!*

*   *   *   *   *   *   *   *   *   *

Thom took a hallway at the opposite side of the bullpen and walked to the end. The only turn he could make was to the left, which was when he was faced with the part of the evening he hated most, walking the gauntlet to the Education Section.

The gauntlet is a long straight hallway, an incredibly long hallway. Even though it is straight, with separations made only by barred doors, it is impossible to see to the end. It is just too far and there are too many barred doors. When walking the gauntlet, Thom felt as if he were descending through the seven levels of Hell. This was one of the few places in the unit where Thom often feared for his safety. There are seventy-five feet between each series of doors, and thus, seventy-five feet of space between stationed guards. Between the guarded doors, a visitor finds himself literally surrounded by nameless convicts, although there is a physical separation of sorts. On either side of the hallway, there is a yellow, painted line. These lines, which are precisely thirty inches from each wall, leave just enough room for convicts to walk in single file. With very few exceptions, when moving in the hallway, inmates stay to their left, and between the yellow line and the wall. This frees up about six feet in the middle of the hallway, and for this, Thom was truly grateful.

As he looked straight ahead, a sea of white enveloped his peripheral vision. A hoard of convicts milled about, some turned their heads, speaking to others directly behind them. Most were merely going through their never-changing circadian ritual, without expression, staring blankly at the floor twenty feet ahead.

The smooth, brick walls were painted a soft shade of sky blue and off-white. The actual walls were only four feet high, above which were one-inch thick, vertical iron bars coursing their way to the ceiling. The bars, too, were painted sky blue, but the paint here was chipped, revealing the underlying black iron.

Glancing through these bars, Thom could see just how expansive the Unit was. The cells and dining areas, the television rooms, and shower rooms seemed to go on forever. And every square foot was crammed with that sea of white-clad humanity.

Thom realized that as he made his way deeper into these bowels of Hell, the ever-present prison aroma remained constant. Initially, he had thought that the further he got in, the stronger the stench should be. But this was not the case. It now seemed to him that as soon as you entered one of the units, the odor was intense enough to make you gag and that the intensity never changed, neither increasing nor decreasing. Perhaps this was because there wasn't a single source of the odor; in this unit there were fifteen hundred sources.

*   *   *   *   *   *   *   *   *   *

Half-way into his trek, an unfamiliar voice called out, "Yo, Doc. How ya doin'?"

"Fine, How you doin'?"

"Jus' the same."

The voice was attached to the typical white prison attire that Thom recognized all too well, but the face remained unknown. Of course, he hadn't been in this particular unit for two years, and with classes averaging forty students, he couldn't remember every face. Actually, he couldn't remember any of their faces, a fact he chalked up to his ability to pretty much repress all of his prison experiences.

To have the appearance of making amends for not remembering the student's face or name, Thom ever so briefly continued the conversation.

"Well, you taking my course this semester?"

"C'mon, Doc, I took that last time. Got a B, too."

Shit. "Oh, yeah, that's right. Well, see you later."

"Hey, remember, just keep cool in there, man."

"You got it."

*   *   *   *   *   *   *   *   *   *

Thom made it through the first set of doors and saw two guards
stopping a convict who was coming out of the cafeteria. He wondered if
there was any rhyme or reason for searching one inmate and not
another. Did the guards have some sort of mathematical system they
were working under, one in every five convicts, every third for nine and
then every fourth for twelve, or were they trained to spot discrete
behavioral traits, much the same as the customs agents at the airport,
who had been trained to notice characteristics of drug smugglers?
Maybe the guy who kept on getting hassled had just been in trouble
before and the guards knew whom to search. Thom couldn't tell and
right now couldn't care less. It was just one of those things—a normal
occurrence in a prison environment.

Another unknown voice greeted him. "Take it easy, Doc."

Must be somebody from a previous class. Who? It occurred to him that
that really didn't matter either.

"Thanks, see ya later."

He continued and continued and continued down the corridor,
through open doors, each with two guards leaning up against the walls,
quietly talking to each other, or telling an inmate he could, or couldn't,
do something. Somebody made a demand and the inmate calmly
clasped the fingers of both hands behind his head; another demand and
the convict turned and quietly returned to his cell; still another and the
convict calmly reported to a third guard station to obey yet one more
demand. It was life in the prison and all seemed the same as it had for
the hundred times Thom had been there before. Looking to the left and
looking to the right, through the chipped bars forming the walls of the
Wynne Unit, nothing had changed—the huge expanse of cells, TV
rooms, and cafeterias, all teeming with white shirts and trousers.

Maybe this was the reason that it seemed to take forever to walk the
gauntlet. It wasn't that it was a prison, and it wasn't the smell, and it
wasn't the fear. It was the complete and constant sameness, that total
lack of variability from one place to the next, like driving across the

desert in the great Southwest as opposed to driving in the Northeast when you passed through a different state in what seemed to be every fifteen minutes.

What an existence, he thought.

Thom made a left into the Education Section, went through the double doors, and descended the staircase. He immediately found the guard, who gave him his room number for the evening, a stack of notebook paper, six sheets apiece for each student in the class, and two copies of his class roster. He then hotfooted it down the near hallway and went into his classroom.

Finally, he really had arrived.

CHAPTER 7

Thom picked up his roster along with a photostatic copy of the original and gave the list a quick once-over. *Thirty-four students. Not too bad.*

Taking roll was Thom's first required task. He believed this to be a complete and utter waste of time, figuring that if an inmate wasn't there then that person probably had a good excuse, such as being in the "hole" for fighting. Rarely on the campus of TSU-C would Thom take roll, but here, in the prison, this was a sacred—and required—duty. The rules were that he had to place a "3", designating a three-hour course, in a small box by each inmate's name if the inmate was in class, add them all up, and put the total at the bottom. He then had to sign the original in ink—only in ink—and place it in the front—only the front—of the special box just to the right of the guard's station. Simple enough, or so he thought.

A year ago, Thom had unwittingly filled out the copy, not the original, and placed it in the box. The next morning came a call from the prison's principal.

"The rules explicitly state that we have to have the original."

"Didn't I fill out the original?"

"No, we only have the copy."

"But that's identical to the original?"

"No, it's a copy."

Exasperated, Thom almost pleaded, "But it's identical to the original. It's a photostat."

The voice on the other end of the line continued with dedicated insistence, "Yes, it's a copy. I must have the original for my records."

"Listen, can't I bring up the original next week when I come up for my class, it's forty-five mile drive up there?"

"We have to have it immediately."

God, what a pain in the ass!

After much haggling, the two finally compromised and the principal agreed that Thom could send the original up with another faculty member who taught the next night. *Perhaps a hope of sanity here!*

Another time, Thom had forgotten to sign his name to the roster. He received a chastising call the next morning along with the command that he come up and sign the roster—no compromise here. As the principal explained, it was the end of the month, and all signed rosters had to be turned in. "Otherwise, we can't close out March."

Without a clue, Thom asked, "What does that mean?"

"We can't release any monies for employees until all the forms are in and correct."

"Can't I do it next week?"

"We need to close out March and people need to be paid. We can't do that until we get your signed roster."

The thought dawned on Thom that he could actually delay the paperwork for the entire prison—Could he really bring them to their knees?—and everybody's pay check, just by not showing up? Of course, the monies for faculty came from the university and TDCJ didn't release anything, let alone money, for university faculty. But, wouldn't it be cool if he really could destroy the entire economy of Huntsville, Texas with his one small omission? What power he would wield.

Nevertheless, he knew he would dutifully drive up the interstate, go in, sign the necessary crapwork, and drive home.

"Hey, why don't you just sign my name?"

"That would be a felony."

"I'll swear it's my signature."

"That would be a felony."

There was no possibility of escaping the inevitable. "OK, I'll be up this afternoon. Any possibility I can get my usual twenty-eight cents per mile for the trip?"

"Be here before four to sign the form, please."

The phone clicked in Thom's hand.

*   *   *   *   *   *   *   *   *   *

On this night, making sure he had the original roster, Thom immediately signed it, then started calling out names.

"Aguilar."

"Here."

"Bruhn."

"Present."

"All right, time to get something straight. As long as we're all in here together and none of us can leave, when I call out your name, you answer 'Yo.' Not 'Here.' Not 'Present.' Just 'Yo.' Understood? Now, Aguilar."

"Yo."

"Good, that's more like it."

"Bruhn."

"Here."

"What?"

"Yo," and muted snickering could be heard from around the room.

When all was said and done, Thom scanned the list for omissions and spotted four names without "3"s beside them. He called out the name of the first absentee.

"Cox."

A Hispanic inmate in the back of the room poked the white guy next to him. The "Yo" was almost immediate. Another student came through the door, another name checked off.

"Name?"

"Johnson."

"Johnson?"

"Here."

"No, 'Yo.'"

"Huh?"

Thom eyed a convict nearest Johnson and commanded, "Wheeler, explain the rules to this guy."

Satisfied with wasting enough time, he counted heads, thirty-four, and again called the absentees' names out. He received two immediate and positive responses.

"Sanchez."

"Yo."

"Sumner."

"Here," followed by a little snicker directed at Cox.

Asshole.

*   *   *   *   *   *   *   *   *   *

Outside the classroom, Roy Palmer dutifully went up the steps to his sergeant's desk and handed in his final count sheet.

"Listen, Sarge. As soon as the Doc let's class out, I'm hittin' the road. Got a date with a fishin' hole."

"I got no problem with that. Just remember to sign out."

"Thanks, Sarge."

    *   *   *   *   *   *   *   *   *   *

At the precise moment Thom had called out the last two names on the roster, in a secluded corner of the Sam Houston National Forest surrounding Huntsville, Philip Kimble opened the footlocker he had retrieved earlier from the Greyhound Bus Station and picked up the contents with his left hand. He then took a honeydew melon he had purchased at the Kroger on 11th Street, and carefully anchored it six feet from the ground into a crook formed by two limbs of a pine tree. Studying the sketch on the legal pad in his right hand, he retreated seventy-six steps, looked at the weapon in his left hand, raised it with the 'scope meeting his right eye, and put the cross-hairs on his target. CRACK! a miss, high and to the right. Kimble calmly lowered the rifle and adjusted the 'scope, aimed again, and let off another shot; a miss, just low and to the left. Adjusting the 'scope one more time, he aimed, lovingly massaged the trigger back, and watched as the melon exploded into a million pieces.

    *   *   *   *   *   *   *   *   *   *

At 8:22 p.m., the last foghorn sounded and count had cleared. Thom figured he'd stop in the lounge, take a whiz, then set sail down the gauntlet and meet Richard for that long-awaited beer. Thank God he had made it through another one. The inmates apparently were excited, too. For the most part, they were out, down the hall and through the double doors into the gauntlet, heading for their own nine-by-twelve homes.

Charles Wilson, a six-foot-five-inch African-American with close-cropped hair and a large scar down the length of his right cheek, followed Thom out of class. He had been in a couple of Thom's other classes and the guy was a good worker. Always polite and respectful,

Charles seemed to be a nice guy and Thom had always wondered what he was in for.

"Hey, Doc. How's about I walk with ya up the stairs?"

"Um, yeah, but wait just a second, I've got to go to the bathroom, it's a long trip home, ya know."

"That can wait," Charles insisted. "I gotta talk ta ya 'bout sompin' important."

"Look, I really gotta go. If it can wait until next week, I'll spend some time before class or during one of the breaks with you."

"It can't wait, it's important."

Thom cut the young man off. "Look, it'll have to wait until next week."

The inmate merely looked down and mumbled, "Yeah, sure."

Charles sauntered away and Thom, feeling a little guilty, pushed his way toward the faculty lounge. *Just what I need, someone to hold me up, right when I was making my escape.*

As he exited Education, the inmate turned to the guard and whispered, "Hey, get the Doc outta here in a hurry. OK?"

The response came with no emotion whatsoever. "Sure, no problem."

And as the last convict climbed the steps leading to the gauntlet, Roy Palmer picked up the phone. "Education is out. Nobody's left so I'm locking it up. See you on Monday."

"Good. And, by the way, catch a big one for me."

"Will do." Silently, Palmer took his keys and secured the door in front of him, locking himself in the wing, then turned and walked down the far hallway, past the lounge and away from Thom. Stopping at Room 6, he turned the knob and carefully let himself in. Immediately, he came face to face with an apparent "comrade in arms" dressed in the identical gray guard's uniform Palmer himself wore. Taken aback for a second, he peered into the guard's eyes and then relaxed ever so slightly.

"Oh, it's you."

"Yeah. Everything set?"

"All the stuff's in place, just where you want it, and…."

The guard never completed his last sentence as he felt a sharp pain just below his sternum and then a twisting in the center of his chest. He gurgled as he slumped to his knees. The pain quickly subsided, the light-headedness disappeared, and all that remained for Officer Roy Palmer was blackness.

CHAPTER 8

Approaching the door of the lounge, Thom heard an unwelcome whine. "Hey, Doc."

Shit, who is it this time?

He turned and saw the student he recognized as Cox standing there. *Oh, great. Now my night is complete.* He looked the inmate in the eye and pleaded, "Look, I really have to go. Can't this wait?"

Cox persisted, "Sir, I want to apologize. Those guys put me up to givin' you a hard time."

"OK. Don't worry about it." *Just get me the fuck outta here.*

"If you have a coupla minutes, I have just a few questions."

GOD!!! "All right, all right, all right. But let's hurry up. I really have to go."

The inmate led Thom back to the classroom and proceeded to ask two or three truly inane questions about things that had been covered quite thoroughly only a half-hour earlier and when it was over, Thom's thoughts were only on getting in the car and heading to the *Hair of the Dog Saloon* in Spring to meet Richard and get that beer. *Finally!*

*　*　*　*　*　*　*　*　*　*

At 8:30 p.m., Ellen Christopher, halfway through her nightly exercise routine on the floor of the master bedroom, had an uneasy feeling. She held out the remote and switched the TV channel, but the feeling wouldn't go away. Finally, to put her mind at ease, she rose, walked down the hallway to Amy's room, and peeked in to see her child hunched over a biology textbook, doing her homework. *No problem here.* She shrugged her shoulders and returned to her own bedroom, still uneasy but not knowing why.

*   *   *   *   *   *   *   *   *   *

Thom got down to the end of the hallway and spied the vacant chair beside the guard's desk. Turning the corner to enter the stairwell, he looked up at the closed door and came face to face with two inmates. He couldn't remember their names but recognized them as Cox's two buddies.

The Hispanic began. "Hey, Doc, we need to talk to you."

"How about next week, guys? I was just about to leave."

"Don't think so, we talk now."

Shit. "C'mon guys, I gotta go, I'm gonna be late gettin' home."

With that, the Hispanic closed in on the professor, placed his arm around his shoulders, and put his sweaty face not two inches from Thom's. "Doc, we gonna talk, *NOW.*"

Nothing like this had ever happened before and Thom started to panic. Without thinking, he bolted, shoving the inmate to the side in a vain attempt to make it to the door. He never saw the butt of the gun before it connected with the side of his face, and when he awoke, his mind was in a fog. His tongue dragged along the jagged edges of several broken teeth and he felt a sharp pain in the side of his face as he rose to his knees. He looked around and immediately saw the figure of the guard sitting at the far end of the room, wrists tied in front of him and a large piece of adhesive tape covering his mouth and chin. He turned toward the inmates, all three together now, and with horror, saw the barrel of a gun pointed directly at his chest. The room began to whirl, he started to sweat, he had chills, and he thought he was going to pass out again. It was a horrible, inconceivable nightmare.

The Hispanic made a motion with the gun and ordered the professor to sit. Thom literally collapsed onto one of the sofas. Staring down at nothing in particular, his gaze was drawn absentmindedly from the bottom of the other sofa to the door of the men's room, from the base of the bookcase to the bottom of the door of the first small closet, and then to the base of the second closet. Perhaps it was delirium brought on by the throbbing in the side of his face or just outright fear, but he started to laugh. He couldn't help but lose control at the fact that some moron had apparently spilled a whole bottle of ink, and red ink to boot, in the second closet. It just seemed to ooze from the base of the door. Then, almost instantaneously, a new wave of nausea overtook him as he realized it wasn't ink.

* * * * * * * * * *

Long after the actual abduction, a phone call was placed to James Vernon's private line in Washington, D.C.

"Yes?"

"Sir, I think there's a problem."

Vernon quickly replied, "Why? What's happened?"

"From what I can gather, there might be a civilian involved."

His interest now high, the Assistant Director responded excitedly, "Who? How the hell did that happen?"

Philip Kimble replied in a matter-of-fact tone, "Some sort of foul-up. Some college or something started their prison classes. From what I can gather, the teacher may be down there. He should've been out by now, but he isn't, and I can't get an answer on the cell phone in the section. What do you want me to do?"

During a brief pause, Vernon grumbled to no one in particular, "Shit, I don't believe this." Then, he spoke into the receiver, "Listen, don't do anything, just stay out of the way. Besides, it doesn't change anything we have to do. Just keep me informed."

Before a response could be offered, the phone line went dead.

CHAPTER 9

In Cell Block A, the eleven o'clock count continued. Guard Lennie Jones counted the convicts, putting a small mark on a legal pad for each inmate. He finished the block, added up the marks, and sighed, "Damn, three shy."

A second count yielded the same result, still three short. Lennie called over his co-worker and drinking buddy, Adam Kessler. "I got a problem, I'm missin' three."

"Count it again."

"I did, a couple of times."

"Shit. OK, who are they?"

"Cox, Sanchez, and Sumner."

"Go call the sergeant and see if she knows anything."

Lennie went to a wall phone, punched in a number, and explained the situation.

"They're Cox, Sanchez, and Sumner."

"Hold on a minute."

After a moment of silence, she came back to the phone and admonished Lennie, "Didn't you check your 'in box'?"

"I was fixin' to."

"Well, check it before the count. All three of these guys are in the infirmary. Cox fell down the stairs going to the laundry, Sanchez was found unconscious in the bathroom with his face half beat in, and Sumner picked a fight with some guy and is recovering."

"We have anything to do with it?"

"Nope, he apparently just picked on the wrong guy."

Lennie breathed more easily. "Thank God for that."

                *   *   *   *   *   *   *   *   *   *

At 11:37 p.m., Charlie Williams was trying to clear the count in Cell Block C. Again, it didn't come out right, three missing.

In twelve years, Charlie had never been shy a convict and was sure that these three jerks were in the shower or had gone to the head or whatever. Two counts later, he called the sergeant.

"Don't you guys *ever* check the 'in box'?"

"Ma'am, I checked it when I came on shift. These guys aren't here."

"All right, names."

"Villareal, Menteur, and Samuels."

"Gimme a minute."

Thirty seconds later a siren went off and every convict throughout the prison was ordered to return to his cell, to sit, and to wait. The entire unit was in a "lockdown."

                *   *   *   *   *   *   *   *   *   *

The simultaneous necessity to both vomit and defecate hit Thom hard. His stomach churned, he tasted the stinging, putrid bile rising in his throat, and knew he wouldn't be able to suppress it. Putting his hand on his forehead, he lowered his temple to the cool metal arm of the sofa and prayed he didn't puke all over himself.

Breathe deeply. Hold your breath for a second. Let it out....slow. Swallow. I'll be OK.

The coolness from the arm of the sofa seemed to help his throbbing head. He felt better and he knew he had passed this crisis. Thom slowly sat up.

WHAM! He raced for the men's room, not knowing if he could make it. *Please, dear God, let me get there.*

In the back of his mind, almost completely masked by the incessant ringing in his ears, he heard the Hispanic yell, "What the fuck?"

A laughing, whining voice blurted out, "Ah, dat fucker's just pukin'."

Amid their chuckles, the third inmate remained silent, seated on his perch at the door of the lounge, looking out.

Thom got to the sink and heaved. He heaved and heaved, then heaved again. When his stomach was empty, he just heaved bile, and when that was gone, he dry-heaved. His head pounded, tears streamed from his eyes. Thom's face was on fire and the after-taste of vomit filled his mouth and nasal passages. The acrid bile burned his throat, making him even more nauseous. The pressure in the side of his face made him feel as if his brains were about to explode, and the aching in his teeth from the acidic saliva caused him to moan out loud.

He stopped, gulped some of the warm, stagnant air, lapped some water from the faucet out of his hand, and then heaved again. This time he wished something would come up, but there was nothing left. As he sank to the floor, he pressed his right cheek and the right side of his forehead against the coolness of the sky blue bricks that surrounded him. He closed his eyes, and in incomplete visual images, his whole adult life seemed to flash before him.

* * * * * * * * * *

The son of a Presbyterian minister and a high school reading teacher from Pittsburgh, Thom Christopher was an adequate, but not outstanding student who had ended up only in the top third of his high school graduating class. A year later he found himself attending a small, private college in St. Petersburg, Florida. Actually, Thom had been accepted by two schools, one in central Ohio and another on Great Tampa Bay. He just had to decide which one he would go to, and on each day of his senior year, the decision was different. Finally, on an early February morning, in the midst of walking to the school bus stop in eighteen inches of snow and twelve degree weather, the decision became obvious: head south and spend the next four years in sunny Florida. His first December of 85-degree weather convinced him that he loved the South and now would be not just a "Yankee," but a "Damn Yankee," a northerner who came down and never left.

Thom treated his first two years of college as an experiment. Not knowing what he really wanted to do, he took courses from as many different disciplines as he could, eventually going through nine majors. Early in his junior year, he was still unsettled but had a bigger problem: he was almost out of cash. As luck would have it, he spotted an advertisement in the college newspaper asking for an assistant in the college psychology lab. Figuring this was easy money and all he'd be doing was watching people look at inkblots, he went in, interviewed with one of the faculty members, and two days later found himself in the midst of watching not inkblots but rats that were on different kinds of drugs. It was interesting work and Thom got more and more involved as the work continued. The excitement was consuming and he found himself spending more and more time studying and less and less time in the more social aspects of college life. Thom Christopher had found what he felt was his true calling.

A year and a half later, he applied to several graduate schools, having the good fortune of being accepted by two or three and managing to pull down a teaching assistantship in one.

In his last year in graduate school, he met Ellen, fell madly in love, and the two were married. After graduation, they both found jobs in the Northeast, but after their first few winters in what they called the "tundra," they couldn't handle the frigid temperatures, and started applying for any jobs they could find below the Mason-Dixon Line. They ended up a year later with the job at TSU-Conroe, a house, and their future in Southeast Texas. Thom truly was a "Damn Yankee."

*   *   *   *   *   *   *   *   *   *

Back in the Education Section of the Wynne Unit, the whining, little inmate who had called himself Cox, belched and Thom was jolted back to the present. *Why're they doing this to me?*

CHAPTER 10

❀

At 12:47 a.m. the lockdown and counting continued and Villareal, Menteur, and Samuels were nowhere to be found. They simply had disappeared. The sergeant called the warden's residence.

"You've checked out the entire place?"

"High and low."

"How'd they get out?"

"Don't know yet."

"Well, find out. And when was the last time they were seen?"

"The eight o'clock count."

"Nobody seen 'em since then?"

"No, Sir."

"All right, contact all the surrounding PDs. Then find out all the locals they've had any contact with in the last couple of years and send guards over to have a look. And make sure they have a deputy with them. If that doesn't pan out, call DPS and get them up here. Ask for some dogs and a helicopter. They can't have gotten too far."

"Yessir."
"We'll get 'em. It's just a matter of time."

*　*　*　*　*　*　*　*　*　*

With the door to the bathroom in the faculty lounge slightly ajar, Thom crouched in his small, four-foot-square sanctuary, the bowl of a dirty porcelain sink directly above him. He rested his pounding head on the wall, letting the coolness of the brick drain the heat from his forehead.

This isn't happening. In a while, I'll wake up, fix Amy breakfast, and take her to school. This is all just a bad dream.

A loud Hispanic voice broke Thom's trance. "What's he doin' in there?" followed by a response tinged with amusement. "He's pukin' his guts up. Want me to get him?"

Oh please, don't let them make me leave here.

Suddenly, a third voice spoke with irritation. "Let 'im go, he didn't do anything and we're gonna need 'im. Just leave 'im be. He sure as hell ain't goin' anywhere."

"C'mon, let's fuck with 'im."

Thom's thoughts raced. *Oh, please, just let me stay in here for a few more seconds. Please.*

"Shut up, Eddie, let 'im alone."

"Yeah, well you popped him in the first place. Lemme have some fun with 'im."

"Sit down over there or I'll break your fuckin' neck."

*　*　*　*　*　*　*　*　*　*

Thom felt he had been in the bathroom for hours, but in fact, it had only been twenty minutes. The Hispanic lost patience, went to the door, and yelled through the crack, "Hey, Doc, get out here. You been in there way too long."

"Let me go get him."

"Shut the fuck up, Eddie."

Thom could only curl into a fetal position and lie there, motionless. Five minutes later, the voice of the third inmate called out, "Doc, time to come out."

A whining voice followed with, "Yeah, and I need to take a leak."

"Shut up, Eddie."

Finally, Thom stirred and raised himself up on his two wobbling legs. He ached. His body was bent over at the waist, but he forced himself to try to straighten up. Every muscle in his stomach contracted; his mouth was ablaze with broken teeth and a shredded tongue; his jaw and temple ached. He struggled to the side, managed to push open the door, and half-crawled out of the bathroom.

Staring at the three inmates, the captive suddenly realized that there weren't any orange I.D. patches on their prison whites. *Why didn't I see this before?* For reasons even he didn't understand, he mumbled more than spoke. "Who are you?"

What seemed minutes passed, when finally the inmate seated on his perch in the doorway quietly said, "I'm Elliott Samuels, that's Jesús Villareal, and he's Eddie Menteur."

"Why'd you tell him that for?"

"Shut up. He has a right to know."

"Why're you doing this to me?"

The response to the question came from Jesús. "Hey!"

Thom's knees quavered as he turned and saw the inmate pointing the barrel of the gun directly at his forehead. "I'm in charge here. You don't ask no fuckin' questions; you don't say fuckin' nothin'. You go over there, and sit the fuck down."

In a trance, he stumbled his way to the sofa, and as ordered, sat in silence, his gazed fixed on the floor directly in front of him. Then he looked up and stared directly at the bound guard while eternities passed.

CHAPTER 11

At 2:03 a.m., officers from the Texas Department of Public Safety
showed up with six German Shepherds, delivered by truck from
Montgomery County. A DPS helicopter, with its intense spotlight, was
already on the scene and was circling the perimeter of the prison. The
pilot and co-pilot knew the routine: "Anything that moves, spot it,"
which, in several cases, momentarily blinded several of the seventy-four
guards and sheriff's deputies who had been called out, but it had to be
done.

On the ground, Joe Leonard and Terry Gilman pushed their way
through the brushy countryside that surrounded the Wynne Unit. One
carried a high-powered automatic rifle, but the other was unarmed.
The intense, directed beams of their TDCJ-issued flashlights scanned
the ground in a 180º arc so that both were always aware of exactly what
was in front of them at any one moment. After three and a half hours in
the still-oppressive heat and humidity, they were becoming more and
more frustrated. Terry had heard the rumor that nobody could find any

breaks in the fence or any holes in the walls of the sheds that were placed sporadically around the unit.

Gilman lost patience. "How the fuck did those shits get out?"

"Ah, you know how it is. Security around here? These sons of bitches can take off whenever they want. They just walk over to the fence and then we get our asses called out in the middle of the night. The whole thing is fucked."

"Man, I don't see it. They were in the block just before the last count. Where the fuck'd they go?"

"Look, just find 'em. You weren't in there when it happened, so you ain't gonna get canned. Ain't our problem."

After another ten minutes, Terry asked, "What'd they do, anyway?"

"Sergeant said somethin' about 'em being lifers but, shit, I was half asleep."

Great. Just what I need, lifers.

*   *   *   *   *   *   *   *   *   *

Back in his cell, Thom tried to think what to do. He tried to remember what the TDCJ training manual had said, conjuring up visual images of the particular pages describing what to do in hostage situations. He could see those pages, the page numbers, the title at the top left-hand corner. He could even envision in the upper right hand corner the message that the manual had been revised in 1993. But he couldn't make out the words in the paragraphs.

His thoughts roamed. *There was something about time. Was it the beginning that was most dangerous or was it later, when they started getting antsy that was bad? No, the first hour is the most crucial. I'm sure that was in there. I made it past then, I'll be OK.*

Something about authority. Did it say to act with authority? Take charge? No, that couldn't be. Nobody could be that stupid.

God, I know there were other things. What were they? Why didn't I at least look at that damn manual?

What would Richard do?

In the midst of these thoughts, Thom dozed off. He dreamed of his daughter, his wife, the dogs. He was back home, enjoying a lazy Sunday morning, working the Chronicle crossword and deciding whether he should go out and run before it got too late. True peace when the clatter of loud voices woke him up. *No. Please, let me go back to sleep.*

But he couldn't go back and all that was left was to stare at the floor. He checked his watch—4:32 a.m.—*they must know I'm here. Surely, Richard knows.*

CHAPTER 12

Richard McClain grew up in the 1950s and '60s in Alvin, Texas, a small town about half-way between Houston and Galveston. Early on, McClain showed promise as both a good student and an even better athlete. In Texas, that meant only one thing: you played high school football—the official state religion. By the time McClain was in junior high, he showed good speed, and even though he wasn't very big, he was solid. Because of his academic record, Richard always figured that if he didn't make it in college football, he at least would get a college degree and succeed in a "real-life" vocation. In high school, several of the small colleges around the state recruited McClain, but coaches from the "big-time" programs at A&M and UT-Austin were put off by his size. Still, he was undaunted; he would get himself a free education, somewhere.

In the summer of 1969, Richard McClain graduated from Alvin High School and set off for Abilene College where he had been awarded a full scholarship to play defensive back for the Javelinas. When he left home for good, the last thing he did was promise his parents that he would return with a "degree in hand." McClain went through the two-a-day summer drills, bulked up, worked on timing and getting used to competing with much larger players, and progressed. The talent he saw on that field in Abilene and the level of competition on the practice field and in games forced McClain to evolve into an even better player, with quickness and finesse that made his coaches proud.

All during his college playing days, Richard kept up with his studies. While several of his teammates opted to major in Phys. Ed., McClain chose a double major in biology and chemistry. It was tough—the studying, the labs—he even got a lot of grief from his coaches for choosing the difficult path. But he didn't care, he had made up his mind to do something useful when he got out of school, and moreover, to keep his promise to his folks. So he worked, earning mostly A's with a few B's mixed in, but doing very good work for what some considered to be just another "dumb jock."

During the middle of his senior year, the coach called him in to his office. From behind the desk, the mentor began, "Richard, you're doing a great job. You've got determination and leadership and I'm very impressed."

"Thanks, Coach. Is that all?"

"Not quite, son."

With a coy smile, the coach got up and announced, "There've been some scouts from the Bengals to our last few games. They came down to look at Lonnie, but you really caught their attention. We sent them some videotapes and it's a long shot, but you never know."

McClain was in a state of near-shock. "They really want me?"

"I didn't say that. I said they wanted to evaluate you. But they did sound interested. Now go hit the showers and have a good game this weekend."

"You bet. And thanks again, Coach."

    *   *   *   *   *   *   *   *   *   *

The following week, the team flew into Hobby Airport in Houston, took a bus north, and prepared to play the Ravens of Texas State University in Conroe. McClain was still on "an all time high" wondering if there might be any scouts in the stands, watching, as he prepared to look like the best defensive back in the history of college football. During the third quarter, Richard managed to swat two short passes out of the air and make four solo tackles, one resulting in a fumble recovery by a Javelina. He played at the top of his game.

The game became a tense see-saw battle between two worthy opponents with defense keeping the score tied at seven. Five minutes into the fourth quarter, the Javelina quarterback threw a long pass down the field; it was snagged one-handed and pulled in by a receiver, who then managed to scramble the remaining twenty yards into the end zone. With a missed PAT, the new score stood at AC 13 and TSU-Conroe 7. The end of the game was rapidly approaching when the Ravens' running back broke free and was in the open field, with only daylight and the end zone in front of him. WHAM! He was hit from out of nowhere, taken to the ground, and fumbling the ball. A few seconds later, Richard McClain got up from under his prey, walked over to the sideline and, turning his head from side to side, mentioned to the trainer, "This doesn't feel right. I can hear some crunching in my ears." A trainer carefully led McClain into the locker room and the paramedics took him to the local hospital. Hours later, x-rays showed he had chipped some vertebrae in his neck. The doctors told him he was lucky not to be paralyzed, and in fact, was lucky to be alive. In the ensuing months, McClain made a full recovery, but the incident forever ended his chances of playing football again.

After graduation—he had kept his promise—Richard McClain took a summer job working for his uncle as a security guard at a motel just outside Alvin. He found he liked the job, it gave him a lot of interaction with people from all walks of life, and more than occasionally, there would be a problem to be solved. One incident involved a loud party in the middle of the night. The manager told McClain to go in and "break it up" and after a quarter-hour of talking and reasoning, the problem was peacefully resolved. In another case, a group of high school toughs assaulted a female guest at the motel. McClain, with his uncle at his side, intervened, and managed to "keep the peace" until the Alvin Police Department showed up, *en masse*. Richard liked it and at the end of the summer he was accepted as a cadet at the Police Academy in Houston.

At the Academy, McClain excelled, receiving outstanding marks in all his classes, both academic and physical. He graduated second in his class and started his career in a patrol car. During the next five years he honed his skills, nearly always getting accolades from his superiors and colleagues. He was a cop who used his head and not his force. A few years later, McClain took the sergeant's exam and was promoted almost immediately. Seven years after that, he found himself promoted to lieutenant, with several men under his charge. Thom Christopher had once asked McClain why he never took the captain's exam. The response was quick and simple. "I like doing police work. I don't want to sit around pushing papers."

In 1986, McClain was called out to a bank robbery. Three gunmen held several civilian hostages inside the bank, and McClain found himself to be the senior office in charge, along with a SWAT lieutenant and the newly ordained head of the SWAT snipers, a Sergeant Pelfrey. McClain calmed everybody down and then got on his cellular phone. Within half an hour, the three crooks came out with their hands held high; nobody had been hurt. The story of the negotiation spread through the Department and as a reward, the Chief ordered McClain to create a new "Crisis Negotiation Team" to work in conjunction with SWAT; the lieutenant would choose all his negotiators, be in charge of their training, and run the whole show. Even though he was still under the direction of a captain, in all practicality, McClain had *his* command.

Throughout the years that followed, Richard continued to select, train, and monitor his men. With the number of incidences requiring negotiations seemingly increasing each year and "call ups" averaging two-and-a-half per week, he eventually got his cadre of men up to thirty strong. During this time he immersed himself in his work, learning and developing new negotiation techniques and strategies, writing two text-books on the art of negotiating, and generally trying to help the victims of the brutality he so often had to witness.

As McClain's tenure in the Department lengthened, he continued to search for new ways of training his men. One night, after an unsuccessful stand-off when the suspect unwittingly pointed a shot-gun at an officer and ended up having his brains splattered all over the wall behind him, Richard drove home wondering how he could have avoided what had just happened. Half-way home it hit him: *Psychology. They have to know some psychology. I can teach them all I know, but they have to understand why they're doing what they're doing. Then maybe we can avoid outcomes like tonight.*

Over the next few weeks, Richard visited the various colleges and universities in and around Houston and finally found one that was receptive, even excited, about helping to train "real, applied psychologists." And that was Texas State University in Conroe. McClain made more phone calls and funding was set up by a charitable organization within Harris County. With everything in place, classes began a year later and all the candidates were enrolled in a master's degree program.

It was a perfect situation; he and his men were being trained in not just "the how" but also in "the why." And they were being rewarded with graduate degrees, to boot. And although he occasionally winced at seeing a particular spot on the TSU-C football field, he was content with how things had turned out.

CHAPTER 13

Purely by chance, the same semester that McClain's officers began their graduate classes, Thom Christopher had an 8:00 a.m. class that didn't have enough students. The class was cancelled and he was assigned to "administrative duties;" in this instance that meant that he became the liaison for the "Police Program."

Thom and Richard fast became friends. McClain was just two months younger than Thom, the same height, and, although his short brown hair had much less gray than Thom's, he was showing the paunch of middle age. Still, those swarthy good looks, in his younger days, might have made women swoon. The two got along well and often seemed more like brothers than just friends.

Over the months, they got into the weekly habit of meeting at the *Hair of the Dog Saloon* in Spring for "fat burgers," table shuffle-board, and beers. During these forays, Thom learned some of Richard's history. He heard about a bank robbery and how McClain talked the three thugs into giving up. He even learned how McClain had saved another

officer's life. In the midst of a "gang-war" firefight, a fellow policeman
had been badly wounded, with blood spewing from his thigh. Ignoring
the ricocheting bullets, McClain had run to him, taken off his own belt,
and used it as a tourniquet to stem the flow of blood. Richard then carried the officer out of the melee to a waiting ambulance. For this act, he
was awarded the city's highest award, the Medal of Honor.

That was years ago, though, and memories fade fast. What McClain
was really known for was his ability to negotiate and run a tight organization. One day every month, he required all of the men to attend
Negotiation School. It didn't matter if an officer had been a negotiator
for one year or ten, if he had just come from the FBI or the ATF, or if he
had spent the previous twelve hours negotiating with a guy high on
crack and embalming fluid who was holding his girlfriend hostage. On
that day he was "in school." As Richard had told Thom, "In any situation, you'll react the way you were trained. That's why my officers will
always be trained, and trained well. And either they train or they don't
work for me."

The idea that Richard was a hostage negotiator intrigued Thom.
Here was a person he was teaching who used psychology every day, not
in the "ivy-covered tower" but out in the "real" world, and whenever
Thom got a chance, he'd ask Richard about exactly how he handled different situations. Usually, it was like trying to pry the lid off a bottle of
ibuprofen: "If I told you that I'd have to kill you," but other times,
Richard opened up and offered what might be good in a particular
instance.

✳   ✳   ✳   ✳   ✳   ✳   ✳   ✳   ✳   ✳

Thom found out later from one of the other negotiators that
McClain was, indeed, a very important officer, not just at HPD but also
around the U.S. and in several parts of the world. He had achieved most
of his fame by his innovative techniques, and with his two textbooks

circulating internationally, he was widely recognized as one of the best "talkers" in the world.

*   *   *   *   *   *   *   *   *   *

Back in the unit, Thom sat, every single muscle of his stomach aching. His eyes wandered over the speckled white tile floor, stopping at the now-coagulated pool of blood that had seeped from the second closet. He stared. The once deep crimson liquid had developed a skin on the surface and the edges had turned a dark, iron-brown color.

His eyes locked on the crack at the base of the door of the closet. The blood there remained crimson and Thom couldn't look away. He was mesmerized; he felt his soul drawn to the results of previous carnage. He stood and walked toward the pool. He couldn't control his actions, and at the time, was not even cognizant of where those legs, someone else's legs, were taking him. Still staring at the floor, he reached his destination and almost unconsciously detected a faint metallic odor. *Is this death?*

His next step was met with a loud "pop" and the whiz of a projectile speeding past his ear. Jolted back into reality, he realized his hand was gripping the doorknob of the second closet.

"Get the fuck away from there."

Oh, God!

Seemingly from nowhere, Samuels stepped up, made some gyrations in the face of the gun-toting Villareal, then turned. "Doc, you sit over there. Don't go messin' with stuff."

Obediently, down-trodden, Thom walked back and sat. Looking down, he realized his shoes were splattered with the dark red, sticky liquid. In his own mind, though, they were someone else's shoes, not his, not in this horrific reality.

CHAPTER 14

After what seemed hours, the bound guard in the corner made a slight movement. It wasn't much, just some muffled struggling and a light grunt, but it was enough that Villareal and Menteur both approached. They asked a few questions to which there were some nods, and then got the guard to his feet and led him toward the men's room. Passing the couch, Villareal pulled the revolver out of his belt and pushed the muzzle into the guard's side, forcing him toward the wall. Moments later, Thom heard the extended splashing of urine, the whoosh of the flushing toilet, and then the slow emergence from the lavatory, head down and eyes focused on the floor. This time, though, the barrel of the pistol was pushed into Thom's face.

"You keep your eyes on the floor, too, asshole. This ain't none of your business." He meant business, there was no life, no emotion, nothing, in those eyes and Thom wanted to vomit. But he knew that if he moved, there would be no reluctance to pull that trigger and end his life.

With the "prisoner" back to his solitary "holding area," Thom tried to think what to do. He hadn't read the manual but he had worked with cops. Surely he could remember some of what they had told him. He recalled that the first hours *were* the most critical; if he survived those initial moments, then he was likely to live. *Why?* It was only because sieges were highly emotional and that, as time passed, the suspects became progressively calmer. As reason and rationality took over, Thom knew that Villareal, Menteur, and Samuels also must be starting to relax, or at least, tire.

*　*　*　*　*　*　*　*　*　*

Thom dozed off, then awoke, still weary. Checking his watch, he saw it was 6:27 in the morning. Still half asleep, his mind wandered. *Time to fix Amy's breakfast, put some food in the dogs' bowl. Oh, God, how's Amy gonna get to school?*

A loud bang resounded through the section.

Thom's head jerked up. Samuels was still on his perch, Menteur curled up in a chair in the corner. *Where's Villareal?*

A moment later, the Hispanic returned with the report that the sun was coming up and that he didn't see any guards outside the Education Section.

Samuels was visibly nervous. "What was that noise?"

"Door slammed."

Thom's heart sank.

Samuels looked at Villareal. "Hey, we got a problem."

"What's that?"

"The guard's gonna be coming down here to open up the place. They're gonna be lettin' those GED guys in pretty soon."

"Fuck. I forgot about that. Let me think." The Hispanic paced back and forth then went over and kicked Eddie Menteur out of his slumber. "Hey, faggot, I got a job for ya."

"Don't call me that. I ain't no fag."

"Whatever. Go down and cram some gum in that lock. Make sure it gets in there good so the lock don't work."

Eddie sauntered off, muttering something about "that little Spic," but the words and meaning were unintelligible.

*　　*　　*　　*　　*　　*　　*　　*　　*　　*

By 7:30 a.m., it was presumed that the escapees had gotten into a waiting car and were well out of the area. It was time to get back to normal. Sergeant Larry Mills descended the steps of the Education Section, put his key in the lock and tried to turn it. Nothing. The lock didn't budge. He tried again, and still, nothing. He tried once more, then looked into the lock and could see that somebody had stuffed something in the mechanism. Mumbling to himself, he checked the urge to curse. "Great! Now I gotta get somebody to unclog that sucker."

Then, without warning, Mills heard some muffled talking.

"Damn, who's in there?"

He went to the desk phone at the top of the stairs and dialed the classroom area. He could hear the ringing, but there was no response. So Larry let it ring repeatedly, figuring that eventually the instructor would get irritated enough to pick it up.

Twenty-two rings later, Villareal was going nuts. "Fuck, take the phone off the goddam' hook."

Menteur again moved down the hallway, lifted the receiver, and in a surprisingly placid voice, asked, "Yes? May I be of assistance to you?"

"Hey, look, this is Larry Mills, that door lock is jammed and we got inmates comin' down for class in five minutes. See if you can get whatever's in there out. OK?"

"I don't believe that's possible today."

"What?"

Eddie's voice dripped with sarcasm, "I'm sorry. Classes won't be in session today, Mr. um. What was your name?"

"Mills, Larry Mills. What're you talkin' about?"

"Well, Mr. Mills, classes for today have been canceled due to Inmate Appreciation Day. So, we'll have to leave the Section closed."

Mills bellowed, "Who the hell is this?"

"Name's Eddie Menteur."

A brief silence ensued, during which the guard collected himself. "Look, Eddie, we've been huntin' for you all night. How'd you get locked in down here?"

Eddie laughed maniacally. "We didn't get locked in, man. We took the place over."

There was another brief pause. "Who's we?"

With a slight chuckle, Eddie answered, "Me, Jesús, and Samuels. Oh, yeah, and the Doc, too."

Villareal, from behind Menteur, heard only the last part of the conversation but grabbed the receiver and slammed it back to its cradle. Glaring, he spat out, "What the fuck you doin', man? You don't talk to nobody without talkin' to me first. Got it?"

Eddie's bluster gone, his newly-found ego deflated, he dejectedly responded, "Yeah, whatever."

CHAPTER 15

At a quarter past five, Friday morning, Richard McClain grabbed the phone on the nightstand, put the receiver to his ear, and heard a dial tone. *God, I must've been dreaming.*

He lay back, unable to dismiss the sensation that something was wrong. Finally, knowing sleep was over for the night, he got up, showered, shaved, and went off to work. All the way to the office, he couldn't shake that troublesome feeling but then realized that he had forgotten to stop off at the saloon the night before. No big deal, it wasn't the first time and it certainly wouldn't be the last.

* * * * * * * * * *

At six, Ellen awoke, reached over for her husband, and found only an empty space. A feeling of dread came over her, then she remembered that Thom was going out with Richard the night before. *Damn him.*

He's probably sound asleep on the McClain's sofa. She was seething. *He knows I hate this.*

        *   *   *   *   *   *   *   *   *   *

In the middle of The Today Show, an anonymous caller phoned the newsroom of the NBC affiliate in Houston and reported a hostage situation in Huntsville. Moments later, the screen went blue, then became active again, showing the flowing auburn hair of an attractive female news anchor, "This is Dominique Villanueva. We have a breaking report from Huntsville where it appears that three convicts have barricaded themselves in a wing of the Wynne Prison Unit in Huntsville. Information is still sketchy, but it appears that at least two persons may have been taken hostage. More on this and other stories at 8:25."

Within minutes, every other Houston news station had been alerted by that same anonymous caller.

        *   *   *   *   *   *   *   *   *   *

As the story broke, Thom took a long hard look at his three captors, sitting across the room, speaking only in hushed whispers. *Why are they doing this to me? Why me?*

CHAPTER 16

Eddie Menteur grew up near Carswell Air Force Base in Fort Worth, in the early 1970s. He had always been a short, pudgy kid who, by the time he entered junior high school, had developed a chronic case of teenage acne and a chronic weasely look about him. Eddie, from the start, had suffered the interminable aggravation of being the brunt of everyone's jokes and endured both the verbal and physical aggression of his class-mates. Given all this, over the years, his self-esteem was as low as it could possibly be. Everything he did turned out badly and when it turned out badly, it only reinforced his feelings of inadequacy. Eddie couldn't win and he became a "victim" of his own arrested physical, social, and emotional development.

When Eddie was in the eleventh grade he made a gamble to enter the mainstream of high school society; he asked the girl sitting next to him in his fourth period class to the Friday night fair dance. She wasn't too pretty, not conceited like the rest, and she even had smiled at him once. In front of the entire U.S. History class and in a voice too loud to be ignored, she responded, "Go to the dance with YOU? You have *got* to be kidding! I wouldn't go from here to the corner with you."

Eddie was devastated. He leapt from his desk, and in a mad dash, ran out, tears of anger and embarrassment welling up in his eyes. He raced home, threw open the door to his bedroom and spent the next three hours lying there on the bed, sobbing at his own impotence and hating the world.

For days he avoided going back, feigning illness or just cutting out on the way. After a week, a letter was sent, informing Mr. and Mrs. Menteur that if their son continued to be absent he would be in danger of not reaching the state's minimum attendance requirement and would have to repeat the eleventh grade. That night, Eddie's father made it painfully obvious to him that he would not miss another day of school.

Going back, tail between his legs, Eddie entered the school fifteen minutes before his classmates. He went to his locker, got his books, then crept to first period class. His ears burned as he heard the silent snickers of the other students filing into the room and taking their seats. He knew they were all watching him, if not through outright ogling, then through their furtive little glances. They were all talking about him and about "the incident." Especially those football players sitting behind him. They always rode him real hard, *cliquish assholes!* After thirty minutes, his mind could no longer take the incessant taunting and he jumped up and screamed, "Leave me alone, you mother-fuckers!" Almost instantaneously, looking at the sea of blank faces, Eddie panicked and, again, raced from the school.

That night, after a call from the principal, Eddie's father used the strap for the second time in two days. This time he wouldn't go back, he couldn't go back. But the next morning, in the midst of arriving school buses, his father, who didn't give a rat's ass what Eddie believed the kids were saying about him, delivered his son to school, no questions asked. As he walked down to his locker, nobody seemed to notice him. Nobody seemed to care. He knew, though, in his heart of hearts, what they were all thinking. Then, out of the blue, he heard that derisive voice. "Hey, faggot, whaddaya think you're doin'?"

The voice and the words hit like a ton of bricks. The blood rising in his ears, he whirled around, only to come face to face with Tim Brandt, James Woodson, and Charlie Johnson, three of the largest linebackers in the entire Dallas-Fort Worth Metroplex. They dwarfed him, his puniness now more pronounced than ever.

He heard their jeers, was pushed up against the locker five or six times, and then was told that they'd be waiting for him at the end of the day. Their sneering chuckles stung him to his very core.

By seventh period, Eddie had a plan. He'd hide out until football practice started, then sneak out the side door and head for home. Son of a gun, if it didn't work. He made it home with no problem and safely planted himself inside his room for the remainder of the afternoon and evening.

The next morning, delivered again to school, Eddie went to retrieve his books and found the word "faggot" scratched into the paint of his locker door. As tears filled his eyes, his face was literally slammed into that hideous word.

"Hey, faggot, we're waitin' for you."

"We're gonna beat that suckin' face to a goddam' pulp."

What could Eddie do?

A bell rang, everybody dispersed, each going to his respective class and the day continued. Once again, Eddie was able to escape.

The assaults continued, and after two weeks, his humiliation was complete. With his father sleeping on the couch, he sneaked into the master bedroom, went to the closet, and got his father's .22 caliber pistol. He'd scare them, all right; he'd scare the shit out of them.

The following day, he again was assailed but this time, when the bell rang and all of the 450 students filed into classrooms, the three linebackers held their positions.

"Fag boy. Like ta suck?" Tim Brandt grabbed his own crotch. "Suck this."

"Hey, queer, we're gonna beat the fuck outta you."

Panicking for his life, Eddie struggled for the gun hidden under his jacket, and turning, pointed the muzzle at Tim Brandt.

"Leave me alone. Just leave me alone."

Wide-eyed and mouths hanging open, the three jocks made an attempt at a hasty retreat, hands outstretched as if to protect themselves.

"Hey, man, don't do that, we were just jackin' with ya."

"Yeah. Put the gun down, man. We were just fuckin' around. We didn't mean nothin' by it."

Eddie screamed, "No! You take it easy. Why don't you leave me alone? I never did nothin' to you guys. Leave me alone."

Still retreating, Tim Brandt pleaded, "Calm down, guy. We ain't gonna fuck with you no more."

Eddie hesitated and the three backed up even more.

Tim Brandt pleadingly looked into Eddie's eyes, "We OK, man?"

"Yeah, just leave me alone."

A cue to get out of the situation, the three turned and scurried down the hallway. But as they made their way, Charlie Johnson turned to Tim Brandt and said, "Jesus, that little faggot scared the piss outta me."

The word "faggot" struck Eddie like a searing iron. He roared, "Hey, assholes."

They turned and saw Eddie, gun in hand, aiming at Brandt's chest.

"Oh shit. That fucker's crazy."

In a series of flashes, the barrel of the gun exploded, again and again and again. Two shots struck Tim Brandt, killing him instantly, one hit James Woodson in the stomach, and the fourth went astray.

* * * * * * * * * *

In the aftermath, Eddie Menteur, then seventeen years old, was taken to the county jail where his state-appointed attorney informed him of the severity of his actions and then told him he was going to be tried as an adult. "Son, I need your permission to make a deal with the District Attorney. They're going go for premeditated murder. You had the gun, they were walking away, and you called them back and fired. Their view is: it's open and shut."

Amidst true sobs, Eddie asked, "What kinda deal?"

"Well, we might get it reduced to manslaughter. The judge may take into consideration the harassment. If it all works out, bottom line, probably five to ten. With good behavior and time served, you'll be out in 36 months."

Eddie was terrified. "Oh my God, three years, I can't do that."

"Son, you killed a kid and crippled another one."

Realizing the truth, he replied, almost inaudibly, "Yes, talk to whoever you need to."

* * * * * * * * * *

At the informal hearing, Eddie Menteur pleaded guilty to manslaughter. The judge remanded him to custody, sending him back to the county jail to await sentencing, and six weeks to the day later, Eddie entered the courtroom. The judge, pounding the gavel, called on Eddie to rise.

"Mr. Menteur, you've pleaded guilty to murder. The act, although performed under somewhat extenuating circumstances, is no less heinous than if you had gone into a shopping mall and gunned down an innocent bystander. You took a young man's life and you've destroyed a family forever. Mr. Menteur, do you have anything to say before I pass sentence?"

The prisoner stared at the floor. "No, sir."

Unfortunately for Eddie, the morning of sentencing the judge had had an argument with his wife over her credit card bills. Whether it was justice or displaced aggression, the judge read the sentence. "Mr. Menteur, I sentence you to forty-five years in the state penitentiary. Bailiff, remove the prisoner."

CHAPTER 17

Jesús Villareal was born in the Glenmont section of southwest Houston in 1970 to an unwed teenage mother. During his first years, he was primarily cared for by an aunt who, although not especially fond of children, doted on her nephew. When he was six, the aunt died, a victim of the random violence indigenous to large metropolitan areas and Jesús was basically on his own. His mother occasionally showed up but was either drunk or high on drugs, and was always with a man. If they had sex, Jesús was left alone, if not, there was Hell to pay. As such, the young Hispanic never had love and never felt in control.

Gangs dominated the Glenmont section of Houston. Graffiti-filled walls, tattooed homeboys, and regular Friday night drive-by shootings were all part of the local culture. It was a dangerous place for anyone but especially dangerous for someone without "friends." Thus, while still a child, Jesús Villareal was thrown into a very harsh environment where he could either swim or sink.

Given Jesús situation, he became a prime candidate for a life on the streets. Spending most of his time hanging out at the Los Estados apartment complex just off Glenmont Avenue, he found a group of older boys he could respect. They sported gold chains, had intricate artwork adorning their biceps, and wore green, the color of money. Sometimes, they were even seen driving big Caddies or BMWs. In this neighborhood, the "Greens" were in charge and Jesús admired that. More importantly, though, they paid attention to their new young friend and it was at that point that Jesús Villareal became a gang "wanna-be."

In a short time, as his association with the O.G.s—original gangsters—continued, Jesús became what sociologists call a "baby gangster." As such, he wore the black and green, his trousers rode low on his hips, and the jewelry he had "purchased," using his five-fingered discount, from a neighborhood pawnshop, adorned his body.

He was a member of the gang. He belonged. He was somebody. Jesús' involvement intensified, going from painting simple graffiti and committing petty theft to intimidation of rival gang members to alleged rape. The violence increased, the danger increased. But it didn't matter; Jesús was protected by the same brothers whom he protected.

By the time Jesús was seventeen, he had reached the middle levels of the gang; he even started calling some of the shots. Tattooed and with his new moniker, El Cid, he now commanded the attention and respect he and his homies so craved.

In a few years he knew he would reach the upper echelons of the organization. His reputation and status would soar and he would be a "high roller." He would be the father figure to these young 13- and 14-year-old recruits and he relished the thought of being idolized, just as he had idolized his superiors.

*   *   *   *   *   *   *   *   *   *

On the afternoon of July 12, 1982, "Chongo," a fifteen-year-old initiate, showed up at Los Estados Apartments. His "greens" were ripped and just underneath his swollen right eye was a large gash.

"Shit, Chongo, what da fuck happened?"

"It was them Skinheads, man. They was layin' for me. I din't do nothin'."

"Where was they?"

"Layin' for me down near Choo's house. I wasn't doin' nothing. They just come after me."

The bloodied state of their homie and the knowledge that a rival gang had invaded their turf signaled that it was time for retribution. What right did these *coños* have coming into this part of town, anyway?

Jesús placed five phone calls, and within fifteen minutes, twenty-two "Greens" descended upon the Los Estados complex. The meeting commenced.

"We got a problem. The 'skins are comin' in tryin' to take over our turf. It ain't happenin'. Look what they done to Chongo. Man, they gotta pay."

So plans were made for a "simple" drive-by shooting at the home of one of the Skinheads. Four gang members would get a car, pack several automatic weapons on the floor of the back seat, and then go over and teach "shit" a lesson. Juan had the address, 405 Hickson Avenue, and would drive. Since Jesús had recruited Chongo, he would personally direct the activity.

At 11:30 p.m. on July 12, the bangers descended upon Hickson Avenue, and with their guns at the ready, opened fire at number 405, placing dozens bullet holes through the door, the windows, and the walls. Speeding away from the scene, they turned onto Travis Avenue and resumed a normal, legal speed.

*   *   *   *   *   *   *   *   *   *

The next morning, the Channel 2 News crew reported an apparent gang-related shooting at 405 Jackson Avenue in the Northwest section of the city. Two twelve-year-old girls had been killed and three others wounded. All had been attending a slumber party.

The city was outraged. The mayor, along with the chief of police, held several news conferences over the next week decrying the incident and announcing progress in the case. Police officers at the scene found a neighbor who had been awakened by the shots. He gave his perception of the incident along with a partial description of the car, a light-colored Oldsmobile 98. A second witness said he saw the driver, a light-complected male with very short hair, and the city's gang task force went into action. They scoured all the hangouts, searching through parking lots, talking to children, adults, teenagers, gang members, gang wanna-be's, and even gang snitches. Finally, they got a break. Somebody had seen four members of the "Greens" driving out of Los Estados in a brown Olds on the night in question. With this information, they took an educated guess as to whom the culprits might be and two of the task force members were assigned to bring them in "intense" interrogation.

✳   ✳   ✳   ✳   ✳   ✳   ✳   ✳   ✳   ✳

Paco Garcia was the youngest member of the "Greens." Thirteen years old, he had never been arrested before and his parents knew nothing of his involvement. He was brought in for questioning along with Juan Gonzalez and Jesús Villareal.

As Juan was separated from the group, Jesús and Paco stayed together in a room with one wooden table and four straight-backed chairs. After forty-five minutes, two police sergeants entered the room and said they had to take Paco to another room for questioning. They led him down the hallway and into a virtually identical room.

"Paco, you want a Coca-Cola?"

"Why, man? What you doin' that for?"

"We just thought since you're gonna be here for a while you might be thirsty."

"Yeah, OK."

So one of the sergeants went and got a can of Coke for Paco.

"Hey, Paco. You hungry?"

Puzzled, the boy looked up. "Why you doin' this, man?"

"I got some pizza left over from lunch. Want some?"

"Yeah, OK."

"Oh, yeah. You smoke?"

"Yeah."

"Go ahead and light up. It'll be OK."

"They took my butts when I came in."

"No problem. I got some in my locker."

The sergeant went out, got a pack of cigarettes and two slices of pizza and brought them back to Paco who ate and smoked to his heart's content.

After forty-five minutes the sergeant said, "Look, I gotta get you back but here's another Coke if you wanna take it with you."

Loosening up, the young gangster responded, "Thanks, man."

An officer led Paco back to the holding room and, again, left him alone with Jesús.

"What'd they ask, Paco?"

"Nothin'. They didn't ask nothin'."

Seeing the Coke and smelling the cigarettes, Jesús spat out, "Bullshit. What'd they say?"

Sweat now surfaced on Paco's forehead. "I'm tellin' ya, they didn't ask me nothin'."

"Yeah? You better be right."

Thirty minutes later, a sergeant came in and escorted Jesús to the second room. This time there were interrogators waiting.

"Jesús, you want a Coca-Cola or something."

"I don't want nothin'."

"All right, but listen and listen good. We have the car with your fingerprints all over it. We have a witness who saw you on Jackson that night. What's the extent of your involvement?"

"I don't know nothin'."

"What were you doing that night?"

"I was at a party."

"Where?"

"Los Estados, man. I got witnesses."

"Who was with you?"

"Choo. Manny. Chongo. All the guys."

"I don't think so, Jesús. Your homies put you at the scene. Now, we figure you're too smart to be the trigger man, but still, if somebody rolls, you're lookin' at a long stretch in Huntsville."

"No way, man. I wasn't there."

After a long pause, the officer continued, "Jesús, how about givin' us something we can work with. Maybe help you out? Can you say that Juan was the driver?"

"Look, man, I wasn't there. Hey, don't I get a lawyer?"

"Why do you need a lawyer? You haven't been charged with anything...yet."

Two more hours of intense questioning took place before the officers escorted Jesús back to the room holding Paco.

"Hey, Paco. *Pedazo de mierda.*"

"What the fuck'd I do?"

"You been talkin', you shit ass."

"I never gave 'em nothin'."

"How'd they know Juan was the driver? Just shut your fuckin' face; *vate al infierno.*"

The interrogators transferred Juan to the room holding the other two gangsters and merely waited and watched from a one-way mirror. Thirty minutes later, Juan again was retrieved for questioning.

"Son, you got a problem. You been rolled over on."

"No way, man. That's bullshit."

"We got enough to go to the D.A. with and get you as the shooter. Understand?"

"I din't do nothin'."

"Well, that's not what we hear. But if you weren't the shooter, then we gotta have a name and your involvement. Otherwise, you're lookin' at twenty-five to life."

Juan knew where he stood. He was the driver but he also knew that that little weasel Paco and, shit, maybe even Jesús had talked and named him as the shooter. The police scam had worked again.

Estoy fregado. Then he spoke, "Look, man. I was there. But I was only drivin'. I din't even have a piece. Paco and Jesús, they was the shooters."

"Would you sign a statement to that effect?"

"Yeah, sure."

Two statements, one naming Jesús and the other Paco as the shooters were quickly typed up and signed by Juan.

The officers returned to the other two gangsters, took one to an alternate room and then both were interviewed simultaneously.

*   *   *   *   *   *   *   *   *   *

"Jesús Villareal, you are under arrest for the murders of Rebecca Hogue and Jessica Thomas. You have the right to remain silent. If you give up that right, anything you say can be used against you in a court of law. You have the right to an attorney. If you cannot afford one, the state will provide one for you. Do you understand these rights?"

"No way, man. That's bull shit."

With that, the two officers produced a photostatic copy of Juan Gonzalez' statement. "You've been rolled over on, man. You're gonna take the fall."

"*Chingate!* That's a fake. He ain't gonna do that to me."

"Yeah, well he did. Now, do you understand your rights?"

Jesús stared at the confessions in front of him and sighed, "Yeah, whatever."

In the alternate room, an almost identical sequence of events occurred. The only exception was getting an additional piece of evidence implicating Jesús, the individual the police *knew* had planned and executed the shootings.

"Paco, you've been rolled over on. You're gonna take the fall for Jesús and Juan."

"That's shit."

Producing the signed statements, the officer watched Paco's eyes drop to the floor.

A moment later Paco muttered, "Juan was the driver. Jesús planned the whole thing. I was just there."

*   *   *   *   *   *   *   *   *

So the three young gangsters were taken down to the bowels of the Houston City Jail, relieved of their personal property, body searched, and then put into separate cells to await trial.

After a brief jury trial, Jesús was found guilty of second-degree murder and the judge pronounced sentence of thirty years. Both Paco and Juan were found guilty of lesser offenses and given lighter sentences. The fourth gangster involved in the shooting at 405 Jackson was never identified.

CHAPTER 18

Elliott Samuels grew in up Ardmore, Oklahoma, the son of lower middle class parents. As a youth, he starred as a halfback for Ardmore High and planned on playing for the University of Oklahoma and then in the pros. During his senior year in high school, several of the Big Ten schools interviewed Elliot, but his SAT scores and grade point average didn't quite make the NCAA cutoffs. Accepting reality, he enrolled in a junior college, after which he would transfer to the "majors."

During Elliott's second semester at the "juco" he fell in love. Carly was all that he had ever looked for in a woman: beautiful, a quick wit, and affectionate to a fault. They dated through the spring and decided to get married in the summer, just before football season. The following January, Carly announced she was pregnant and that the baby was due in August, just when Elliott was due to report to Norman for summer football drills.

They had little money; she worked in a beauty salon while he picked up extra jobs whenever he could. The pregnancy proved difficult, and toward the end, Carly had to quit her job and spend several weeks in bed. Deeper and deeper into debt, Elliott saw his career with OU starting to fade into oblivion. He called the offensive coach in Norman and explained that he would probably have to delay entering their program; he had a wife, a child on the way, and no money.

"Listen, son. You just get you and your wife up here and we'll see what we can work out."

"But, sir, I just don't have any money."

"Just get up here. We can work it out."

Elliott and Carly spent their last few dollars on a bus ride from Ardmore to Norman where they were picked up by an assistant coach in a university van.

"Coach says he's real happy you're here. Wants me to take you over to campus."

"Sure, let's go."

When the three arrived at the field house, the coach came out, greeted Elliott warmly, and then told him he had arranged for him and his wife to stay in an apartment complex for married students. Two small bedrooms with a small living room and kitchenette for a mere $330 a month.

"Sir, I can't afford that. It took just about all our money to get up here."

"Don't worry about it, it's all part of your scholarship. The university provides dorm space for you and pays your tuition and fees. Plus you get some laundry money every week. All you have to do is play football and keep your grades up. Oh, and, you have an appointment with a businessman in town to discuss a part-time job. He's a good man and a real fan."

Elliott was amazed. "That's great?"

"Don't think nothin' about it. It's all part of the package."

*   *   *   *   *   *   *   *   *   *

The coach delivered the couple to their new apartment and then drove Elliott over to a car dealership on the north side of Norman. As they left the van, a tall, bald man with a beer gut greeted them. In a jovial voice, he called out, "Hey, coach. Is this that fine young halfback you was tellin' me about?"

"Sure is. This is Elliott Samuels, all the way up from Ardmore. Elliott, this is Big Ed Monroe. He owns the place. Now I'm gonna go back to my office but I expect to be hearing from you later on, Ed."

"We'll work things out, don't you worry none."

The coach turned, walked back to the van, got in, and drove off.

"Elliott? That *is* your name isn't it, son?"

"Yessir."

"Let me show you around the place. The showroom is over there. Around over yonder we got most of the used cars."

"Yessir. Sir, the coach said you might have a job for me. I got a wife and a kid about to be born and I could sure use the work."

"Sure, son. But your main job here is to play football and keep your eligibility. As for working here, I don't want you worrying too much about it. You'll be a repo man."

"Isn't that dangerous?"

"Nah, easy as pie. I got a list of procedures to go through so if anybody ever asks what you do you can tell 'em. Also, we got some other guys working here doing the same thing, so you won't be making too many calls."

"If I'm not working that much, can I make enough money for Carly and the baby?"

"Well, here's what we'll do. The NCAA says you can't work during the season or during the academic year. You'll need money all year long, especially with a little tyke on the way, so what we're gonna do is stretch out a pretty nice salary for your summer work. Over the course of the whole year, that is. That seem fair to you?"

"Yeah, but am I gonna make enough to last for a year?"

Big Ed Monroe pulled out a small notebook and wrote down a figure. "Will that be enough?"

"Well, yeah. We can probably get through a month on that."

"Son, that's for a week."

Elliott stammered, "Geez, thank you, sir."

"There is somethin' else I do have to talk to you about."

Aha, the catch was coming. "Yes?"

"We been havin' a little problem with the IRS. They seem to be screwin' around with us 'cause they don't understand how we keep our books."

"What's that have to do with me?"

"Well, once a week, you come down and pick up your pay. And it's gonna be in cash, if that's all right."

"Sure, I guess so."

"And don't worry about the taxes and all that other crap, we take all that stuff out from the beginning. That figure I showed you is after taxes.

"Now, when that baby comes, the company'll pick up all the expenses. We treat our boys right, make sure they're taken care of and make sure they can play. And by the way, boys working for me usually get the use of a company car. I'm gonna set you up with one of them pick-ups over there." Big Ed pointed toward the back lot.

"Gawd, That's great."

"Just remember, though, with these feds on our tails, you can't tell nobody about it. OK?"

"Yessir."

So Elliott was on his way. Carly gave birth to a bouncing baby boy, the job was great, and he was averaging 96.2 yards per game for the University of Oklahoma. Life couldn't be sweeter.

✶   ✶   ✶   ✶   ✶   ✶   ✶   ✶   ✶   ✶

During the spring semester of Elliott's first year one of his teammates was caught going into an airport with a .357 Magnum under his jacket. Another was charged with the rape of a cheerleader. Still another was pulled over and charged with DWI. The press demanded an investigation, allegations against the coaching staff and administration were made and the NCAA was alerted. In the ensuing investigation, numerous rules violations were uncovered. The coach was forced to resign and the university surrendered several scholarships; the athletic program was falling apart.

Many of the team members had, in fact, brought on their own demise and suffered the consequences. Some were victims of a coaching staff and public which demanded eleven wins and no ties each season, and of course, a berth in the Orange Bowl. Still other players were also guilty, guilty of naiveté, guilty of blindly accepting what they were told, and guilty of ignoring what common sense would say was wrong.

* * * * * * * * * *

On a Friday morning in early August, Elliott Samuels opened the newspaper and saw his name on the front page

NCAA DECLARES SAMUELS INELIGIBLE

Elliott was stunned. Sure, he had talked with the investigators but he hadn't told them anything of consequence. He certainly hadn't done anything wrong.

Putting the paper under his arm, he quickly left his apartment to go to the field house and consult with the coach. *Shit, where's the truck?*

Going back into the apartment, he woke Carly. "Hon, did you move the truck last night?"

"No. It's in the parking lot right where we left it."

"Well, it's not there. Somebody must've stolen it. Shit, I'd better call Big Ed."

     *   *   *   *   *   *   *   *   *   *

"Mr. Monroe, this is Elliott Samuels."

"Sure, son. What can I do for you?"

"I gotta apologize. Somebody stole the truck."

"Uh, actually, son, we had to repo it. One of my boys picked it up last night."

Elliott was incredulous, "What?"

"Buddy boy, it was a repo, you didn't do your job."

"But you never called me. I'd a gone out. You never called."

"Not that job, Bud." And the receiver in Elliott's hand went dead.

     *   *   *   *   *   *   *   *   *   *

In mid-August, Elliott Samuels was formally notified that he had been banned from collegiate football for accepting money from a booster. His scholarship was gone, his education was down the drain, and now he was faced with supporting his wife and raising his infant son on virtually no income whatsoever.

Elliott made several calls around Norman asking for employment. No one would touch him, he had brought shame on OU, and in many minds, was the sole reason the team had been sanctioned. He even contacted every team in the NFL but was rejected by all. It was a bad time, the draft had occurred the previous April and all of the teams were involved in exhibition games with the express intent of paring down and eliminating players from their rosters, not adding them. Therefore, with no place else to turn, Carly, Elliott, and their son, James, returned to Ardmore, where Elliott found a job in the Western Auto.

Despite having his dreams dashed, Ardmore was not all that bad a place for Elliott. He was still somewhat of a "local hero" and he could pal around with some of his former teammates from Ardmore High. He was a good father and a good husband, dutifully depositing his checks in the joint account for his wife to spend on rent, food, and clothes for the baby. Still, Elliott was depressed. He could have done so much but because of stupidity or gullibility or greed, or perhaps a little of all three, he was destined to this life he could barely tolerate.

Every now and then Elliott would take a few dollars from his paycheck and go out and have a few beers with his buddies. It usually occurred on a Friday night, and with Carly and the baby asleep by the time he got home, no one was the wiser.

After a year and a half at the Western Auto, Elliott went out with two former offensive linemen and got plastered. Drinking tequila with beer chasers, the three were barely able to walk when the bar closed. They got into the car and wove their way south along Interstate 35 hunting for a package store that was not only open but irresponsible enough to sell three drunks more liquor. Past Lonesome Grove, past Overbrook and Marietta, they finally crossed the Red River. Seven more miles and they entered the outskirts of Gainesville, Texas where they pulled into an all-night mini-mart to buy gas. As Elliott went to pay, he saw the display cases containing beer. Grabbing two six packs, he staggered over to the counter, "I'll take these, too."

The seventy year-old man behind the counter, barely one hundred pounds with slicked back gray hair, responded, "Sorry, Bud, too late."

"Whaddya mean?"

"C'mon, Bud, it's after midnight. Just pay for the gas and hit the road."

With this, Elliott felt anger and frustration overwhelm him. "I ain't your fuckin' bud and you sell me the fuckin' beer."

Stepping on a button below the counter, the clerk responded, "Sir, it's state law. I can't sell it to ya, it's after midnight."

Rage took over. "I don't give a fuck about state law. Sell me the goddamn' beer."

Standing face to face over the counter, a DPS officer entered the market, a 9 mm automatic in his hand. "Hey, Buddy, what's goin' on?"

By this time, Elliott's "pals" saw what was happening and fled the scene, heading north toward the Red River and safe haven.

Elliott spun around, flailing his arms, and managed to catch the agent firmly on the shoulder, knocking him to the ground. In an instant, the officer came up, his gun pointed directly at Elliott's chest, and commanded, "Freeze."

Elliott just reacted. He grabbed the barrel of the gun, pushed it aside, then slugged the officer in the face. The two wrestled for control of the weapon that finally discharged, depositing a bullet in the linoleum floor less than an inch from the DPS agent's right ear. The din from the blast surprised Elliott so much he jerked his right hand, causing the gun to slide across the floor. As the officer scrambled for the weapon, he was tackled and hurled into the frozen meat counter, shards of glass covering the floor. At this point, Elliott retrieved the pistol and pointed it squarely at his adversary. And the next thing Elliott felt was a sharp pain at the base of his skull.

* * * * * * * * * * *

The next morning the local paper reported on the incident.

> …the hero being the store clerk, Pops Martin, who managed to subdue the attacker by striking him on the back of the head with a twelve-inch-long hard salami. The suspect was taken to county jail where he is awaiting arraignment.

The former Ardmore High School phenomenon and Oklahoma star running back survived for the time being. He was charged and convicted of the attempted capital murder of a police officer and received fifty years to life in the state penitentiary at Huntsville.

        ✶   ✶   ✶   ✶   ✶   ✶   ✶   ✶   ✶   ✶   ✶

Four weeks prior to August 16th and the beginning of the siege in Huntsville, Elliott wrote a brief letter to his wife:

> Carly,
> Whatever happens to me, I want you to know that I love you and am truly sorry for what I did. I may be in here for longer than we thought but I made up my mind. I made some arrangements for you and James to be taken care of. Don't ask about it, just remember that I love you.
>
> All my love,
> Elliott

CHAPTER 19

❁

Thom Christopher sat quietly on the couch, occasionally brushing his shredded tongue across his broken teeth and then fully realizing the gravity of the predicament in which he had been thrust. Still, though, he couldn't understand how it could have happened—why God had let him become a victim at the hands of three violent felons. He hadn't done anything to these people. Hell, he didn't even know these people. Why were they doing this to him? The only possible explanation was that they were just cruel, vicious thugs with no emotions whatsoever.

In the midst of these ruminations, Samuels hopped off his perch and approached. "Doc, you doin' all right?"

The bile again crept into Thom's throat. He swallowed hard. "Why? Why are you doing this?"

Samuels looked down at the bench. The professor looked pathetic. "I'm sorry, it just turned out this way."

"But why? Why do you want to kill me? I never did anything."

Elliot stammered for a second, not sure what to say. "It, it's just that you were in the wrong place at the wrong time."

"Then let me go. I never did anything to you. I have a wife and daughter. They depend upon me. You don't understand."

"Yes, I do. Believe me."

Thom bristled at the convict's words. "You don't understand. I come here to help you people and you do nothing but hurt me. You don't know what it's like to be a victim."

Now it was Elliot Samuels' turn to bristle. "You people?…victims? Yeah, I know what it's like. And as for having a wife and kid, well, I know what that's like to. I been there. And don't give me that crap about coming in here to help us out. You come in here to get paid. Sure, you act like you care and act like you're all buddy-buddy with us, but that's bullshit. You leave after class is out; we go back to our cells and sit in the fuckin' heat and humidity, listenin' while the guards go and play their fuckin' little games. We're no more than animals to *you people*, so don't talk to me about that bullshit *victim* crap."

"You're not a victim, you're a thug." Thom couldn't believe his words.

Samuels spat back, "Yeah, well let me tell you a little story. You outsiders always say you don't want to know about what we did, but deep down, you're dyin' to know. So, I'm gonna let you know."

And with that, Elliot Samuels told Thom about his days at OU, the job, the NCAA sanctions against him, and how his entire life revolved around Carly and young James. When it was over, Thom stared blankly. He felt a tear come to his eye as he dropped his head. "I'm sorry."

"You're sorry. Right. None of y'all are sorry. And look at Villareal over there. Mother's a crack head, grew up on the streets where if he didn't join the gang, he'd a been dead a long time ago. And Menteur over there. The reason he's in here is he lost it and shot a couple of kids who were beatin' the shit out of him every day. His folks don't even ever come to see him. He's got nothin'. So, don't think you're the only victim here."

"But you broke the law. I never did anything."

"Hey, Doc. Ever been out at a bar and had a few too many? Then tried to drive home?"

"What?"

"Drunk! You ever drive drunk?"

"Yeah, maybe."

"Well, did you or didn't you?"

"Yes, I did, all right? What's your point?"

"The point is, you broke the law. You just didn't get caught."

"That's different."

"No it ain't. There's a guy two cells down from me in the wing. Nice guy, real gentle. Used to work for a computer company, some sort of bigwig or somethin'. Well, he stopped off for a drink on the way home one night, had a few too many, and ran a red light. Killed an old couple and now he's doin' ten to twenty for intoxication manslaughter. Never been in trouble before, but now his whole life is down the shitter.

Difference between you and him, Doc, is that you're just lucky. Or maybe he was unlucky. Point is, don't give me that bullshit about you bein' a victim and never doin' nothin' wrong. As I said, you just didn't get caught."

Without another word, Samuels turned, looked toward the door to the outside, then sauntered back on over to his perch. Thom remained, stunned, still registering all that the convict had said. The logic and the truth behind the inmate's words had stopped him cold. He knew all of it was true and that, somehow, there was perhaps a very fine line between him and the men who had taken him hostage.

CHAPTER 20

Just before noon on Friday, Janice Garling paged her husband, Brian, a volunteer member of the Crisis Negotiation Team, at his office in the Homicide Division of the Houston Police Department. Sergeant Garling immediately dialed his home phone number.

"Jan? Everything OK at home?"

"Brian, have you been watching the TV monitor?"

"No, what's goin' on?"

"Just turn on Channel 2 and watch."

"Can't you tell me what this is all about?"

Insisting, she reiterated, "Really, Brian, you'll get more exact information by watching for yourself. Now hurry up and see what's going on."

The officer went into the vending area of the precinct and flipped on the TV. He saw one of the Channel 2 reporters, Susan something or other, with a microphone held up to her mouth.

"...Several minutes ago authorities released the names of the two hostages. One is Dr. Thom Christopher, a professor at Texas State

University in Conroe, who was teaching at the unit at the time of the siege. The second, a guard, has been identified as Roy Palmer, a fifteen-year veteran of the prison system. There is no word as to their conditions at this time. Stay tuned for more on the siege in Huntsville at noon. This is Susan Lennon, reporting live for Channel 2 News."

Stunned, B. C. Garling sat mesmerized, unable to take his eyes off the screen. Then, slowly, as if in a dream, he rose from his chair and walked back to his desk where he picked up the phone and dialed.

* * * * * * * * * *

The phone at the Crisis Negotiation Center rang with the usual response. "CNT, Calabro."

"This is Garling. Is Lieutenant McClain in?"

"Just a moment, sir."

There was a double click, after which a voice responded, "McClain."

"Lieu, Garling. Did you hear what's goin' on up in Huntsville?"

"No. What?"

"I just caught it on the TV. Thom Christopher is up in Huntsville. Some assholes took him hostage in one of the prisons up there.

"What?"

"We gotta do something about this."

Richard, a large knot in his stomach, kept his cool and forced calm into his voice. "Look, B. C., stay where you are. I'll find out what's goin' on and give you a call back."

He punched a button and cut off Garling, not waiting for a response.

* * * * * * * * * *

McClain flipped on the TV next to his desk and watched for a few seconds. *Ricki Lake. Shit.* He then called the Channel 2 News Bureau and explained that he was a police officer and needed to find out about the situation in Huntsville.

With as much information as was available, McClain calmly dialed the Wynne Unit and asked to speak with Jim James, a TDCJ negotiator he had once trained.

"I'm sorry, sir, but he's very busy at the moment."

"Tell him Richard McClain's on the phone."

The operator immediately put McClain on hold, no elevator music, no commercials, just a few, almost-inaudible clicks.

Three minutes later, "Lieutenant?"

"Yeah, Jim, how ya doin'?"

"Could be better."

"I heard. Listen, this teacher they took is a friend of mine. Any way we can get invited to help out?"

Rather tentatively, James responded, "Well, maybe. Let me make some calls and I'll see what I can wrangle. We really could use you."

"Thanks, I'll be waiting."

McClain and James both hung up at virtually the same moment.

*   *   *   *   *   *   *   *   *   *

Jim James made a quick call to his warden and explained that Houston's CNT had offered to assist in the negotiations. He also reminded him that McClain had trained the TDCJ negotiators and that the textbooks for continuing education in negotiations were all written by McClain. Reluctant, the warden finally relented and gave his permission, and James made the call to McClain.

*   *   *   *   *   *   *   *   *   *

At 12:20 p.m., forty-eight minutes after Janice Garling had phoned B. C., Richard McClain informed his captain about the invitation to assist in Hunstville.

"Sure. What are you going to need?"

"A team of snipers, a CP."

There was a momentary pause, then, "All right, we can do that, we'll still have three teams down here. Anything else?"

"I think that's it."

"Then call Jinks and set it up."

∗   ∗   ∗   ∗   ∗   ∗   ∗   ∗   ∗   ∗

Richard immediately phoned Brian Garling. "B. C.? We're assisting in Huntsville. Head out and I'll meet you up there."

"Great! We takin' anybody with us?"

"Portable CP and a couple of snipers."

"TDCJ's not gonna let us use 'em, are they?"

"They don't know about it. If we just show up with them, what're they gonna do?"

Garling smiled to himself. "OK. See you there."

∗   ∗   ∗   ∗   ∗   ∗   ∗   ∗   ∗   ∗

McClain left his office and sped up Allen Parkway toward I-45. Still within the Houston city limits, he reached over, grabbed the cell phone, and started punching in numbers. The first call was to Jinks Conrad, the captain in charge of the SWAT team.

"Cap'n, this is McClain over at CNT."

"What's up?"

"We got a call to go up to Huntsville. Cap'n here said to call you to set it up."

"What d'ya need?"

"A couple of your best snipers along with a mobile CP."

"All right, this's been cleared. Right?"

"Right from the top."

"Good. Anything else?"

"Nope, that's it."

"Hang on."

Thirty seconds later, Jinks got back on the line. "McClain?"
"Sir?"
"I'm sending Pelf up. He'll choose a coupla others from his team."
"Thanks, Cap'n. Listen, is Pelf there?"
"Hold on."

＊   ＊   ＊   ＊   ＊   ＊   ＊   ＊   ＊   ＊

Sergeant Adrian Pelfrey was the best marksman HPD had. After three tours of duty in Viet Nam as a sniper, he returned to an uncongratulatory American public and realized he couldn't do anything better than shoot. Thus, he signed up as a cadet with the Houston Police Department, went through what the other cadets felt was an excruciating six months of agony and then became a patrolman. After two years of chasing down speeders, dealing with spousal abuse cases, and directing traffic at auto accidents, Pelf was ready to pack it in and get on with his life.

Frustrated, he went to his lieutenant with the complaint that he wasn't being allowed to do what he did best. In only a slightly condescending tone, the lieutenant asked, "And, Adrian, what *do* you do best?"

"I'm a marksman, Sir."

Going over Pelf's files, the lieutenant did note an unusually high score on the rifle range although his score at the pistol range was only adequate. Since he had been an exemplary officer, never having made an "unclean" arrest and never having had any complaint placed in his personnel "jacket," the lieutenant told him just to hang in there a while, that things usually worked themselves out.

Two months later, the lieutenant summoned Pelf into his office.

"Adrian, there's a position coming open at SWAT in a few weeks. You might want to put in an application."

Pelf waited for the formal announcement, then, with a strong letter from his lieutenant, got an interview with Jinks Conrad. He outlined his experiences in Viet Nam, mentioned his Bronze Star, and directed Conrad's attention to his scores on the rifle range.

Jinks was impressed, and after the intense psychological screening that every potential SWAT officer receives, Pelf was placed in training. Three months later, thirty days of climbing barricades, hurdling through the obstacle course, being tested on the rifle range, and being repeatedly harassed by Conrad and others, Pelf became part of the SWAT team.

It was not an easy task. As Pelf noted, all the other SWAT team members were young, lean, and mean. Children of the '60s who had been too young to serve in Viet Nam, they were not yet daunted by the advent of adulthood, they still possessed the exuberance and energy of their youth. Realizing this, Pelf competed with extra effort, and with his scores on the rifle range, had ended up close to the top of the class. He was assigned as a marksman, what he had been years before, and now reveled in what he felt was his true calling.

Two years after his assignment to SWAT, Pelf was promoted to sergeant. A year later, because of his abilities and also the normal matriculation in and out of SWAT, his captain put him in charge of all of the marksmen on the team. At the time of the siege in Huntsville, Pelf was fifty-eight years old, an old man in a young man's game, but as McClain and Conrad both knew, he was the best. In thirteen years as a "sniper" Pelf had never made a mistake, had never missed a suspect, and had never wounded a hostage.

In all honesty, Adrian Pelfrey had grown to hate his job. He loathed being both judge and jury to suspects who were in their own reality. They were, without exception, either high on drugs, mentally incompetent, or stressed beyond the limit. And he was their executioner. What he loathed more, though, was the assault on, and all too often, the demise of an innocent victim—an estranged wife, a girlfriend caught cheating, or just an innocent bystander in the wrong place at the wrong time. Pelf hated this more, so he performed his job and performed it efficiently. As he viewed it, the job was a necessary evil, perhaps even *he* was a necessary evil.

*   *   *   *   *   *   *   *   *   *

The phone in Richard's hand clicked and Adrian Pelfrey came on the line.

"Lieu, I hear you got a job for me."

"Yeah, we need you and two of your snipers up in Huntsville. Wynne Unit. You up to it?"

"Yeah. When?"

"Right away, I'm already on 45 headin' north."

"All right, we'll leave in a few minutes. If you get there before we do, get me all the usual stuff. Maps of the compound, vantage points, a description of where they're holed up. Everything. We'll be up there by, say, two-thirty."

"The other two snipers, make sure they're very good."

"Lieu, they're all good."

*   *   *   *   *   *   *   *   *   *

A second call was to McClain's wife, Jennifer.

"Hey, Babe, I just got a call-up. So don't hold dinner."

"Richard, when do you think you're gonna get home?"

"Don't know, but it's probably gonna be late."

"All right. There'll be a casserole in the fridge. If I'm asleep, just throw it in the microwave."

"Jen, I want you to do something. Go over and see Ellen Christopher. I think she's gonna need someone with her tonight."

Jen was puzzled. "Why? What's goin' on?"

"Just do it. Please. I'll explain it to you later."

"Richard, what's going on?"

"Um, Thom's had a problem. And I've gotta go and help straighten it out."

"What happened? Was he in a wreck?"

"Hon, I can't talk about it right now. Just go over and see Ellen."

"But…."

"Do it." And Richard hung up before she could continue to argue the point.

∗   ∗   ∗   ∗   ∗   ∗   ∗   ∗   ∗   ∗

Ellen Christopher jumped when the phone next to her hand blared out.

"*Hello*," she nearly screamed.

"Ellen, this is Richard."

"Oh, God, Richard, did you hear?"

The officer slowly spoke. "Yes, but calm down. He'll be all right. I'm on my way up there right now and I'll get him out and bring him home."

The young woman choked forth her words, "Richard, I don't know what to do. Please help him. "

"He'll be all right. We'll get him. You stay where you are. As soon as I have him out, we'll have him call you. So don't leave the phone and don't worry."

She became even more frantic, "What do you mean 'Don't worry?' He's my husband."

"Ellen, just take it easy. I'm going to bring him home."

"Richard, *please* be careful with him."

"Oh yeah, Jennie's on her way over. She should be there in a half-hour or so. You just stay where you are."

She was crying softly now but agreed, "OK, Richard, and thank you."

"You just stay calm and stay put."

∗   ∗   ∗   ∗   ∗   ∗   ∗   ∗   ∗   ∗

A final call was to B. C. Garling's cell phone.

"McClain here."

"Yessir."

"Where are you right now?"

"Just past 1960 on 45."

"All right. You're about thirty minutes ahead of me. Get off at Exit 118 and wait for me at the DPS station. We'll rendezvous in the parking lot and then go in together."

"I'll be there."

"Hey, B. C.?"

"Sir?"

"We're gonna get him out."

"Let's hope so."

"See ya there."

As Richard pressed the cellular's "OFF" button, the little voice in the back of his mind repeated B. C. Garling's last words, "Let's hope so."

CHAPTER 21

Ever since the argument between Menteur and Villareal about the phone, Thom could hear the running footsteps above him, the indecipherable voices of guards, and the muffled whop-whop-whop of helicopters over the unit. He occasionally saw the bound guard glancing at the ceiling. This was a good sign. They knew where he was and common sense told him it was only a matter of time. And they certainly weren't going to let one of their own get hurt.

Menteur and Villareal appeared more agitated while Samuels remained the same, serenely sitting on his perch, blankly staring into the corridor.

* * * * * * * * * *

Thom thought about the computer wiz living in the wings near Samuels and how that could have been, could be, him. These thoughts were broken off by the twangy voice of Eddie Menteur who complained, "Fuck I'm starved."

Villareal immediately yelled, "Shut up, faggot."

"No! *You* shut up, motha-fucka. I'm hungry."

Samuels slowly turned from his perch and matter-of-factly told Eddie to quit bitchin'.

Eddie blurted out, "Hey, they *gotta* give us food."

Samuels responded. "They don't *gotta* give us shit."

"Yeah? Well, they're gonna feed *their* guard, ain't they? And what about the Doc?"

Turning, Eddie yelled, "Hey, Doc, you hungry?"

"Leave him alone. We'll need him later."

Thom only stared at the floor.

"No! We need him now. What's gonna happen if he asks for food, anyway?"

"…Yeah, maybe."

Villareal then entered the conversation. "Let him do it, whatta we got to lose?"

Under Samuels' watchful eye, Villareal, with the gun barrel pressed sharply into Thom's back, marched the hostage down the corridor to the guard's station and handed him the phone receiver.

"No fuckin' around. Short. Sweet. We want food. Got it? You fuck around and you get hurt real bad."

A nod was the only response.

As Jesús dialed four numbers, an elation took over as Thom heard a voice on the other end say, "Who's this?"

He started to speak but couldn't utter a word. The knot in his throat grew so quickly he thought it would explode. Finally, Thom managed to get out an almost inaudible squeak, just as Villareal ripped the phone from his grasp.

"That was the Doc. Him and the guard are hungry and want food down here. He says send enough for all of us."

"Who is this?"

"Don't you worry about who this is. If Mrs. Palmer's up there, put her on the phone."

The guard on the other end of the line signaled his sergeant who quickly got Shirley Palmer to the phone. She spoke quickly and in a shaking voice. "How's Roy? Is my husband all right?"

Villareal thought, *Your old man's a goner, honey,* then answered, "Yeah, Mrs. Palmer, he's OK but we want you to get some food down here. Otherwise who knows what we might do?"

Pleadingly, the woman said, "Please don't hurt my husband."

"Ma'am, just get the food down here, pronto and he'll be all right." And then the phone went dead.

Thom turned and, with Jesús on his heels, slowly trudged back to his own living Hell. When he sat down, he realized for the first time, tears were streaming down his cheeks.

CHAPTER 22

By mid-morning, Friday, the press had arrived, *en masse*, at the Wynne Unit. Reporters came from Houston, Dallas-Fort Worth, Austin, and San Antonio. Even CNN had dispatched a representative with a camera crew. Earlier in the day, the entrance to the unit had been sealed off with the order that members of the press were to be kept at arm's length. Thus, the news vans arrived and the drivers were directed to the parking lot of the County Sheriff's Office, just across FM 2821 from the prison. Here, the *major* reporters sat in their air conditioned vans nursing their cold Perriers, waiting for something, anything, to happen. Outside, the cameramen, the lighting crews, and the news gofers were busy scurrying around in the oppressive heat and humidity, setting up all the equipment needed to get not only the first but the best video of the siege.

＊　＊　＊　＊　＊　＊　＊　＊　＊　＊

As the day wore on, activity around the compound became more and more chaotic. There were several news helicopters in the vicinity of the prison although none was permitted to fly directly overhead. Most circled the unit until they were low on gas, then landed at the Huntsville Airport, directly north of the prison, to refuel. From here, they re-ascended, hovering for a second, then quickly darting to the right or left as if they were part of a swarm of dragonflies preparing for the feast.

A few of the airborne crews toured the town from air and filmed file footage of several of the other units. Who knew when something this big might happen at the Walls, Estelle, Goree, Holliday, or Ellis? Best to be ready, get the scoop, and beat the competition. For the residents of Huntsville, the constant whop-whop-whop of the news crews served as a consistent reminder that something major was happening in town.

Traffic along FM 2821 was almost at a standstill. Every high school kid in town had his pick-up parked either on the shoulder across from the prison, in the parking lot of Kate Barr Ross Park that abutted the western edge of the Wynne, or along one of the little dirt side roads scattered throughout the vicinity. Each pick-up came with its usual assortment of ornaments: two teenagers in the cab, three or four standing in the bed peering over the roof of the passenger compartment, all with high-powered binoculars just to get a better look, a case of Busch carefully hidden behind the driver's seat, and more than occasionally, a .22 caliber pistol in the glove box. Intermixed among these vehicles were the blue and red pizza delivery trucks, trying to make their way to the hungry news crewmen who had placed their orders via cellular phones hours before. And then there were the rubber-neckers, those who just happened to be traveling down 2821 and had to take a long, piercing look to the right or to the left, thus failing to see the car directly in front of them that had just come to a complete stop. It was a nightmare.

*   *   *   *   *   *   *   *   *   *

All day, as shifts of employees arrived and left, guards, civilian workers, and anyone else with a right to be at the prison were fair game for the media.

"Sir, do you have any information about what's going on inside the compound? Can you give us an interview?"

"Ma'am, we'd like to interview you for Channel 26. Could you give us a few minutes of your time?"

"Can you give us an update?"

"How much longer do you think it's going to be?"

The reporters were always rebuffed, though, either because the employees didn't know the answers to their queries or they knew the consequences of giving out sensitive information. Regardless, anytime anyone entered or left the compound, the newsmen tried anew.

✳   ✳   ✳   ✳   ✳   ✳   ✳   ✳   ✳   ✳

The media also swarmed onto the campus of Texas State University in Conroe. Members of the press requested interviews with the various university vice presidents, several deans, the Psychology Department chairperson, and a number of Thom's colleagues and current and former students.

The official university approach to the situation was "No comment," but after some prodding, Thom's chairman granted his one and only interview.

"Dr. Bryant, what do you think about the hostage situation up in Huntsville?"

"What do you mean 'What do I think?'? It's awful, of course."

"Can you tell us a little about Dr. Christopher?"

"Sure. He is well-liked by the students and has some of the highest teaching evaluations in the department. He has published several very good articles and he has several students working with him."

"Can you tell us about his emotional state?"

A flash of anger now surfaced. "Well, what *exactly* do you mean?"

"He's probably undergoing a lot of stress. Do you think he can handle it?"

Dr. Bryant finally snapped, "He's a psychologist! Of course he can handle it! And this interview is over."

   * * * * * * * * * *

In the University Administration Building a low-level payroll clerk made a call to his immediate superior.

"Mr. Swanson, this is Greg down in records."

"Yes, Greg. What's the problem?"

"Well, I don't know what to do about this Christopher thing. He's not here and probably won't be for a while. How do I handle it?"

"Handle what?"

"How I'm supposed to fill out his forms? Do I deduct hours from his vacation account or should it go on sick leave? I'm really not sure how to do this, it's never happened before."

"You idiot! What the hell's wrong with you? We've got a lot more things to worry about than balancing your damn budget sheets."

The young clerk was immediately cowed. "Yes, Sir. I didn't mean anything. I just didn't know what to do."

"Well, try *thinking* for a change."

Swanson slammed down the phone and his subordinate went back to his budget sheets.

   * * * * * * * * *

At 4:00 p.m. Friday, the president of the university issued a brief statement.

"The University and the community are very concerned that one of our own has been placed in a situation such as has occurred in Huntsville. We all pray for the safe return of Dr. Christopher and for the safe release of the guard. We have every faith that the police and other law enforcement agencies are doing their utmost to procure a peaceful end to this event. As far as the University is concerned, all classes will meet as scheduled and all offices will remain open. Thank you for your time."

*   *   *   *   *   *   *   *   *   *

By evening word of the siege was widespread. The amount of news coverage and several anonymous phone calls from the Post Oak section of Houston had alerted every "social action" group in the state and almost all had descended upon Huntsville for a chance at free publicity. As the 6:00 p.m. news programs gave the latest updates and scanned the compound, viewers could read amidst the sea of placards in the foreground the messages, "Abortion is Murder," "Capital Punishment is a Crime," "It's a Woman's Right to Choose, NOW," and "Fry the Cons." One group of heavily tattooed Hispanic males from the Glenmont section of Houston even carried a home-made sign saying, "Free El CID;" all of this merely because of the free air time unwittingly donated by the local affiliates.

The next morning the scene remained much the same with a few exceptions. The news vans still crowded the parking lot of the Sheriff's Department but the caravan of pick-ups was missing; the deputies, in all their wisdom, closed FM 2821 to all but emergency and police traffic. But this action merely diverted the mainstream of chaos to Kate Barr Ross Park where curious onlookers peering through binoculars spent their time pacing the outer limits of the prison itself. Some had erected tents, some had slept in their cars or in the back of pick-ups. Most had gone home late the night before and managed to arrive before dawn the next morning. In addition, as one scanned the area around the compound, he noticed the "new" entrepreneurs. Several young adults now opened up businesses selling T-shirts with slogans such as, "I Survived the Siege in Huntsville," or "Huntsville, Home for Hostages." Some hawked cold drinks while others offered Polaroid pictures of the buyer with the Wynne Unit in the background. The chaos of the preceding day's carnival had evolved into a full-fledged circus.

CHAPTER 23

Jennifer McClain pulled into the Christopher driveway just in time to see a near-hysterical Ellen dashing from the house.

"Jen. I have to do something about Amy. Before she hears what's happened. Please."

A moment later, the two sped up I-45, exited at Tamina Road, and made a right into Oak Ridge High School where Jennifer pulled her Chevy mini-van up to the southwest entrance, amid several orange school buses. Urgently, Ellen screamed out, "No, it's over at the other side."

"OK, Ellen, we'll get there. Just hold on."

When they arrived at the south entrance, Jen's five-foot-seven-inch svelte frame had to spring from the car to catch Ellen before she got to the front door. Putting her arm around her friend's shoulder, she said softly, "Ellen, let *me* explain the situation. Then, we'll get Amy and everything will be all right."

Ellen acquiesced but the tears welled up again as they went into the building.

"The office is on the right."

"It's OK, Ellen. Let me handle it."

When they opened the door to the office, Joan Blalock, the secretary, jumped up, "Mrs. Christopher. Um...I'm really sorry. Amy's down with the counselor. I'll have her here in a minute."

Ellen again felt the panic. "What does she know? What did you tell her?"

Leading her to a chair, Jen said in a measured voice, "Ellen, it's all right."

"No, she's my baby. I have to explain it to her myself." Then, turning to the secretary, "What did you tell her?"

"When we heard the news we felt she'd be better off in the counselor's office. She doesn't know anything. She'll be down in a second."

Ellen stared straight at the floor, a glazed look in her eyes. When she looked up, Amy was there, standing at the door.

"Momma, why're you here? What's wrong?"

She went to her daughter and placed her hands around her shoulders. "Everything's all right, Baby. We're just going home."

"*Why?* What's going on? Why can't I go back to class?" The girl's eyes searched her mother's face and Jennifer immediately intervened. "Honey, your mom needs you at home. Everything's all right, but we're going to take you back to the house."

Seeing the tears in her mother's eyes, the young girl sensed danger. "What's happened? Something's very wrong. What is it?"

Jennifer turned to the frightened child, "Let's just go. We'll talk about it in the car."

"No. I need to know. Let me know. *Now!*"

"Please, Jen, let me handle this. Amy, Dad was at the prison and he ran into some trouble. But he's OK."

"Is he home?"

"No, he's still in Huntsville."

Tears streaming down her face, she screamed, "No! He's dead, isn't he?"

Ellen, suppressed all the stress of the past few hours, and with a firm resolve, looked at the girl. "Don't *ever* say that. He's OK. He's coming home. He has to." And then she hugged her child and both broke down.

✳   ✳   ✳   ✳   ✳   ✳   ✳   ✳   ✳   ✳

Nearing the house, Ellen, Jen, and Amy spotted several vans, sporting TV and radio logos, along with the usual paraphernalia: cameras, microphones, spotlights, and those ever-present, curious gawkers. In the driveway, Ellen couldn't move and Jen, jumping out of the car, went to the passenger door, pulled both her and Amy out, shielding them from the media onslaught. By now, both Ellen and Amy were again in tears.

Ellen collapsed onto the sofa but was jolted upright by a ringing phone. Jen leaped, grabbed the receiver, and spoke. "Mrs. Christopher has nothing to say. Please don't call here again."

Hanging up, Jennifer placed a hand on Ellen's shoulder. "Just a reporter wanting to talk."

"Can't they understand?"

"Ellen, they only understand making their deadlines. This is a big story."

The phone rang repeatedly, each time with the same result. Finally, Jen said she was going out to put an end to this, once and for all. She left through the side door where the press mobbed her.

"Is Mrs. Christopher all right?"

"Will she talk to us?"

"When was the last time she saw her husband?"

"Has she spoken with the guard's wife yet?"

Jennifer stood there for a second, and composing herself, appealed to their sense of decency, "Please. Mrs. Christopher is going through a traumatic experience. She cannot speak with you right now but when her husband is released they'll both come out and answer all your questions."

"Would she like to make a plea to the prisoners on TV for her husband's safe return?"

Jen snapped back, "Not now. It's not the time."

She then muscled her way through the masses to her car where she opened the passenger door and took out a small attaché case. Amidst numerous microphones and cameras, Jennifer knifed her way back to the side door where she pushed aside two photographers and entered.

"Ellen, take the phone off the hook."

"What? Why? What if they call?"

From the attaché, Jen pulled out a cellular phone, dialed Richard's beeper, then punched in a code for him to call her. Five minutes later the mini-phone beeped and Jen responded.

"Yes?"

"Jen, is Ellen OK?"

"No, but she's hanging in there. Are you in Huntsville yet?"

"No, another half hour or so."

"Well, this place is a zoo down here. Reporters everywhere. We took the phone off the hook, so call us on the cellular."

"OK. But I probably won't say much."

"Understood."

Both Richard and Jen knew that various members of the media, along with not-so-well-meaning private citizens, could easily tune in on scanners and monitor calls from cellular phones. Unfortunately, the fourth amendment didn't protect these conversations so the two were always especially careful when they spoke on the cellular.

"OK. I'll talk to you later."

"Bye, Hon."

                *   *   *   *   *   *   *   *   *   *

Jennifer turned to Ellen. "Richard'll keep us up to date through the cellular."

"What did he say? Is Thom all right?"

Contriving something reassuring, Jen McClain told a small white lie. "He isn't there yet but he said he'd take care of everything. Don't worry, he'll have Thom out as quickly as he can."

Ellen trembled as she turned to Amy and held her close.

CHAPTER 24

McClain sped down the ramp at Exit 118 and spotted B. C.'s city car sitting in the DPS lot. Honking once, he rolled down the window and asked, "You ready to go?"

"Yeah, let's do it. I'll follow you in."

McClain pulled onto Highway 75, drove the requisite half-mile, and turned into the Wynne Unit driveway where an armed sheriff's deputy flagged him down. He showed his I.D., quickly explained who he was, and entered the compound with B. C. close behind.

Both men pulled into the employee parking lot, locked their cars, then walked up to the picket.

"Ma'am, I need to speak with Jim James. He told me to call him when I got here."

"Name?"

"McClain."

She checked her logbook. "Hold on, I'll have to call in."

Five minutes later, in the stifling heat and humidity, Jim James walked briskly out of the main building, across the yard, and through the gates. "Lieu, thanks for coming up."

"Thanks for inviting me. How's it look?"

"Not bad. They're holed down in the Education Section."

McClain was a little impatient. "And?"

"Well, they're in the lounge area. No windows, but it is surrounded by glassed-in classrooms. It's absolutely indefensible."

"So why haven't you done anything yet?"

"We were gonna use flash grenades, but we got the guard and that civilian down there. We figure if we can talk 'em out we can keep everybody in one piece."

McClain sighed, "Yeah, well, let's end this shit in a hurry." He then motioned toward B. C. and said, "Oh yeah, this is Sergeant Garling. He's with me."

     *   *   *   *   *   *   *   *   *   *

The three officers proceeded through the gates, up to the main building, and through the glass doors. Upon entering, Garling reeled. "Christ, what's that smell?"

"Sorry, it's just prison."

After arriving at the warden's office they sat down to discuss the situation.

"How long they been in there?"

"Since eight last night."

"Then they gotta be gettin' hungry."

"Well…." The word hung in the air.

"Well *what*?"

"They called out a couple hours ago and asked for some food."

"So?"

James was almost apologetic. "Well, a guard took 'em something to eat."

McClain just shook his head. "That's just great. Fire the fuck."

"Can't. Her husband's the guard they grabbed."

"Ah, shit, that's all we need."

"Look, as soon as we realized what had happened, we got her over to Psych Services."

"Good. Keep her there. Now, have they got any weapons down there?"

"Don't know."

"All right, let's play it safe. We need maps of the entire compound. Locations of the pickets, all the doors in and out of the building, windows, every stinkin' bush, tree, everything."

"No problem. That's all in the next room."

"Also, the psychological profiles. Do you know these guys at all?"

Now James appeared more than a little irritated. He muttered, "Profiles are on the way, I called for them right before you came in."

Well, everything looks pretty much under control. How do you want to handle it?"

"Sir, you trained me. You do what you need to. It's your call."

"Then let's get to work. Oh, by the way, some friends of mine are gonna be up here early this afternoon. Can you make sure they pass through without any problem?"

"Sure, who are they?"

"Just some officers I work with."

"HPD?"

"Yeah."

James made another call informing the officer at the gate to wave anyone from the Houston Police Department into the compound. James, McClain, and Garling then walked over to the office next door where the sergeant dug out the maps of the compound from an ancient file cabinet and handed them to Richard. McClain took a quick look at them and then started walking out of the building, back into the yard.

"Man, it's hot. They don't have air conditioning down there do they?"

"No, Sir, we cut that off this morning."

"Let's keep it that way."

Garling, virtually silent during the whole meeting with McClain and James, suddenly chimed in, "Hey, Lieu, there's the CP."

"Good. Go tell Pelf I need to see him."

B. C. went over, talked with the driver momentarily, and three heavily armed men, dressed completely in black, with bulletproof vests and SWAT caps emerged from the van.

James stared at the menacing figures. "Richard, those are *your* guys?"

"Yeah."

"They're snipers."

With only the hint of a very faint smile, McClain quietly said, "Well, yeah."

             *   *   *   *   *   *   *   *   *   *

Washington, D. C.

FBI Assistant Director James Vernon answered the phone on the first ring. "Yes?"

"Sir, they've brought in some hired help. Looks like a SWAT team from Houston and some guy who's a negotiator."

"All right, just stay out of everybody's way. Did you reconnoiter the area, pick an appropriate position?"

"Yes."

"Then just lay low for the time being. Nothing happens until Monday anyway. Tell me, what was the effect of the list of names you passed on to your man?"

"Worked like a charm. It's been a zoo up here."
Vernon smiled. "Good. Keep me informed."
"Will do."

CHAPTER 25

Jennifer McClain closed all the window shades, locked the doors, and took the phone off the hook. Thom's two Westies, Daisy and Beau, stood nervous guard at the front door, agitated by the mob of strangers on the other side. The media circus on the front lawn continued and the "prisoners" inside the house sat and waited. Amy, upstairs in her bedroom, was restless. With nothing else to do, she picked up the remote, aimed it at the television set, and hit the "ON/OFF" switch. Her first inclination was to press the "SCAN" button, for Thom had long since taught the child the necessity of channel surfing in the age of cable TV and satellite dishes. As he had always told her, "Who knows? You might be able to get a never-before released episode of Gilligan's Island." So, Amy surfed.

On her third sampling of channels, Amy's eyes became as large as saucers. She raced to the top of the stairs and screamed down, "Mom! Turn on Channel 2. It's our house. We're on TV."

Jennifer jumped, ran to the tube, and pushed the "ON" button. The two women sat and watched as a reporter summarized the day's events with a view of Ellen's home in the background. "…a tragedy unfolding. The two hostages, one from Huntsville and the other from this home in The Woodlands, have been held since early last evening. We do have a confirmed report that a Houston Police SWAT team has been requested to intervene in the situation and that they are on the scene at this time. We switch you now to Susan Lennon in Huntsville but we'll continue our live report at six o'clock. Until then, this has been Rob Johnson with our News 2 Team coverage."

The scene quickly switched to an attractive reporter standing in a parking lot. Several large buildings loomed directly behind her. "Behind me is the Wynne Unit of the Texas Department of Criminal Justice and the large building in the background is where the two hostages are being held. There's no word yet as to their conditions, and prison officials, along with the police, are refusing comment at this time. We're going to return now to our news desk but will keep you updated as the situation up here unfolds. This is Susan Lennon, reporting live from Huntsville."

Ellen stared directly at the TV, captivated by the image on the screen. Even when the commercial came on she didn't move, she only stared, fixated by what had just been there. After several seconds, she said out loud to no one in particular, "Please turn it off. I've had enough."

Pulling herself up from the couch, Ellen Christopher, for one of the few times in her life, felt inadequate; her husband needed help and she was incapable of doing anything to alleviate his suffering. What *could* she do?

"Look, Jen, this place is driving me nuts. I can't stand it. The walls are closing in on me. I have to do *something*."

"I know how you feel…."

Unexpectedly, she spat back, "No you don't. No one can know what it feels like."

Jen defensively retorted, "El, I was there six years ago when Richard got shot. We didn't know if he was going to live or die. You weren't here then, but it was really horrible."

Tears welled up again. "I'm sorry. You've been great. I just don't know what to do."

"Listen, it's going to be OK. Richard will have Thom home in no time and everything will be back to normal."

"Do you really think so?"

"Absolutely. Richard's a pro."

As Ellen paced furiously around the room, Jennifer did her best to alleviate the tension, "Hey, isn't it time for dinner? How about we scramble up some eggs for us and Amy?"

"Thom won't let her eat eggs. He says the cholesterol will kill her."

"Yeah, well, we'll do it anyway."

Ellen relented and the two went to the kitchen and prepared three omelets loaded with cheese, mushrooms, peppers, and whatever else they could find. During dinner Amy looked up and said, "When Dad gets home we better not tell him about this. He's really gonna be mad."

Ellen managed a wry smile. "We'll just keep it our little secret."

After dinner, with the plates neatly lined up in the dishwasher, the *angst* hit again. "Jen, I have to get out of here. Can't we go up to Huntsville? Maybe Thom needs me."

"*NO!* Absolutely not. What are you going to do up there? That's the worst thing you can do."

"Well. I can't just sit here and do nothing."

"Going up there will only cause problems." She then immediately changed the subject. "How about the gardens around the pool? It's still light enough outside. Why don't we go out and rip out some weeds?"

Again Ellen bristled. "I got rid of the weeds three days ago."

"All right, calm down. Then, let's just go and sit out there. You need some fresh air and quiet. Come on."

Ellen relented and the two women, with Amy upstairs watching *Wheel of Fortune,* went through the sliding glass door and sprawled on the lounges next to the swimming pool, the two dogs protectively at their feet.

Outside, Ellen seemed to relax, just a bit. "Jen, you know, Thom was dead set against this pool. He always said it was too expensive, that the dogs would be drinking out of it all day, and that he'd . . ." her voice broke, "he'd probably be the first to drown in it."

Jennifer picked up the mood. "Yeah, but he always bragged to Richard that he had a lot less grass to cut."

"He was always the first one in there after work, sitting in his stupid floating chair with his Coors Light in the armrest until the middle of the night. Last summer he spent virtually every day just getting tanned in the stupid thing."

"Do you remember that time he sat out there all summer then tried to pass himself off as a Native American just so he could get a government grant to pay for his research?"

Jennifer McClain laughed out loud, and a second later, Ellen let out a long sigh. "What am I gonna do?"

"Well, you're going to get through this. By tomorrow it'll all be over and everything will be back to normal."

The pleasant, soothing conversation was abruptly interrupted by a bright spotlight coming over the wooden fence, the growling of Beau, the shrill barking of Daisy, and the loud voice of a newsman yelling. "Mrs. Christopher. Mrs. Christopher. Can you give us an interview?"

Jennifer bolted out of the chair, furious with this intrusion, and screamed, "Look, *why* won't you people leave us alone? What do you expect us to tell you?"

Oblivious to Jen's plea, the reporter yelled, "Mrs. Christopher, we'd like to talk to you."

Jen raced toward the fence and, with fire in her eyes, shouted, "Get out of here. NOW!"

As several more spotlights now reflected off the top of the water in the pool, Jen, grasping Ellen by both shoulders, hustled her into the house.

"God, Jen, is no place safe?"

＊　＊　＊　＊　＊　＊　＊　＊　＊　＊

On the ten o'clock news, the Christopher house again served as the backdrop for the lead story. The report was much the same as before, although during this broadcast the newsman was interviewing the slightly stooped, retired Mr. Sumter, from across the street. Ellen's whole body felt numb as she watched the broadcast.

"Again, we're coming live from the home of Dr. Thom Christopher in The Woodlands with an exclusive interview. This is Russell Sumter, a neighbor of the Christophers.

"Mr. Sumter, what's been the response around the neighborhood to the events of the past twenty-four hours?"

"Well, of course, we're all just heartsick. Both Thom and Ellen are good friends of just about everyone on the block and we pray for his safe return."

"Have you had any contact with Mrs. Christopher since this tragedy started to unfold?"

"No. Shirley, my wife, tried to call several times but the phone's been busy."

"What can you tell us about Dr. Christopher?"

"What do you mean?"

"Was he well-liked? Did you spend a lot of time with him?"

"Oh, yes. Everyone in the neighborhood liked him." Turning to the camera, Mr. Sumter spoke directly, "Ellen, if you're watching this, we're all praying for you and know that Thom will be home safe and sound in no time at all." And then turning back to the reporter, he quipped, "Now I have to go."

"Thank you for your time, Mr. Sumter."

With that, the neighbor turned, and shaking his downcast head, walked back into his house. The camera again zeroed in on the reporter who quickly added, "This has been an exclusive interview from Channel 2 News. We return now to our newsroom. This is Rob Johnson reporting live from The Woodlands."

Tears streamed down Ellen's face and a moment later Jennifer disappeared into the kitchen and brought out a small plastic bottle with the words *Diazepam, 5 mg* on the label. Handing Ellen a small yellow tablet along with a glass of water, she ordered her friend to take it, saying it would relax her. Ellen did so, and thirty minutes later, in her own bed, she mercifully drifted off to sleep.

CHAPTER 26

❀

When Richard had finished setting up the microphones in the vents leading to the Education Section, he walked outside and saw Jim James, who was in the midst of positioning a TDCJ marksman. After James completed his instructions, McClain approached.

"Look, Jim. Who are those assholes down there, anyway?"

"Just regular convicts."

"Not students?"

"No."

"Then what were they doing down in Education?"

"Best guess is that they took the place of three guys who are now in the infirmary."

"Jesus, didn't anybody figure this out?"

"I don't know what happened. Whether the guard miscounted or didn't recognize what was going on. I just don't know."

Exasperated, Richard pressed on, "Didn't somebody figure that three guys in the infirmary couldn't possibly be in class?"

"It's a screwball system. The civilians who work in the Ed Section leave at four. Class lists typically aren't checked until the next morning. There're lots of little gaps."

"Wouldn't the guard have known there were extra people in the class?"

"He should have."

"What about the teacher? Wouldn't he be told there were people in the class that shouldn't have been there? Or that three of his inmate students were in the infirmary?"

"No, he wouldn't have had any idea. Unless an inmate told him."

You're kidding?! Look, I'm sorry to tell you this but this system up here is really fucked." Then he shook is head and relented ever so slightly. "I guess what's done is done, let's get to work. What's the phone number where these guys are being held?"

*   *   *   *   *   *   *   *   *   *

Richard McClain went to the top of the front picket and dialed the number. Jesús Villareal answered.

"Yeah, whaddya want?"

"This is Lieutenant McClain. I'm in charge of our operation out here so I'd like to talk to you about your situation. Who am I talking to?"

"This is Jesús Villareal. But anyway, what's to talk about? We're runnin' the show."

"Well, Jesús, I'm runnin' it out here and I need to know some things."

"Like what?"

"Like how the hostages are. Is anybody hurt?"

"The Doc and guard are fine. For right now."

"Can I talk to the Doc? What's his name?"

"I don't know. We just call him the Doc."

"Well, could I talk to him?"

"Not yet."

"Why 'Not yet.'?"

"Not yet 'cause he ain't comin' to the phone right now."

"Then when *can* I talk to him?"

"Fuck! I don't know. Later maybe."

"Well, how do I know he's OK?"

"Christ! You gotta take my fuckin' word for it."

"Well, I'm trying to work with you but until I know that the professor and the guard are all right, I can't do anything. You have to give me proof that they're OK."

Villareal thought for a moment, then told McClain to hold on. He went back to the lounge and retrieved Thom and said that someone wanted to talk to him.

The ensuing thirty seconds were interminable to Richard as he sat and waited. Finally, he heard the voice of his friend, "This is Thom Christopher."

"Thom, this is Richard. You all right?"

Thom's heart leapt. "Richard?!"

"Are you all right?"

"Oh, God, please help me."

McClain asked for the third time, "Are you all right?"

"Yeah, yeah, I'm fine."

"What about the guard?"

"He's OK."

"Do they have weapons down there?"

"I don't...."

With that, Villareal jerked the receiver away from Thom's ear and spoke. "OK. You got your proof. Everybody's all right. Now, how about we talk over our demands."

McClain paused, and said, "What demands?"

Pulling out a wadded-up piece of paper, Villareal read, "Here's what we want: an armored car. And make sure it's the real thing, not one of those fake ones. Safe passage to the Houston airport where you get a private jet waitin' for us. You got that?"

"Yeah, Jesús. Is that it?"

"Fuck, no. You nuts? We need passports. Use our TDC pictures, but the passports better be good. And money. Two-hundred-fifty-thousand dollars in U.S. bills with another quarter-mil in gold."

"Anything else?"

"No, that's it."

"Well, Jesús. All that stuff is gonna be tough. I'll have to pull a lot of strings."

"Hey, you don't meet our demands, the Doc and guard is gonna die. And those people on the outside is gonna die, too. And they're real important people."

McClain was stunned. "What are you talking about?"

"Yeah, man. You heard me. We got a guy on the outside holding some TDC family members. You don't get us what we want and they're goin' down, too."

Very calmly, Richard responded, "Jesús, exactly what are you telling me? Who's being held?"

"Hey, we ain't fuckin' around with this shit. Like I said, they're important. Also, don't try comin' down here. We got a bomb. Anybody tries to take us out, we let it blow. You get all our shit done by one o'clock on Monday or everybody dies."

"I don't know what you're talkin' about—these other people. You have to give me more information."

"You're gonna hear about it. Just wait."

"Are you gonna tell me about this or what?"

"Just meet our demands."

"Take it easy. I'll do what I can but you have to give me some time. It's Friday afternoon and the banks are gonna be closed for the weekend. We need more time."

"Look nothin'. We got a deadline. Understand?"

"Yes, I understand. Let me see what I can do and I'll have to get back to you."

Abruptly, the phone went dead.

*   *   *   *   *   *   *   *   *   *

Richard McClain, veteran of hundreds of hostage situations, sat in the small picket for a second, thinking. *A kidnapping? Nah, it's gotta be a bluff, these assholes aren't that smart.*

At that moment, Sergeant David Mays of the Huntsville Police Department jolted McClain from his thoughts. "Lieutenant, we just got a call on the radio. Somebody said he was holding Beth Singleton and her daughter at an undisclosed location."

"Who's she?"

"She's the wife of the warden over at the Goree Unit and the daughter of the Director of TDCJ."

"Shit. Well, did they get a trace?"

"No. It was all too fast."

"Maybe it's just a scam, a crank call."

"I called the warden's house. He doesn't know where they are. They were supposed to be over in College Station but they never showed up."

Richard slowly rubbed his temples. "Listen, Sergeant, you got the FBI alerted, right?"

"First thing we did."

"Does the TDC Director know?"

"Yessir, he's on his way."

"How's the warden?"

"About like you'd expect, I guess."

"OK, let me think about this for a while."

"Anything I can do to help out, Lieutenant?"

"Just make sure you bring the FBI guys to me as soon as they get here."

"Sure, Sir."

Sergeant Mays then descended the tower to await the arrival of the federal agents.

     *   *   *   *   *   *   *   *   *   *

From his office in the J. Edgar Hoover Building in Washington, D. C., James Vernon screamed into the phone, "What the fuck do you mean they snatched a woman and her kid? That wasn't in the plans. Has Garubba gone nuts?"

"Sir, all I know is what they're saying in the compound. Garubba's apparently decided to play this out with a few tricks of his own."

"Doesn't that asshole know our agents are gonna be all over the fuckin' place? You get a hold of your informant and you put a stop to this shit."

"I tried. He's not responding."

The Assistant Director blared again, "Well you keep on tryin' and for Chrissakes, stay away from anybody from the Bureau. Got it?"

Before he could answer, the phone in Philip Kimble's hand went dead.

CHAPTER 27

Richard called down on his cellular phone to the portable command post and B. C. Garling, who had been listening intently into a set of earphones. "B. C., did you get the whole conversation with that asshole?"

"Are these guys serious?"

"Looks like it. Somebody just grabbed a warden's wife and kid. B. C., we got a real problem here. Did you pick up any noise in the background from the mikes?"

"Not really. A couple voices. It was hard to tell what was goin' on. There wasn't much, they were talking real low."

"All right, did Psych Services deliver the profiles yet?"

"They just got here."

"Then get on the phone with anybody who might know these jerks. Parents, wives, girlfriends. Anybody. Get whatever you can so we can break 'em down. We gotta do somethin'. And soon."

"I'm on it."

*   *   *   *   *   *   *   *   *   *

Richard thought for several minutes, then punched in a number on his cellular phone. Villareal answered almost immediately. "Yeah, who's this?"

"This is McClain again. We need to talk."

"I told you, man. We got a deadline."

"Jesús, I'll do what I can do but I gotta have more time. If we take you to the airport we're gonna have to go through ten or fifteen different jurisdictions, I have to get their OKs to do that. I also have to have time to get the passports. It's just too complicated. There are too many problems. And the money's another bitch."

"That's you're problem, man. You do it or people are gonna die. One o'clock Monday."

Once again, the phone went dead.

*   *   *   *   *   *   *   *   *   *

When Villareal got back to the lounge, he turned to Samuels and Menteur. "I gave some cop our demands: armored car, half a million bucks, passports, and safe passage."

"And?" responded Menteur.

"He's workin' on it."

Eddie whined, "Well, what'd he say?"

"He said he needed more time and I told him he's got until Monday afternoon."

"Shit, Jesús. Give him more time."

"Hey, Menteur. That's not in the fuckin' plan and we're stickin' with the fuckin' plan."

*   *   *   *   *   *   *   *   *   *

Jim James, after checking with several his snipers around the compound, walked into the picket. "Lieu, you heard about the Director's daughter?"

"Yeah. Listen, I need a camera down there. I gotta take a look around. See what the set-up is. What kind of weapons they got."

"All right. I'll have some of my guys run a camera line down into the vents. We'll hook it up to a monitor in the warden's office."

"How long?"

"An hour, at most."

"Good."

"You think they have weapons?"

"They say they have a bomb."

"Shit."

"Yeah. So let's get goin' on the cameras."

Forty-five minutes later, Richard turned on a remote monitor and immediately saw the face and frame of Thom Christopher, sitting placidly on an old, worn couch. McClain hit a button and the figures of the three convicts came into view. Scanning the room, he also saw a large black briefcase on the floor next to Villareal. It wasn't Thom's, he always carried a small attaché. This piece of evidence was what chilled Richard McClain.

*   *   *   *   *   *   *   *   *   *

With the abduction of the two civilians, the FBI immediately helicoptered an agent in from Houston. Upon arriving, he was quickly ushered into the office where Richard McClain sat, gazing at a TV monitor.

"Lieutenant, I'm Ratley Mace from the FBI. I've been called in to handle the kidnapping case."

McClain looked up and asked, "So what're you doin' so far?"

"We're covering Highway 30 between here and College Station. We've got twenty field agents out there with choppers, bloodhounds, the whole nine yards. We have a lot of open pasture but the problem is there's a lot of forest out there, too. I'm not even sure we'll be able to find the woman's car right away. What kind of time line are we working on?"

"Deadline is one o'clock Monday afternoon."

"Or what?"

"Or they blow themselves up and have the woman and the little girl killed. Or so they say."

Ratley Mace breathed a sigh. "What are they asking for?"

"A Brink's truck, passports, jet waiting at Intercontinental, gold."

The agent gave Richard a rather incredulous look. "Right. And they think that's gonna happen? Put me on the phone, I'll straighten 'em out."

The sarcasm was not lost on Richard as he stood, got into the face of the FBI agent, and calmly, but with an air of authority, said, "Listen and listen good. These guys are serious. They're not fuckin' around. They got a bomb down there, they got hostages, and if it's true, somebody they're workin' with on the outside kidnapped a woman and a little girl.

"Now, I've been talkin' to one of 'em and I got my boys workin' on their backgrounds. We can probably bring this to a peaceful solution but if you're gonna go and 'straighten them out' over the phone, you're gonna get somebody killed. And that ain't happenin' on my watch."

"Lieutenant, this is Federal now. I need to talk to them."

"They're not gonna give you anything. They're not fuckin' around. They're dead serious."

Obstinately Mace looked at McClain, "Give me the number, Lieutenant."

"Look, I'll dial and set it up but you be goddam' careful."

McClain punched in the numbers on the phone, watched the monitor as Villareal looked up and left the room, and then waited for a response.

"McClain?"

"Jesús, I need to talk to you for a second. We have a guy here from the FBI. He wants a few minutes on the phone."

"What's he want? He workin' on our demands?"

"Just let me put him on for a second."

"Yeah. OK."

The policeman handed the receiver to the agent who, assuming a haughty tone of voice, said, "Villareal, this is Agent Mace of the FBI. We're investigating two possible kidnappings in this area and we have reason to believe you know something about them. Give us information for the safe return of the two civilians and we can help you out. Otherwise I cannot guarantee your safety."

"Hey, man, I don't give a fuck about your FBI shit. We give up those two people, we ain't gettin' outta here anyway. I figure as long as my buddies are holdin' 'em, you ain't gonna do squat. Now put McClain back on."

Ratley Mace handed the receiver back to Richard who said, "Yeah, Jesús."

"McClain. I don't wanna talk to that asshole no more. I talk to you and only you and that's it. If he calls here again I'm gonna blow this whole fuckin' place sky high. Got it?"

"I got it. Don't worry."

"You workin' on our demands?"

"Yes, Jesús, but it's taking time. I don't know if we can meet all your demands by Monday. We'll need more time."

"No way, man. That's the deadline."

An abrupt click ended the conversation.

McClain turned to the agent and spoke. "Mace, he says he doesn't want to talk to you anymore. I'm in charge up here right now and I can't put the hostages in any more jeopardy than they are already in."

Mollifying his tone, Richard said, "How about this? I'll deal with these guys in here, get whatever information I can, and you get whatever leads you can on the warden's wife. That way, we're attacking from both sides."

"Yes, you're probably right," Ratley conceded. "I'll keep in contact," he grumbled over his shoulder as he walked out the door.

CHAPTER 28

Twenty minutes after the departure of Agent Mace, the Director of the Texas Rangers walked into the warden's office and extended his hand.

"McClain, I'm Del Promeneur, Texas Rangers. Anything we can do to help you fellas out?"

McClain, taken aback by the Director's sudden appearance, looked up. "No, I appreciate it but things are pretty much under control, Director."

"Listen, call me Del and if you need any help I'll give you *carte blanche* with the Rangers," then turned and started to leave the small room.

"*Wait*, Sir."

"What is it, Lieutenant?"

"We got a real problem down there. First of all we got the hostages in the prison itself. They probably have a bomb down there and, since they didn't ask for any weapons in their demands, I figure they've got some guns. Then we have these two civilians that have apparently been kidnapped."

Del Promeneur stood quietly, considering this information as McClain continued, "I've seen the psych profiles of these guys and, except for Samuels, I don't see how they could have pulled something like this off. We've been watching the monitors and it looks like Jesús Villareal's in charge, but he's not all that smart. He's just an asshole gang banger. Besides, these guys are too goddam' calm. They ought to be climbing the walls by now but the fucks are just sittin' down there relaxin.'"

He paused. "The other thing is there's somethin' fishy goin on."

"How so, Lieutenant?"

"I've never been in a situation before where I couldn't buy more time. I've talked to Villareal several times and explained to him all of the logistical problems in meeting their demands. The asshole's adamant. One o'clock on Monday. He won't budge an inch. They *always* bargain and we get more time, but this is different. It makes no sense."

"All right, as I said, you have *carte blanche* with me and my Rangers. What do you need?"

"I could use a few very good snipers....And I'd like to get another armored personnel carrier."

"What?"

"That's one of the demands."

"You're gonna meet them?"

"No. They'll never make it but maybe we can get them out into the open."

"All right. Let me make some calls. I should have the snipers here by tomorrow morning and the vehicle by Sunday."

"Thanks, Sir."

"It's Del."

"OK, Del. Thanks."

CHAPTER 29

That evening, a few minutes after he and McClain had downed some cold fried chicken, Garling was back at the portable CP. The TDC Director and his son-in-law, the warden of the Goree Unit, both arrived and headed for McClain's quarters. The Director, a very large man, clad in a white cowboy hat and lizard-skin 'shit-kickers,' with a chaw of tobacco stuck in his lower lip, demanded to know what was happening with his daughter.

McClain shook his head in despair. "The FBI's taking care of that, Sir, an agent named Mace, Ratley Mace is in charge. He was here a while ago but went back out into the field."

"Did *he* question those assholes down there?"

"Tried to but they wouldn't talk to 'im."

In a tone conveying more threat than command, the Director demanded, "You get those little fucks on the phone right now cause I'm gonna find out what they did with my little girl and my grandbaby."

"Can't do it. Besides, it's somebody from the outside that got them. I doubt those shits even know anything."

The Director spat back, "Get 'em on the phone, *Lieutenant*."

The son-in-law quickly intervened, "Sir, Sergeant James says that the Lieutenant here is the best man to deal with this. I think we ought to trust him."

"Well then, Lieutenant, what exactly *is* your plan?"

"Sir, it would be best if you just went home."

He was irate. "Christ, we can't just leave. This is *my* fuckin' prison and we're gonna do somethin' to get my baby back."

Then, McClain saw the beginning of tears welling up in the Director's eyes. "All right, there is something. I need as much information on these guys as I can get. I have their psychological profiles and TDC histories right here. Sergeant Garling also has a set down in the command post, but he's busy doing other things."

"You want us to read their jackets." It was a statement.

"I want *you* to do that. Find out anything that shows a weakness, help us make one of 'em crack, or drive a wedge between 'em. You got that? And I want your son-in-law here to go home and sit by the phone. If the woman and child are released, or if the assholes who took them want to make a deal, that's probably the first place they're going to contact."

The Director turned and commanded, "Do as the man says, boy, go on home. I'll do what I can here."

McClain immediately responded, "Good," and pulled the three files off the top of the desk. Two minutes later, the Goree Unit warden was on his way home while his father-in-law sat in an office in the Wynne Unit, meticulously going over the information he had just received, looking for a clue, any clue, that would bring his family safely home.

Richard, alone again, was left to formulate his plan.

*   *   *   *   *   *   *   *   *   *

The late evening continued. McClain eventually got a few hours of fitful sleep on a couch in the Warden's Office while the Director of TDCJ dozed off with his head resting on the desk in front of him.

CHAPTER 30

Ellen Christopher dreamily awoke at 6:15 a.m., out of habit, reached for Thom. The void jolted her back into reality. *Oh, no, please don't let it be true.*

A few moments of disbelief later, she rose, went to the closet and pulled on a pair of jeans, socks, sneakers, and a clean white t-shirt. She slid her hair through the back of a baseball cap into a ponytail then peeked out the door and silently went to Amy's room. There, curled up in a heap of blankets, was her child, sound asleep and dead to the world.

Ellen only mouthed the words, "Be good, Amy. We'll be home later. I love you."

She descended the steps leading to the foyer, glanced into the living room and saw Jennifer, sound asleep on the couch, her hand cradling the cell phone. She tip-toed to the right, into the dining room and then on into the kitchen, where she took a small pad of paper and wrote a note.

Jen,
I had to run some errands. Please take care of Amy for
me, I'll be home later.
    Thanx,
    Ellen

She attached the note to the front of the refrigerator with a magnet and carefully left through the side door. Maneuvering her car around Jennifer's mini-van and the news trucks, now devoid of any signs of life, she set off, heading directly into the sun toward I-45. After a quick stop at Whataburger for a large coffee, she went under the overpass, made a left onto the feeder road, another left onto an entrance ramp, and then joined the fast-moving traffic heading north. Setting the cruise control at 80, Ellen was now dry-eyed, and her emotion had gone from despair and fear to determination and anger.

Fifteen minutes into the trip, the radio set on the oldies station played Rod Stewart's *Reason to Believe*. The song was high on the charts when Thom and Ellen were about to be married and just hearing it brought back a flood of memories. She remembered when she and Thom had first met. Both were students attending TCU, he in graduate school, she a senior French major. It was at a party just before spring break when they happened to bump into each other, going for one of the last few bottles of light beer. She had always described that moment when their eyes first met, when Thom's hand brushed against hers, when both were irretrievably smitten, a pure and simple *un coup de foudre*. The next day, both canceled their plans for spring recess and spent that week, and for that matter, the rest of their lives, as inseparable components. Two weeks later, they were married and the next fall, they moved, to where they both had found jobs, she as a French teacher and he as an Assistant Professor in a small, liberal-arts, college. During their first year there, Ellen discovered she was pregnant and eight months later, little Amy was born.

Passing FM 1488, Ellen thought about their honeymoon—how they had walked down the beach at dusk and at dawn, how they browsed through the small shops along The Strand, window shopping but not buying anything, and how they spent all night, every night, making love. As she thought of this, the indignation brought on by the idea that someone was about to take this away boiled over in her. *No! I won't let that happen.*

*   *   *   *   *   *   *   *   *   *

Ellen had only been to Huntsville five or six times in the past and had never taken the so-called "tour of prisons" touted on the highway billboards. Her sole purpose in going was to browse the various antique shops, where there were incredible bargains to be had. She knew, as did only a few others, that the prices of curios in Huntsville were always about fifty percent less than for the same collectibles in Galveston. Ellen had always kept this a secret, guarding her little "find."

When she passed the giant statue of Sam Houston, she realized she wasn't sure where the Wynne Unit was. So, at Exit 116, she pulled off the interstate onto the feeder, and then turned directly into the *Kettle Restaurant,* where sat the usual assortment of cowboys, shopkeepers, secretaries, and retirees. Approaching the counter, she waved down the waitress, a middle-aged woman with short blonde hair, who had a name tag identifying her as "Sally." "I have to get to the Wynne Unit?"

"Sorry, Hon, you can't get there from here."

"What?"

"It's all closed up. Ain't you been watchin' the news?"

Exasperated, Ellen pleaded, "Look, my husband's in there. I have to get there."

Sally studied Ellen's face. "You that teacher's wife?"

"Yes. How do I get there? *Please.*"

"Hon, they won't let you in."

At this point a young, man dressed in gray guard's attire came up and tapped Ellen's shoulder. "Ma'am, I can take you out there but, like Sally said, it's locked up tighter than a drum."

Ellen pleaded, "Please…I have to see for myself."

"OK. But there's nothin' you can do out there."

"But I have to see."

The guard gave a sigh, "All right. Where you parked?"

"Just outside."

"All right. I got that blue Chevy pick-up over there. Just follow me."

Involuntarily, she hugged him. "Thank you. Oh, thank you so much."

The two left and headed down the feeder, past the DPS station and onto 75N, all the way to FM 2821. At the intersection, the blue Chevy stopped at a DPS roadblock, the driver said something to the officer on duty, and both vehicles were waved through. As they made their way down the farm-to-market road, an arm came out of the driver's window of the truck and directed Ellen right, into the parking lot of the Sheriff's office. Both pulled in, weaving around the various news vans, and parked.

Ellen looked across the road, recognizing the scene immediately. It had been a thirty-second clip on the TV but the image was burned into Ellen's memory, never to be forgotten. She got out of her car and went up to the pick-up. "I can't tell you how grateful I am."

"Ma'am, you have a right to be here."

"Thank you again."

"You be careful."

And with that, the guard rolled up his window, pulled out onto the road, and was gone.

Ellen stood for a second and took in her surroundings. With the various political action groups and hawkers now banned from the immediate area, all she could see across the road were numerous police cars, a large, egg-shell blue van with the symbol of the City of Houston painted on the side, and what seemed now to be a collection of small, relatively insignificant buildings. From behind her, she heard a stern demand. "Lady, what the hell you doin' here? This place is off limits."

She turned and found herself face to face with a large, intimidating figure dressed in khaki brown and green. The insignia on his sleeve and the nameplate on his pocket immediately told her that this was a Walker County Sheriff's deputy.

"I have to get over there. My husband's in there." With an unmistakable smirk, the officer chided, "Well, Missy, that place is all locked down. I guess you'll just hav'ta visit hubby next week."

"No, you don't understand. My husband's being. . ."

Ellen was interrupted in mid-sentence by a familiar voice, "Deputy, I'll take care of this."

The young officer, a kid really, looked at Richard, then at lieutenant's bars, and then at the ground "Yessir. I didn't realize...."

* * * * * * * * * *

Richard hustled Ellen into the Sheriff's Department and then into an out-of-the-way alcove, gently pushing her into a chair. He looked down and asked, "What are you doing here?"

"I had to find out if Thom was all right. How...?"

"Jen called. And you can't stay. If the news media find out, they'll broadcast that you're here, and if those fucks down there hear of it, it'll be a lot harder."

"I can't leave. I have to be here. What if Thom needs me?"

"We're taking care of it. I've been talking with them and I'm pretty sure we can get Thom out without too much trouble. Your being here only complicates matters."

She locked eyes with him defiantly. "I'm not leaving. I'm not going back home. You can't make me."

He knew he was in a battle he couldn't win. "Christ, all right. You know anybody who lives in Huntsville?"

She groped, "Yes, I think so. There's some people who live over in that subdivision, Forest Hills or whatever. We went to a Christmas party at their house a couple of years ago."

"Who are they?"

Ellen groped again, "David and somebody Nelson."

"Good. Then I'm gonna call 'em. If they agree, you can stay there.

"But I have to stay *here*."

"Ellen, you got no choice."

She knew he meant business and relented with a weary sigh. Richard found the number and made the call. Since the subdivision was only two miles away, he packed Ellen into his own city car and delivered her personally to the Nelson household.

On the ride over, Richard explained the situation. "We'll get Thom out. We're negotiating and they're pretty receptive. We may do some things you don't understand but we've got the whole thing figured out. You have to just sit tight."

"I can't just sit there and wait."

Richard shot back, "Look. You do it my way. I know what I'm doing, done it a hundred times before. You'll sit in the goddamned house and you'll wait."

As Ellen began to cry, Richard eased off. "Listen, I'm sorry. I *can* do this but you have to let me do it my way."

CHAPTER 31

❀

With McClain seated behind the desk, B. C. strode to the office, sweating, but with a smile. "I got through to Samuels' wife, she's all upset. Says it can't be her hubby, he's not like that."

"Yeah, a wonderful guy. Exactly why the asshole's in prison."

"Anyway, Oklahoma State Police are picking her up. They'll transfer her to a DPS helicopter up near Gainesville and she'll get here late this afternoon."

"Good, we'll put her on the phone with "hubby" tonight, let the asshole sleep on it, and then work it out early tomorrow. Anywhere we can stash her?"

"Already done. They got a trailer for conjugal visits."

McClain shook his head. "Jesus, guess they can't let their little assholes get horny." Then, after a pause, he said, "Make sure it's all cleaned up and she's comfortable."

"I'm on it."

Garling was about to leave when McClain called and motioned him to sit. Richard picked up the phone, dialed a number, and a cellular unit in the portable command post rang.

"Pelfrey."

"This is McClain. Can you get over here with your guys?"

"Gimme a minute."

"Get that guy from the Rangers, too. Name's Promeneur."

"Yeah, all right. What's up?"

"I got a plan."

* * * * * * * * * *

Pelfrey, with three SWAT officers, clad all in black, along with Del Promeneur, entered the office. McClain motioned to the chairs then rose from behind the desk. "Here's the problem. We've got these three fucks down there holding Thom Christopher. Let's assume they have explosives and that they're armed. They've also gotten somebody to snatch the woman and her kid and the fibbies can't seem to locate them. Then we've got these bomb threats so that most of the TDC guys are running around like a bunch of fuckin' lunatics.

"Now, these assholes aren't smart enough to pull somethin' like this off, alone. And they're so fucking adamant about the deadline that its gotta be someone else pulling the strings. But who?

"Somebody wants one of 'em out. Ain't Menteur, he's a worthless piece of shit. Samuels? I don't know, he doesn't fit the bill. And Jesús? His gang ain't smart enough to pull something like this off. No. There's gotta be something else, something we can't see. Any ideas?"

No one said a word.

"All right. I've come up with a plan. The first thing we do is make sure we don't fuck this up and get Christopher, or the guard, killed.

"Samuels' wife might help, but if that doesn't pan out, we're goin' to let the whole thing play itself out. See what happens."

B. C.'s eyes widened. "You're gonna let 'em walk?"

"Yep. I don't really give much of a shit about those assholes but I want the hostages. Alive. Besides, worst case scenario, they ain't going very far, anyway."

Then it was Pelfrey's turn to speak. "So what's the plan, Lieu?"

"One o'clock on Monday, the assholes walk out, probably holding onto Christopher, the guard, and the bomb. Nobody bothers 'em." Nods came from the men around the room.

"They get into the back of the truck and we drive 'em down the interstate toward the airport. I'll be in the lead car."

"This is nuts, we're gonna let 'em walk outta here?"

"Shut up, B. C."

A moment of silence, and Promeneur asked, "What about all the traffic on 45?"

"We'll close it just north of Huntsville and south of Willis. DPS can divert all the traffic onto the feeders or other secondary routes."

"Why Willis?"

"There's a stretch around Exit 92 where the lanes divide. Both left and right are heavily wooded. There's also an overpass. They get just past the exit we hit a remote kill switch and the truck dies. Same time, we blow the doors open, and take 'em out.

"Del, can your bomb squad guys rig the truck? Make sure the kill switch works and have all the doors blow *out*?"

"Not a problem."

"Good. Anything else? Anybody?"

Tensing, Garling spoke slowly, "What about Christopher?"

"We make sure where he is and Pelf takes out whoever's closest."

"Pelf? You go down and map the area out, get the best vantage points, everything."

"First light tomorrow."

"Good. And take a few Ranger snipers with you."

"You guys do a dry run tomorrow, get everything worked out. For the real deal, set it up for Monday morning. Twelve-thirty DPS will shut down the interstate.

"Questions?"

"What about the woman?"

"Fuck, B.C., we can't control everything. And besides, maybe the Feds will come up with something."

McClain again turned to Promeneur. "Can you talk with Mace from the FBI, see if he can set up a scam with passports and all that shit? However they do it."

"Sure."

"B. C., call up the various jurisdictions for traffic control. But don't breathe a word of the plan."

"Yessir."

"OK. Let's get to work."

As the men left the office, the TDCJ Director was summoned. "Sir, we're getting a visitor in a couple of hours, Samuels' wife."

"Yeah, I know. Your sergeant told me."

McClain winced. "Could you have someone go in and clean up the trailer? Make sure the air conditioning works, put in a color TV? Let's try and make her comfortable, at least. Even get somebody from Psych Services come over and keep her company."

"I'm on it."

"Oh, sir. Any word from your son-in-law?"

"Not yet."

"You might send someone over there to talk to him."

"I already did."

"Good. We're gonna get this thing settled. No casualties."

CHAPTER 32

Barely five minutes after the meeting, McClain's beeper went off. He immediately called Jen's cell phone. "What's up?"

"Richard, what did you do with Ellen? She's calling here every five minutes."

Shit. "OK. I'll call her. How's Amy doing?"

"Stressed but hanging in there."

"Well, tell her I have everything under control."

"Do you?"

"Jen, you're on a cellular. It can be monitored."

"Sorry."

"Call you later. Bye."

"Bye, and I love…."

The phone went dead before the sentence was completed.

   ✶ ✶ ✶ ✶ ✶ ✶ ✶ ✶ ✶

McClain reached for the phone book, found the number of David and Laurie Nelson on Cherry Lane, and dialed. A male voice immediately came on the line. "Nelson residence."

"This is McClain, I have to speak with Mrs. Christopher."

"Yes, sir. Just a minute."

In a split second, Ellen's voice was on the phone. "Richard, is that you?"

"Yeah, we got everything under control over here."

"How's Thom?"

"I spoke to him. He's fine. Don't worry."

"Can I talk to him? I have to talk to him." The voice was almost pleading.

"No! You can't. We're negotiating and I've gotta keep everything under control. Just sit tight, we'll be done by tomorrow morning."

"Oh, God, not another night?"

"El, these things take time. He'll be OK, believe me."

Her voice cracked, "All right."

"Now put Nelson back on the line."

A disheartened Ellen merely said, "Just a second."

"This is Doctor Nelson."

"Listen, Doctor, keep her off the phone and keep her under control. At least until tomorrow. Can you do that?"

"Yes, sir."

"And keep her off the goddam' phone." Then with a slight smile, "Otherwise, I'll have to kill you."

"Yes, sir. "I'll do it, sir."

The conversation ended with a near-silent click.

*   *   *   *   *   *   *   *

Four hours later, McClain's phone rang again. "Samuels' wife's on her way in."

"Good, hey, what's her first name, anyway?"

"Carly."

B. C. led Carly Samuels, her eyes red and puffy, in to meet Richard. Motioning for her to sit, he started, "Mrs. Samuels, I'm Lieutenant McClain. Your husband is in a lot of trouble and we need your help."

She immediately blurted out, "It's not Elliott. It can't be him."

"Mrs. Samuels, Carly, it is your husband and we need your help. Can you talk to him on the phone for us?"

"It's not him. You've made some sort of horrible mistake."

McClain's tone became stern. "Can you do it?"

Carly wiped the tears from her eyes with the back of her hand and answered, "Yes, but I swear, it's not Elliott. I know it isn't."

Richard briefed Mrs. Samuels on what to ask, then punched in the numbers for the Education Wing. Ten rings later, he heard the response, "Yeah?"

"Jesús?"

"No, this is Eddie. Who da fuck is this?"

"This is Lieutenant McClain, Eddie. Can you put Samuels on the line?"

"Sure."

In the background, Richard heard a whining, "Hey, Samuels, phone's for you."

Without a blink, the voice of Villareal came out of the receiver. "McClain, whaddya want?"

"I need to talk to Samuels."

"Why?"

"His wife's here. She wants to talk to him."

"I don't think so, man."

Then, almost instantaneously, a voice unknown to Richard came on the line. "Who's this?"

"This is McClain. Are you Samuels?"

"Yeah, why?"

In the background, Richard heard the voice of Villareal, "You give anything up, man, and you're dusted." Then he heard some muffled whining, "I didn't do nothin'. They asked for him. Quit hittin' me. Leave me the fuck alone."

"I oughta brake your fuckin' neck, you little queer."

Richard leaned back and smiled, then said into the phone, "Elliott, your wife's here."

He handed the phone over and the first words out of her mouth were a sobbing, "Elliott, how could you do this to me? How could you do this to James?"

"Hon, don't worry about it. It's all planned out. Y'all are gonna be all right. Everything's gonna be all right."

She reiterated, "How can you do this to me. I love you."

"I know, Hon. That's why I'm doing this *for* you."

She implored, Please, give up. I want you alive."

"I will be, Babe. Nobody's gonna be hurt. And everything will be taken care of."

After a pause, she regained some of her composure. "Elliott, does this have anything to do with that letter you sent me."

Richard's ears perked up.

"No, Hon, everything's all right." And the line went dead.

Even Richard had forgotten that she hadn't asked the crucial questions and could only say, "What letter?"

Her cheeks wet with salty tears, she turned and stammered, "A month or so ago, he wrote me. He said we'd be taken care of, not to worry."

"Where's the letter."

She again started to cry, "I don't know, I threw it away. He never wrote anything like that before."

Finally, Richard broke and screamed, "What was in the goddam' letter?"

This brought Carly to near-hysteria as she cried, "I don't know, I don't remember. He just said everything would be all right."

McClain looked down, then almost apologetically, said, "I'm sorry, Mrs. Samuels, Carly. It's just that I have to know about everything, in order to save your husband." After a pause, he continued, "Listen, we have a room for you. You stay there tonight and tomorrow, we'll talk to him again. Agreed?"

She looked at Richard through those large, engaging eyes, and near-silently acknowledged, "Yes, sir."

McClain motioned to Garling and Carly Samuels was escorted out of the office.

CHAPTER 33

❀

The next morning, Sunday, Richard awoke with a cramped neck, sore muscles, and praying that today was perhaps the day the siege would end; he had already seen the signs of some dissension between at least Villareal and Menteur and he hoped Carly's input would instigate even more. Today was the day he was going to get to the bottom of it.

McClain called Garling and asked him to bring Carly back in; moments later the two sat across the desk from each other. Carly was dressed in the jeans from the previous day but with a clean, white, short-sleeved blouse. Her hair was combed into an attractive style and he could see that she really was good-looking. A guy wouldn't want to go to prison and leave a woman like that on the outside.

"Mrs. Samuels, I'm sorry about yesterday. We really need you to contact your husband again, and this time, I'd really like to keep him on the line."

She had given in and her response was only a whimper, "Do you want me to call him now?"

"No, not yet. We need to discuss a few things before we make the communication."

Again, a whimper, "All right."

"When you talk to him this time, ask him about the conditions down there. Is anybody hurt, everybody getting along all right?"

"Will this help Elliott?"

"Yes."

"Then, I'll do it."

"Mrs. Samuels, we also need to find out some other things."

"What things?"

"Do they have any weapons? Will your husband tell you that?"

"I don't know."

"Can you try?"

"Yes."

"We have to find out who is behind all this. Who is helping them? You can understand that we're very concerned about the little girl and her mother who were kidnapped. I mean, imagine if it was your son."

Carly, was visibly shaken. "I'll do my best."

"Mrs. Samuels, I just have one other thing."

"What?"

"Find out what's in the briefcase." McClain had erred and he knew it. "No! Forget that. Ask your husband if they have any explosives."

Her face went white and her hands began to shake. "You mean a bomb?"

"Yes."

*   *   *   *   *   *   *   *   *   *

Richard, once again, dialed the phone.

"Who's this?"

"McClain, Jesús. You guys need anything?"

"How about some more food?"

"Sure. Same procedure as before? We send Miller down with the grub and then give you a call?"

"Yeah. How're you comin' on our demands?"

"The armored car'll be here this afternoon. We got the passports and the money but the gold is difficult. We gotta have until Tuesday."

Villareal spat out, "Don't bull shit me, man. We got a deadline. You meet that or you got a problem."

"Jesús. I'm doin' my best. I'm bending over backwards. We just need more time."

"What part of this do you not understand, man? Monday, one o'clock."

"I'll try." Then, without a breath, McClain said, "Samuels' wife is out here. Can he talk to her?"

"I don't know. Well, yeah, OK."

McClain then quickly added, "Listen. If you need to talk to me, my number is 1174. Just dial it and I'll be here."

He handed the phone to Carly who took the receiver and spoke.

"Elliott?"

"Yeah, Babe. I'm here."

Her voice again cracked. "Elliott, please come out. You're going to get yourself killed. James and I need you. We want you here with us. We love you."

"I love you, too, Hon. It's all gonna be over soon, I promise. Then you won't have to worry again."

"Elliott, what do you mean by that? How can I not worry?"

"Carly, I can't explain it to you. Just don't worry."

Watching her actions and hearing half the conversation, McClain hurriedly scribbled a note. "Get the information. Guns. Bomb!" He shoved it in front of the woman.

In a choked voice, she continued, "Elliott, I need to ask you something."

"What?"

"Is anybody hurt down there? Is everybody OK?"

"I'm fine. Don't worry."

Her eyes filling with tears, she whimpered, "Elliott, they want me to ask you if you have a bomb down there."

"*What*? Who wants to know that?"

"The lieutenant. He wants to help you."

"I can't talk about that, Carly."

Tears flowed and her voice broke even more, "They have to know to help you, Elliott."

"You tell 'em to fuck off."

At that point, Carly Samuels completely lost control, and amidst sobs, pleaded, "Elliott, please tell them. Is there a bomb in that briefcase?"

"What briefcase?"

Hearing that last word, Jesús Villareal grabbed the receiver and the conversation abruptly ended.

CHAPTER 34

Jesús' first words were, "How the fuck did they know about the briefcase?"

"I don't know. They just did."

"Well, nobody said nothin', as far as I know. The only way is if they'd a seen it and there's no way except...Shit! They been watchin' us."

The two scrambled back to the lounge and Villareal ordered Menteur to start taking down the ceiling tiles.

"Why the fuck I gotta do that for?"

"Cause you're an asshole, that's why."

"Why me?"

"We're all doin' it. Just pull that shit down.

"Doc, you help."

* * * * * * * * * * *

McClain stared for what seemed to be eternities at Carly Samuels, now holding a dead phone. In disgust, he threw his pen down on the desk. "Goddamn it! You told them about the briefcase."

Carly started to sob. "Was that wrong?"

All he could do was look down, shake his head, and say, "Forget it."

Dejectedly, he shoved his chair back and grumbled, "B. C., take her back to the trailer."

As Sergeant Garling led the woman from the room, the only words Richard heard were her pleas, "What did I do wrong? He told me to say it. Please, what did I do?"

Sitting in front of the monitor, he watched. There were Menteur and Villareal, savagely ripping tiles out of the ceiling, tossing the remnants helter-skelter over the floor. He saw Samuels coming at the air conditioning vent and jerking it off and then yelling to Villareal. The last thing he saw was a dark shadow of a hand followed by the wildly jumping screen. Then, there was just snow.

*   *   *   *   *   *   *   *   *   *

Menteur was the first to find a tiny microphone lying over one of the tiles. He grabbed it, pulled, and threw it on the floor. Forty-five minutes and seven microphones later, McClain's eyes and ears to the lounge no longer existed.

*   *   *   *   *   *   *   *   *   *

As Villareal dismantled the last apparent microphone, Thom thought to himself, *they must've been watching the whole time.* Then a new fear struck him to his core.

He sat back on the couch while the three inmates, now tired and worn, wandered among the debris. Villareal spoke first. "Man, we got a problem. How much fuckin' shit do they know?"

Samuels remained calm. "It's gonna be all right."

Then, without warning, the young Hispanic pulled the gun out of his belt, walked over, and placed the barrel against Thom's head. Peering at the ceiling, toward any cameras as yet undetected, he screamed, "No more fuckin' around, or the Doc gets wasted. Understand?"

Thom couldn't breathe, he couldn't blink. All he could do was feel the cold circular barrel of the pistol pushing firmly into his temple.

Samuels reacted; he came over, carefully pulled Villareal out of the way, and spoke in an urgent, whispered tone. Villareal lowered the gun, put it back in his belt, and sat down in the midst of the shredded ceiling tiles.

In the meantime, Menteur, roaming aimlessly around the room, got all their attention. "What's that smell?"

Everyone in the lounge, Thom and the guard included, sniffed the aroma, a peculiar odor, which had been so slow in coming that nobody had thought of it, now emanated through their senses, the stench of death.

Villareal only lowered his head and murmured, "Fuck, I don't believe it." Menteur vomited. Samuels, realizing what was happening, quickly picked up some of the now-destroyed pieces of tile and pushed them up to the bottom of the door. The guard did nothing, and Thom, for the first time in what seemed to be a week, ran to the bathroom and threw up. Again, the taste of bile filled his mouth. The acid of his own mortality seared his tongue. He lay there, knowing his life was over. Through the door, he heard Menteur's incessant whining. "You'd better do somethin' about this—I ain't gonna put up with this crap."

And with resignation, Jesús responded, "Yeah, it's time to straighten shit out." And the door slammed.

CHAPTER 35

In the luxury penthouse in Houston, the patriarch, dressed in a three-piece suit, looked down at his subordinate and asked, "How's the situation?"

"Everything's going according to schedule."

"Our contact on the inside is still good?"

"Yes. All information seems very reliable. Right now it's a zoo up there. What with the 'nut' groups and the bomb threats, the cops are running around like a bunch of chickens with their heads cut off." He chuckled, sardonically.

"Good idea shipping all those idiots with their placards up there."

"I'll take credit for that. The call about the bomb was even better, though. Now everybody's scared shitless and we can thank Mr. Vernon for that."

The older gentleman took on a serious expression and asked, "What about the woman and child?" He didn't much care about the woman, but his "organization" had a hard-and-fast rule: Never go after the kids.

The tone in his command made sure there was no mistaking. "See that nothing happens to them."

"They'll be released. Unharmed."

"When?"

"Just in time."

"Good. Now, that cop, McClain. What's his next move?"

"He had a big meeting yesterday with his SWAT team. This morning the snipers were gone. We figure they're resting up until Monday."

"All right. One more thing, our contact inside."

"Yes?"

"Well, when this is all over, get rid of him."

"Sir, it's already been worked out."

CHAPTER 36

Jesús Villareal punched in 1174 on the phone at the guard's station; the response was immediate. "McClain."

The response was angry. "Man, you fucked us."

"Jesús?"

"Yeah, and you fucked us."

"What are you talking about?"

"You had a camera down here and a bunch of microphones. Man, you fucked us."

"I don't know what you're talking about. I didn't do anything. What's the problem? Oh, by the way, I got some food on the way."

Villareal was caught off guard. "What? Food?"

"Yeah."

"Good, but what about all the microphones?"

"I don't know anything about any microphones. It must've been somethin' TDC already had in place long before all this came down. You

166

know how those assholes are. We're just waitin' for you guys to come out. That's all."

"Yeah? Then how'd you know about the bomb?"

"You told me you had a bomb."

"Yeah, maybe, but how'd you know it was in a briefcase?"

"You told me that. Said you were going to blow everybody up if we didn't meet your demands. C'mon, Jesús, I've been straight with you from the get-go."

"Man, you a cop. You like fuckin' with us."

"Jesús, I'm not fuckin' with you. I just want to see everything resolved and nobody get hurt. Wait a minute…the food's here. I'm sending it down and I'll call you in an hour and a half—two-thirty. OK?"

"Yeah. OK."

McClain knew he had narrowly averted disaster and decided it was time, finally, to get Jesús Villareal to play his game.

＊　＊　＊　＊　＊　＊　＊　＊　＊　＊

Between 1:15 and 2:00, McClain placed several calls, the first to B. C. Garling who now sat in one of the prison's out-buildings. "Any of the mikes still work?"

"No. Assholes found 'em all."

"Fuck. All right, we'll just let it play itself out, see what happens."

"You're the boss."

"Shut up, B. C."

The phone abruptly went dead.

＊　＊　＊　＊　＊　＊　＊　＊　＊　＊

McClain then called Adrian Pelfrey.

"Yeah, Lieu?"

"Everything in order?"

"Yessir."

"Good. A little past one tomorrow."

"Got it."

"See you then."

∗　∗　∗　∗　∗　∗　∗　∗　∗　∗

The call to Ratley Mace confirmed one of McClain's biggest fears. "Still no word, Lieutenant. Lots of leads but nothing substantive. You have anything from the convicts?"

"No, but you and I need to talk. How about four?"

"I'll be there."

"Oh, yeah, you talk with Promeneur?"

"Yes. Everything's being set up."

"Good."

"See you at four."

∗　∗　∗　∗　∗　∗　∗　∗　∗　∗

McClain's last call was to the home of David and Laurie Nelson. "Is Mrs. Christopher there? This is Lieutenant McClain."

"Yessir, right here."

Ellen's voice was excited and full of hope, "Richard, is Thom all right?"

"We're making progress. Probably have him out tomorrow early afternoon."

She was deflated and began sobbing, again. "You told me today."

"I'm sorry, Ellen, it didn't work out."

"Richard, I want my husband back."

"We'll *get* him back. We've made a deal for his release tomorrow. One o'clock."

She was stunned. "What?"

"It's true. Tell absolutely no one. Not the Nelsons, not Amy, not Jen, not anyone."

She now rallied, "You're sure?"

"Yes."

"Then I won't say a word. And, Richard, thank you."

"I gotta go."

"Richard, wait. I have to be there when he comes out."

"*No!* Absolutely not. And if you try, I'll have you detained by the marshals. When this is all over and everyone's safe, you can have your husband back."

Reluctantly, she sighed, "OK. I understand."

She hung up the receiver, looked at the clock on the mantel, and prepared to wait the longest twenty-three hours of her life.

✷   ✷   ✷   ✷   ✷   ✷   ✷   ✷   ✷   ✷

In the basement of the Wynne Unit, Villareal prepared for McClain's promised phone call. He had made the decision soon after the last call that nobody other than he, not Menteur, not Samuels, nobody, would be allowed to speak. They were just too close to the end.

At two-twenty-five, Jesús headed down the hallway to the guard's station, where sat and waited for the ring. He decided he was going to make sure everything was still on schedule, that the money and car would be waiting, that a jet was ready to whisk them away for parts unknown, that the gold was being delivered. Yes, just as on the outside, Jesús Villareal was now the man calling the shots. He was once again in charge.

At 2:33, Villareal sat, stared at the receiver. He glanced at his watch and then glared back at the receiver. For ten minutes he sat and waited. *Why ain't he callin'?* Finally, at five before three, he could stand it no more and punched in 1174. Richard, his hand a mere four inches from the receiver, didn't move. The phone rang, and rang, and rang and on the seventh ring, he picked up. "McClain."

"What the fuck is goin' on? Why didn't you call me like you said you was gonna do?"

"Sorry, Jesús, we just got a bunch of other things happenin' up here and I sort of lost track of time. What're you doin'?"

"I'm waiting for you to call."

"Oh, yeah. So, what ya need?"

Jesús muttered a curt, "Fuck," and then continued, "McClain, you got the armored car and the money?"

"It's all set."

"What about the gold?"

"We got some of it but not all. What we figure on doing is just loading the rest on the plane at the airport. At least that saves you the time of transferring it."

"Yeah. That's good. I didn't think about that."

"We're tryin', Jesús."

"Well, try harder. And any more bull shit and somethin' happens to the Doc."

Quickly, McClain responded, "Don't do it, Jesús."

"Yeah? Why not?"

"Cause he's your card outta there. Anything happens to him and you'll never make it to the gate."

A pause later, the gangster came back in a tough-guy voice. "Yeah, well, he ain't my only card."

CHAPTER 37

❀

At 3:55, Ratley Mace walked into the Warden's office and sat down. "McClain, we can't find the woman and kid, and my guys are going nuts out there. Plenty of leads but everything's a dead end."

"Any ransom demand?"

"Nothing. You get anything out of the convicts?"

"Not a word since the original implication. But no way they could have pulled this off. Someone else has gotta be callin' the shots."

"Who?"

"Fuck if I know. None of these guys is worth a shit. It doesn't make any sense"

"So what're you gonna do?"

"Deadline is 1:00 tomorrow."

"And?"

"I'll try to get them to release the teacher up here. If that doesn't work then we let it run its course."

"What's that mean?"

"It means we let it run its course. They'll never get away—trust me on that."

Ratley Mace was more than a little agitated. "McClain, I'm concerned about the woman and girl. What happens to them when this is all coming down."

"Could be when we let these guys out of the compound it'll be enough that they'll release them."

Mace shook his head, "Doubt it. Maybe. Perhaps we'll just get lucky and find 'em before the whole thing goes down."

*   *   *   *   *   *   *   *   *   *

Adrian Pelfrey arrived back at the compound early Sunday evening, went into the Warden's office, and laid out the maps of the area surrounding the Seven Coves Drive Exit on Interstate 45.

"This is where I place the snipers—three on the left, two on the right. My two guys and I'll be on the overpass, so when the doors blow, we'll have a clear shot with a good angle."

"Where's it detonate?"

The sniper pointed to a spot on the map, one-hundred-two yards from the overpass. "They pass the first Ranger on the right, here." His finger went to a point just south. "As soon as they get here, we hit the kill switch and that automatically sets off the charges. At forty-five miles per hour, that size van with that much weight will coast to a stop between seventy and seventy-five feet down the interstate. With the hundred-two yards, we can get the best angle into the back of the van to pick out our targets. We did a few quick dry runs last night. Basically, it all came out the same. I do need to know where the hostages are located—in the back or in the cab, who's driving, and what everybody's wearing."

"I'm gonna lead them down the interstate, but Garling will call you with all the information."

"When we blow the van, you better get the hell outta there in a hurry. There ain't nobody, other than the two hostages, walkin' away. You have the paramedics set up?"

"Two teams with ambulances about a hundred and fifty yards from the overpass. There'll be a Med-Evac helicopter at a landing site just off League Line Road, north of the Outlet Mall.

"If that's it, I'm gonna go get some sleep so we can be there bright and early. By the way, what time is DPS shuttin' down I-45?"

"We'll make it noon; just north of Huntsville. You probably won't see the effect until one o'clock or so. We'll get there about one-thirty, quarter of two."

CHAPTER 38

Monday at 5:30 a.m., McClain put on a clean shirt, brushed his teeth in the warden's private bathroom, and then called Garling into the office. "Get on the phone with DPS and make sure that 45's gonna be shut down at noon. Around nine, bring in the Samuels woman and we'll give it one last shot. Then, call Pelfrey and make sure he's all set up."

Garling hurried out, leaving McClain, once again, to make sense of the whole mess. *Why would anybody be tryin' to get the asshole's out? It doesn't make sense; none of 'em's worth a shit. Why?*

He decided it was fruitless thinking about something that might not even be, and went back to preparing to put his plan into action. He left the building, went over to his car, and pulled out a portable light bar, anchoring it securely to the roof. He then pulled out the two spare guns he kept in the trunk and prepared to load them. As he looked at the bullets he was about to insert into the chamber, he thought of the stopping power of those steel-jacketed, hollow-nosed shells and hoped he wouldn't have to use them. He moved the pistols to the front of the car and placed them on the floor—just below the passenger's seat. Richard then went back to the office to check and recheck the maps of both the unit and the area surrounding the Willis exit.

✳   ✳   ✳   ✳   ✳   ✳   ✳   ✳   ✳   ✳

At 8:55, Garling ushered Carly Samuels into the office where McClain sat, staring at the snowy TV monitors. He turned, offered the woman some coffee, then began, "Mrs. Samuels, I'm sorry about yesterday. It was all my fault, and I apologize."

Stonily, she replied, "It's all right, Lieutenant. I understand."

"Would you like to talk to your husband this morning?"

She dryly answered, "Yes, but will he be allowed to talk?"

"Let's give it a try."

"I don't want to ask him any more questions."

"Mrs. Samuels, just ask him to come out. It's as simple as that."

"All right, but that's all I can do."

Richard then asked B. C. to take Carly to an alternate room while he, McClain, set up the call. He dialed the number, and after fourteen rings, a voice said, "McClain?"

"Yeah, Jesús."

"You got our shit ready?"

"It's all set."

"How you gonna make sure we get to the airport in one piece?"

You fucking asshole. "Jesús, I'm gonna lead you down there in my car. The interstate's closed so that nothing unexpected happens."

"Like what?"

"Like some drunk driver hits you or something." *You idiot.*

"Oh, yeah. OK, what else?"

"A guard's gonna drive the armored vehicle."

"Cop?"

"No, of course not. You're too smart for that."

"Yeah." And Jesús grinned to himself. "Then what?"

"We get you to the airport, drive you right up to the plane, and you're off."

"The pilot a cop?"

"Jesús, give us a break, we're not that stupid to try to put something over on a guy like you."

Villareal again smiled to himself. "Good."

"How about you release the teacher and guard up here, when you come out. Deal?"

"No way, man. You crazy?"

"All right. Then just one of 'em? Say, the teacher."

"Not until we're outta here."

"All right. What about your releasing them as you're getting on the plane?"

After a long pause, Jesús responded. "Sure, I guess we can do that."

"Listen, Jesús. What about the woman and child?"

"Who? Oh, yeah, don't worry about them. They'll be OK."

"How do you know?"

"I just do. Now how're we gettin' to the airport, again?"

"You're just going to follow me all the way down."

"Good."

McClain then signaled Garling to bring in Carly Samuels to speak with her husband.

"One more thing, Samuels' wife wants to talk to him.

"No way."

"What's it gonna hurt?"

"He ain't talkin'."

"But his wife just wants to say she loves him."

"I said no."

"Then can you tell him something from her?"

"What?"

"Tell him she'll be outside waiting for him."

"Yeah, whatever. McClain? One o'clock. Got it?"

"I got it."

*　*　*　*　*　*　*　*　*　*

And now, having done as much as he could have under the circumstances, he sat back to wait out the next few hours. At noon he packed up his gear out of the Warden's office, loaded it into the car, grabbed a bullhorn, then climbed the picket in front of the entrance to the main building.

*　*　*　*　*　*　*　*　*　*

Forty-five yards from where McClain sat, Philip Kimble positioned himself atop the unit's red and white checkered water tower. From here, he had a perfect view of the front of the unit and was completely hidden from anyone on the ground. He carefully loaded six hollow-nosed projectiles into his rifle, sighted the weapon at the door, and made a few minor adjustments of the 'scope. He then sat and waited.

CHAPTER 39

Forty-five minutes before the one o'clock deadline, an agitated Villareal paced the entire circumference of the lounge. Each time he passed Thom, he waved the gun in the air then menacingly pointed it at the instructor. On his fourth pass, Samuels stopped him, hustled him to one side, and took the gun away. Samuels then slowly turned and walked toward Thom, looked squarely into his eyes, and quietly said, "Doc, I'm sorry. You're not gonna get hurt. You stick with me and you'll be all right."

"Is it true?"

"Is what true?"

"What you told me about your wife and kid and all that stuff in Oklahoma?"

A tear came into Elliott's eye and he muttered, "Yeah, it's true."

Thom lowered his head. "I'm sorry."

Without another word, the former football star from the University of Oklahoma made a hand gesture to Villareal and both men walked over to the guard. There, Elliott pushed the barrel of the pistol at the guard's forehead while Villareal removed the tape from his mouth.

Thom Christopher watched, instinctively knowing he was about to witness a brutal murder. He showed no emotion, though. He was just glad it wasn't him. Thom had become part of a surrealistic movie and, as Villareal, Samuels, and Menteur were playing parts, so was he. And maybe it was true that every player was a victim.

Samuels started in a near-inaudible voice, "Look, Sal, you said nobody would get hurt. Everybody was gonna be safe. We played along, did our part. Why'd you kill Palmer? He was going along. He even got us the gun."

The bound man responded, "Palmer turned. He was blowin' the whistle on you guys. He told me. I was only protectin' your interests. If he'd a talked, then you'd a been in here forever with nothin'. No money. No retirement fund. No little nest egg. Nothin'."

"That's bull shit. Why would he tell *you*? Why not just go to the Warden?"

"How the fuck do I know? He just did."

"Yeah? You're gettin' away with murder and we're takin' the rap for it. You fucked us."

Samuels cocked the hammer and the bound Vizziani started to sweat. "God, don't do it. I swear it's true....I'll even sign a confession. Just get me some paper."

Samuels thought for a second, slowly pulled the gun away, and yelled over to Menteur, "Hey, Eddie. Bring over some paper and a pen."

"OK, ok, ok. But what the fuck's goin' on?"

"Shut up, you idiot. Just do it."

"Yeah? Well, where you *propose* I get that shit?"

"Look in the Doc's briefcase. He's gotta have somethin' in there."

So Eddie Menteur dutifully went over to Thom's attaché case and pulled out a legal pad and a newly-filled fountain pen.

Thom watched, trying to figure out what was going on but could only surmise that the guard was being allowed to write his last will and testament. *Oh, Lord, am I next?* Villareal snatched the pad and fountain pen from Menteur, and Samuels ordered Sal to write the message:

"I, Sal Vizziani, killed Roy Palmer. Elliott Samuels, Jesús Villareal, and Eddie Menteur had nothing to do with it. It was my plan from the beginning and I forced them to participate."

Calmly, he wrote the words, just as was dictated. He paused, Samuels again cocked the trigger, and then screamed, "Now sign it, you son of a bitch!"

The name penned and the sheet handed back, Samuels wadded up the document with his free hand and placed it inside his shirt. He then turned and called out, "Hey, Doc. Time to go."

Another wave of nausea hit Thom but in a foggy unreality, he rose, slowly looked bewilderedly around the room, and for some reason, reached for his briefcase.

"Leave it, Doc. We don't walk out with anything."

Thom stopped, looked at Samuels with the gun, and murmured the question, "You're not going to kill me?"

The inmate merely shook his head, then turned to Villareal and handed him the pistol. "Here. You take it. You know the plan. Just don't get the Doc hurt."

For once, there was relief; he wasn't *supposed* to be killed and freedom was now perhaps just a few steps away.

*   *   *   *   *   *   *   *   *   *

Eddie Menteur and Elliott Samuels flanked Thom Christopher while Jesús Villareal held the gun just behind their hostage's right ear. The four emerged from the lounge with the guard, oddly enough, at the back of the group. Thom couldn't see him but somehow knew that the second hostage was apparently no longer part of this thing; he had become a non-entity.

Thom glanced to his right and saw for the first time in what seemed to be weeks, the light of day peeking through the venetian blinds of the classrooms. Taking half-steps, they moved quietly toward the guard's station and the bolted door where the professor wearily stared straight ahead. *This is where it's going to happen. When they open that door they're gonna blast these guys. Are they gonna shoot me? It doesn't matter, if they take out Jesús, he's gonna pull the trigger and I'm dead.*

By now, the guard, now with his hands free, had caught up. He reached behind the desk, picked up a cellular phone, and punched in a number. "Five minutes."

What the hell?

Samuels unlocked the door, pushed, and the five started their ascension out of the Education Section. At the top of the stairwell, turning into the gauntlet, Thom could see the entire Unit—vacant. The basketball courts in front of him, usually teeming with convicts, were empty, no inmates walked against the yellow lines, not even a guard was to be seen, and all the barred doors of the gauntlet stood wide open.

Thom heard some muffled talking but couldn't determine if it was from the convicts or the police. It didn't sound like someone giving orders, but it was too muted to tell. In the vacated hallway, with no soft surface to absorb the sounds, the hushed voices reverberated, coming eerily from all sides and making it impossible to determine their source. It was a presence hanging in the air, as if a supernatural being were mysteriously enveloping the group.

As they moved down the hallway, Thom heard the shuffling of his own feet and those of Villareal, Samuels, Menteur, and the guard. These sounds, too, quietly echoed throughout the prison. The unit had never been so dark, so ominous. Perhaps the abundance of white-clad convicts had always managed to direct Thom's attention away from the gloom of the gauntlet; perhaps it was his sullen, dour mood that made his perception all the more macabre; perhaps it was the closeness of death.

The barrel of the gun remained firmly behind his ear and he didn't dare move his head. Forced to take in his surroundings using only the movement of his eyes, he saw on the right what appeared to be a thousand pairs of hands, most with small pocket mirrors protruding, as if they were mere extensions of the barred doors. These were the inmates confined to their cells during the lockdown. There would be no help here. He noticed their dark, foreboding eyes reflected in the glass and wondered anew if it was just his imagination or if it was a sign that something even more sinister was about to go down.

The smell remained, a permanent fixture of TDCJ. It would always be there, even long after the prisons had been shut down and the last inmate moved to new quarters, as if it were a virus, always residing in the cracks and crevices of the system. The scent of prison life was one thing that would always remain. And through that acrid smell, the five walked, slowly, heedful of any surprises, any unexpected actions by someone not in on the plan.

He could still hear the gentle shuffle of his feet and the feet of his captors. But one set of footsteps seemed to be getting further and further away, as if they were fading into the background of the hushed whispers that enveloped the group.

Half-way down the gauntlet Samuels stopped and turned to Villareal. "I gotta talk with the Doc."

"No. Let's get this thing over with."

"Gimme a second."

The convict lowered the gun and Samuels took Thom aside. "Doc, the guard fucked up. He was supposed to wait until you left and then lock the door. Things just got outta hand."

The only response was an incredulous stare.

"When we get outside, just stand there. Don't make a move. Don't do anything."

The response was a near-silent, "*What?*"

"Just stand there. We're all gonna raise our hands and surrender. They come in, take us away, and you go home."

Violently, Elliott Samuels was jerked from his position, and slammed against the wall, the back of his head crashing against the painted iron bars.

"What the fuck are you doin'?" The voice was the guard's.

"Nothin'. I told him not to move once we got outside. Nothin' else. He doesn't know anything."

"You screw this up," then he looked at Thom, "and you're both goin' down. Understand?"

Samuels spat back, "Listen, you little asshole, you got your deal. You just come through on your end."

Then, for the first and only time, Thom got a good, hard look at the guard's face, and the realization hit him that the "captive" guard was one of *them*. Why hadn't he seen it before?

The confrontation was ended by the whining voice in the background. "Hey, let's get this fuckin' show on the road. I gotta take a piss."

"Shut up, faggot!"

Seconds later, they continued their trek, Villareal holding the gun at the base of Thom's skull and the guard seemingly falling farther and farther behind. At the end of the gauntlet they turned right, through the sky-blue iron door, and headed into the bullpen. Thom looked up, seeing the numerous levels of tiers now vacant....*Never again.*

They walked the next forty feet through the dimly lit area and then entered another dark, dank hallway, the last until the foyer and freedom. Side by side, Villareal, still looking straight ahead, whispered, "Samuels, why not go for it? Think of the money the cop got us, think of gettin' outta here."

"You're nuts. There isn't any money and even if there was, Sal's family'd hunt us down and kill us all. At least this way we got a chance to get somethin' outta this deal."

"We can *hold* Sal, make a deal for him. Why not?"

"Because it's too goddam' late. We've come too far, and there's no turnin' back."

Dejectedly, Villareal relented, "Yeah, OK."

At the next turn, into the foyer, Thom stopped and turned his head toward Samuels. "What's in the closet?"

"What? What're you talkin' about?"

He was now insistent. "In the closet…in the closet in the lounge…who's in there? I gotta know."

"Forget it. It's over."

"No! It's not over, I gotta know."

Shaking his head, the inmate responded, "Doc, it's a guard. We didn't have anything to do with it, I swear. I have proof."

"Then who's the *other* guard?"

Samuels glanced back at Sal and calmly said, "Doc, we're almost out. Don't ask, it's better you don't know."

Looking up, into the foyer and the blinding noontime sun, Thom realized that tears now freely flowed down his cheeks.

CHAPTER 40

Outside the gate, TDCJ snipers and a few remaining Texas Rangers dutifully stood and sighted their high-powered rifles. Pelf was gone from the compound and McClain was in constant communication with his replacement, a Ranger marksman who commanded all those itching to free the hostages and end the lives of the three felons. But the word came over the walkie-talkie to anyone and everyone, "Thirty minutes. Nobody, *absolutely nobody*, is to shoot unless I give the order. Understood?" Silent nods returned agreement to the voice on the radio. Still, safeties had been removed, fingers were on triggers, and every sniper awaited a live target.

        *   *   *   *   *   *   *   *   *   *

Along the interstate, twenty-five miles to the south, Adrian Pelfrey deployed his men then punched in a series of numbers on his cell phone.

"McClain."

"Lieu, everything's in place. It's your call, now."

"Good. How's the highway look?"

"DPS did a good job shuttin' it down. Some of the locals are comin' around but the Willis and Panorama P. D.s are keepin' them outta the way. At least it's not gonna be one of those O. J. slow-speed chases with everybody eggin' 'em on."

"God, let's hope not. Listen, Pelf, hang in there, it's probably gonna be another hour and a half or so before we get down there."

"Understood."

✳   ✳   ✳   ✳   ✳   ✳   ✳   ✳   ✳   ✳

McClain turned and scanned the scene from atop the picket. He felt the heat, smelled the rising humidity, and heard the far-off rotating blades of the ever-present news helicopters. With another thirty minutes to go, he worried for the safety of the Director's wife, for the life of his friend, and for what might happen in the case of that ever-present, unexpected glitch. But, everything that could be done was done, and so, he sat and waited.

As he was about to pull a stick of gum out, his cellular phone went off.

"McClain? Mace. We got 'em."

Richard's spirits soared. "What?"

"Picked 'em up a few minutes ago."

"They OK?"

"Yeah, fine."

"And the pricks who grabbed them?"

"Gone. No sign of 'em."

"Why now? They still have twenty-five minutes."

"All I know is that it's a happy ending, at least for us. Is the Director still over there?"

"Yeah."

"Why don't you give him the news? Tell 'im we're bringing them up here for debriefing."

With a sigh of relief, Richard breathed a, "You got it."

CHAPTER 41

The inexplicably-louder sound from a wayward helicopter annoyed Richard to no end but the release of the woman and the child was a great relief. Still, some nagging questions would not go away—*Why before the deadline? Did they just make a mistake? Maybe they got the times screwed up.* Regardless, he was happy to have everything drawing to a close.

He punched a number on his cell phone and gave the Director the good news. "Sir, the FBI just called. They found your daughter and granddaughter, both safe and sound. They were in a cabin down near Navasota. FBI's bringing them up…."

The loud whop-whop-whop of a helicopter landing in the parking lot behind him drowned out his last words and everyone in the compound, McClain included, involuntarily turned and looked as a small, white and red helicopter attempted to land.

McClain yelled first, "What the hell's goin' on?"

Garling, squatting next to him, screamed, "Christ, it's a Med-Evac chopper."

"Well what the fuck are they doin' here? Tell 'em to get outta here."

While McClain tried to order the chopper out of the area with his bullhorn, B. C. screamed above the din into his walkie-talkie, "Somebody, get that goddam' thing outta here."

But it was too late. Distracted by the landing, nobody appeared to notice as four figures approached the door leading out of the main building of the Wynne Unit. Slowly pushing on the glass, Menteur stuck his head out. Then Thom, with the barrel of the gun still aimed against the base of his skull, emerged, followed by Villareal and Samuels. They entered the open yard, and blinded by the brightness of the sunlight streaming down on them, paused for a split second.

*   *   *   *   *   *   *   *   *   *

Richard McClain caught the movement out of the corner of his eye, turned quickly, and saw four figures standing there, motionless. "What the fu...?"

And as the attention of all the officers shifted back to the front of the building, there was nothing to do but stare. Where did they...? How long...? *It wasn't time yet!*

*   *   *   *   *   *   *   *   *

In the midst of all this silent confusion, the barrel of a high-powered rifle emerged from the small side window of the helicopter and an eye behind its telescopic sight took careful aim. Three loud cracks rang out. The ensuing impact literally raised Eddie Menteur's body off the ground, sending a million pointed shards of glass into the air. In the slow motion of disbelief, Elliott Samuels turned to look at the bloodied body of Eddie Menteur as two projectiles ripped through his own body. With shots echoing from everywhere, Jesús Villareal, flailing his arms wildly, discharged his gun several times before receiving a fatal shot to the head.

It took Thom millisecond to realize what had happened; he lunged forward and collapsed to the ground, trying in vain to shield his body from the stinging projectiles. As he dropped, though, he felt his whole body explode. Mercifully, the burning sensations quickly subsided and all that remained was an iron-like metallic taste in his mouth. That, too, soon faded into the distance.

Over the din, all anyone could hear was Richard McClain frantically screaming through the bullhorn, "No! No! No!"

       *   *   *   *   *   *   *   *   *   *

Three seconds of chaos, an eternity to those involved in the carnage, and four bullet-riddled bodies lay at the entrance to the Wynne Unit; a hushed stillness settled over the prison.

       *   *   *   *   *   *   *   *   *   *

Philip Kimble, sitting atop the water tower, continued to wait. Smiling to himself, he took a sip of bottled water, then pressed the rifle's 'scope against his left eye, caressing the trigger with his index finger.

CHAPTER 42

❀

When the smoke cleared, another type of chaos took over with paramedics, guards, and police officers descending upon the scene. As the
pandemonium gathered steam, Richard McClain and B. C. Garling
raced from the picket into the yard. Jim James ran toward the building,
searching for the second hostage. Through the shattered doors and
purely by accident, he ran right into a guard.

He searched the face and excitedly asked, "Where's Roy Palmer?"

"Who?"

"Palmer! The second hostage!"

Sal excitedly responded, "Thank God you're here. He's still down in
Education. He's wounded."

Over his shoulder, running full tilt through the bullpen and down
the gauntlet, he screamed, "Call the medics!"

Sal, on the other hand, calmly walked out of the entrance, carefully
stepping around the shards of glass, medical personnel, and seemingly
lifeless bodies.

* * * * * * * * * *

From his perch, Philip Kimble took careful aim, placing the center of Sal's forehead directly in the sight's cross-hairs. This would be very easy, but also a little chancy, now that all the firing had ceased. Well, there was a mission to carry out and he was the "man". He thought fleetingly about how he might escape after he had dealt with the problem, then decided he'd just wait atop the tower until all the commotion had died down.

Re-sighting his prey, Kimble slowly pulled the trigger of the high-powered rifle just as Sal stepped over one of the wounded men. When the hammer released, he heard a simple click and nothing else. *Nothing else!* He pulled his eye away from the 'scope and stared numbly at his rifle, saying to no one in particular, "Shit, the fucker misfired."

*　*　*　*　*　*　*　*　*　*

When Sal passed Elliott Samuels, one of the paramedics looked up and shouted to no one in particular, "Get that chopper ready."

"I'm on it. Just keep these guys alive."

Now running, he sped through the open cyclone gates and made his way to the helicopter. He knocked twice on the passenger door, paused, and knocked again. The hatch opened, Sal climbed in, and the whop-whop-whop of the blades began in earnest.

As the helicopter rose into the air, Richard McClain looked up from the bloodied, still body of Thom Christopher and quietly asked himself, "Where the hell are they *going*?" Then he screamed, "What are you *doing*?"

*　*　*　*　*　*　*　*　*　*

Within moments, a second Med-Evac helicopter landed; two medical doctors leapt out onto the blacktop and ran into the yard. The lieutenant stepped back from Thom, listened to the physicians momentarily, then, slowly walked to his car.

B. C. Garling, still in a state of shock, just sat with his head up against the cyclone fence. McClain walked over to him, leaned down, and quietly said, "Hey, Brian. It's over. We've done all we can. Go home and get some sleep."

CHAPTER 43

While the doctors worked on Thom, Richard punched in the number to the Nelson residence. "This is McClain. Have Mrs. Christopher ready in five minutes."

Excitedly, the man asked, "Why? Is it over? What's happened?"

The response was a terse, "Just have her ready."

"Yessir, I will."

"And another thing, *don't* turn on the TV."

* * * * * * * * * *

A second call went to his wife. "Have Amy ready to go to Hermann Hospital. I'll be there in forty minutes."

"Is he all right?"

"Just get her ready."

Jennifer pleaded, "Is *Thom* OK?"

"He's been hurt. Just get Amy ready."

The phone went dead and Jennifer McClain looked at the receiver in her hand and said out loud, "Ready for what?"

McClain then started the ignition and sped out of the compound.

✳   ✳   ✳   ✳   ✳   ✳   ✳   ✳   ✳   ✳

Hemostatic forceps were clamped to decrease the flow of blood from Thom's side. Compresses and bandages were applied and he, along with Eddie Menteur, was placed aboard the helicopter. Elliott Samuels was transferred via ambulance to Huntsville Memorial Hospital just three miles away.

✳   ✳   ✳   ✳   ✳   ✳   ✳   ✳   ✳   ✳

As he raced into Forest Hills, down Normal Park to Peach Tree, then left onto Timberline, Richard saw Ellen running out of the house on the corner of Cherry Lane, screaming and waving her hands wildly.

"He's been shot. Richard, he's been *shot*."

McClain pulled up to the curb, jumped out of the car, and, wrapping Ellen in his arms, led her to the passenger seat. He re-took his position in the driver's seat, and looked at Ellen. "I saw Thom. He's been hurt but he'll be all right. He's on his way to Hermann Hospital right now."

A new wave of fear hit Ellen Christopher. Hermann Hospital meant only one thing to the citizens of Greater Houston—The Shock Trauma Unit.

She was now wailing even louder as she gripped his arm. "How bad? How bad is it?"

Richard whipped away from the curb, through the subdivision, toward the interstate, and told her, "Ellen, he'll be all right. He's in the Med-Evac helicopter right now."

"I saw it on the TV. They said there were two helicopters. Why didn't the first one take him?"

The sigh was immediate and without emotion. *That asshole Nelson.* "Ellen, I don't know. There was some sort of foul-up. I called Jen. She's got Amy ready and we'll pick her up on the way."

"*How bad is it?*"

At this point, Richard was pleading. "He'll be all right. Just try to stop crying, please."

"We have to go straight to him. There isn't time."

"Gawd, all right, just let me call Jen."

McClain grabbed the cellular, punched in several numbers, and relayed the message to his wife. He then asked her to make sure she stayed with Amy in the waiting room until he and Ellen arrived.

With some amount of success, Ellen was able to regain her composure. "What happened to those convicts? Did they die?"

"I don't know. I didn't see them."

With loathing in her voice, she said, "I'll kill them. I'll kill them myself. I hate them."

"Ellen, they'll be dealt with, one way or the other."

"Oh, God, please hurry."

She nervously pulled a cigarette from her purse and lit up. Richard gave her a sidelong glance and opened his mouth to say something, but he knew instinctively not even to start.

With the sirens blaring and lights flashing, Richard pulled left off the feeder and onto an empty interstate highway.

Looking around, Ellen asked, "Where are all the cars?"

"We shut it down."

She pounded his arm, screaming, "You *knew* he was going to be shot. *You knew!* Didn't you?"

Now, Richard was almost screaming, "No! And be quiet. Just for a minute."

He picked up the cell phone, punched in Adrian Pelfrey's number, and quickly brought him up to date. Then said, "Pelf, see if you can keep the highway clear for a little while."

"Yeah, Lieu. I'll call DPS."

Fifteen minutes later, Richard and Ellen raced past the Exit 92 in Willis. She noticed the white cross, nailed to a towering tree there and knew it commemorated the driver of a tractor trailer who had misnegotiated the sharp curve of the treacherous exit ramp and died upon impact there. *Oh, God, it's an omen.* Peering out, she saw the blue and white portable command post sitting on the shoulder of the road along with four or five police and sheriff's cars. Pelfrey stood there and gave the speeding car the "thumbs up" sign.

"Who was that?"

"He's just an officer I know."

"Those were SWAT!"

＊   ＊   ＊   ＊   ＊   ＊   ＊   ＊   ＊   ＊

The traffic almost immediately became congested, just as on any other weekday afternoon—people driving to the grocery store, going to the dry cleaners, cutting out from work a little early for a warm evening on the golf course, doing ordinary, everyday errands. It was as if this were a different world, where life went on as usual. Here, life was untouched and unaffected by the carnage that had just taken place only a few miles up the highway in Huntsville.

＊   ＊   ＊   ＊   ＊   ＊   ＊   ＊   ＊   ＊

Fortunately, Adrian Pelfrey had alerted the DPS that had, in turn, called the various jurisdictions on the way to Houston and most of the traffic had been forced to the shoulders by the local police departments and sheriff's agencies. Still heading south, McClain glanced in his rear view mirror and saw B. C. Garling, speedily keeping pace. He tapped the mirror. "B. C.'s right behind us."

Ellen turned and glanced, then sat, facing forward, still silent, a stony silence she had kept since Exit 92.

The two cars sped down I-45, through The Woodlands, past Spring, and into the city itself. Turning onto the Southwest Freeway, they exited at Fannin and then zipped into the parking lot of Hermann Hospital.

The officers, along with Ellen, raced into the lobby and found Jennifer and Amy. The young girl leapt into her mother's arms, "Mom, where's Dad? Is he OK? Where is he, Mom?"

In the meantime, Richard was at the desk getting the information from the receptionist. He turned to the doctor on call, quickly explained the situation and who Ellen was, and then all five, Richard, B. C., Jennifer, Ellen, and Amy, were led to a private waiting room.

"Doctor, I have to see my husband."

"Mrs. Christopher, he's in O.R. right now. As soon as the surgery is over, and he's stabilized, we'll take you to him."

"He'll be OK, won't he?"

He stammered for a second. "Mrs. Christopher, we're confident that we're doing all we can for him."

"But he's not going to die?!"

"As soon as I have more information, I'll be back."

She could do nothing but stare as he left the room. The only sound anyone could hear was his asking a nurse to prepare a mild sedative and to make sure the chaplain was nearby.

Ellen collapsed in the nearest chair. *Oh, God, no.*

*   *   *   *   *   *   *   *   *   *

Six hours later, a nurse came in, asked for Ellen, and then led both Ellen and Amy to the Intensive Care Unit. There, lay Thom, a heart monitor beeping next to him, tubes coming out of his chest, an intravenous bottle dripping into his arm, and an oxygen mask attached to his face.

When she saw his condition, Ellen paled, staggered for a second, and then reached down and tenderly stroked her husband's head. Tears fell from her face to his forehead. Amy only stood and stared.

"It isn't him. It can't be him."

The surgeon then put his hand on Ellen's shoulder. "Mrs. Christopher, we've repaired most of the damage, but right now, he's comatose. We want you to talk to him."

"Is he going to be all right?"

"You can talk to him. He might be able to hear you."

With her voice breaking, Ellen started, first with a whisper, and then, slightly louder. "Thom, we love you. Please stay with us. We need you. You're going to be all right. Please come back to us. Amy's here and wants you to come home."

Ellen looked at her daughter who, now sobbing, pleaded, "Daddy, please wake up. We need you."

*   *   *   *   *   *   *   *   *   *

In his own private world, the light in Thom's eyes continued to brighten and dim as the pressure on his two hands pulled him closer and closer. As he lay there, he could hear his mother's voice, still cracking and wavering as it had in the last few days of her life, "Thom, come out. Please, squeeze my hand. We're here, and we love you. We need you."

The light again became bright and then faded; he couldn't help but know he was being drawn into it. As it once again brightened, Thom Christopher knew he was at the end of his ordeal.

"Doctor, we've got a pupillary reflex."

"Let me see. Good. And blood pressure's coming up. Mrs. Christopher, keep on talking to your husband."

That bright light still in his eyes, he again heard the voice of his long-departed mother, "Thom, come out, it's Ellen." *Ellen?* "Thom, squeeze my hand. Can you hear me? Everything's going to be all right, Honey. You're going to make it."

CHAPTER 44

The official government report on the siege at the Wynne Unit stated that Jesus Villareal had received a single gunshot wound to the head and died instantly, Eddie Menteur received three shots to the chest and died while in transit to Hermann Hospital and Elliott Samuels, shot twice in the chest and shoulder, survived. Within days, he was pronounced stable and awaited transfer to the Galveston Unit for further recovery and debriefing. Prior to his transfer and the possible disclosure of his knowledge of the situation, he took a sudden turn for the worse and died. Although an autopsy was performed, the actual cause of death was never determined. Sometime after the siege, Sal Vizziani was reported missing and was assumed to have escaped prior to his transfer to the Houston Office of the FBI.

Thom Christopher spent the next three and one-half weeks in Hermann Hospital. Upon his release, he convalesced at his home in The Woodlands, under the watchful eye of his daughter, Amy, and the tender caring of his wife, Ellen. By the following January, he had recovered

well enough to return to work, teaching a reduced load and slowly getting back into his research. When he heard that Elliott Samuels had
died, Thom wept, a response that his wife wrote off as a manifestation
of the Stockholm Syndrome.

Two days following the siege, an inmate collecting litter in the compound happened across a crumpled up wad of paper. He tried to read it
but the ink from a fountain pen had run as a result of the morning dew.
The inmate merely tossed his find into his trash can and deposited it in
the unit incinerator.

PART 2

The Search for Sal

CHAPTER 45

He was jolted awake by pure, sweat-drenching terror. His heart raced until he was certain it must explode in his heaving chest. The nightmares, which tormented his sleep, came almost every night. The very idea of sleep brought feelings of dread and he purposely avoided yielding to it.

In spite of physical and mental exhaustion, Thom Christopher forced himself to stay awake, fighting sleep until it invariably overtook him, until it patiently but insistently wielded its irresistible power over his mind.

The images were always the same. It began with his walking, against his will, down a seemingly endless, narrow corridor; footsteps reverberated and echoed hollowly. A crowded gauntlet, so filled with men that he could taste their foul body odor, loomed menacingly. As he approached, the men, all inmates, clad completely in white, dissolved before he could get close enough to distinguish any of their leering faces. This part was always in monochrome, a sharp contrast to the

subsequent colorized segment of the haunting dream, in which, paralyzed, he sat in a stifling lounge on a patched naugahyde sofa, watching
fresh blood ooze and pool from an unseen source behind a locked
closet door. The cold metal of a gun barrel pressed into the hollow
where his head met his neck, incongruously burning like molten lava.
Then, came the distant voice of his dead mother, calling his name, as a
bright and blinding light obliterated all else.

He looked over at Ellen, sleeping peacefully, like an angel, next to
him. Quietly getting out of bed, Thom went silently to the living room
and stared through the window to the deserted street in front of the
house and he wondered if life would or could ever be normal again.

The toll had been great on the whole family. Ellen was still nervous
whenever he left the house, and Amy made a ritual of checking every
lock in the house twice before going to bed.

Thom was glad they were going to Costa Rica. Maybe a change of
scenery and a little escapist adventure would allow them all a measure
of tranquility. With the focus on fun and relaxation, maybe they could
forget—if only for a respite.

It had been a long time since the Christophers had taken a vacation.
The lack of time or money had prevented such self-indulgence, but
Thom and Ellen had had plenty of time in recent months to reorganize
their priorities. They were both painfully aware of the fragility of life.
Tomorrow was no longer a certainty.

Thom looked at the grandfather clock. Four o'clock. It was useless to
try to go back to bed, where he knew he would just toss and turn. He
went to the kitchen and turned on the coffee machine, then unlocked
the front door and walked outside. The porch light illuminated the
front walk and the driveway; and he could see that the Houston
Chronicle had already been delivered. He picked it up, glanced at the
headlines, and walked back to the house.

*   *   *   *   *   *   *   *   *   *

That December, on the first day of the semester break, the Christophers drove to Intercontinental Airport, boarded a Continental jet, and winged their way directly to San José. Here, they caught a bus for the three-hour ride to Tamarindo, a small resort community in the Guanacasta Province on the west coast of the country. Arriving at the Tamarindo Diriá Hotel, Thom checked in, got the keys and the three climbed the steps to the third floor to their rooms, Thom and Ellen's on the corner and Amy's just across the hall. Thom threw back the window shade and stood and marveled at the azure blue Pacific. Amy's room looked out upon the high mountains and lush, green jungles for which Costa Rica is famous. This really is Paradise.

After settling in and unpacking, the trio donned their swimsuits and made their way down the steps and out to the beach where they relaxed in the placid Pacific surf and the cooling breeze. As she walked in the knee-deep water, Thom eyed his wife and once again realized how lucky he was. That long, lean, sensual frame; the face of an angel surrounded by her highlighted golden tresses; it drove him crazy. And then there was Amy, a beautiful, but younger, version of her mother.

That evening, they found a small, out of the way café where they dined on some of the regional specialties. After dinner, they again headed out to the beach where they walked, shoeless, in the still calm Pacific surf. The next morning, Thom made several reservations with a local travel company for day trips for him, Ellen, and Amy. Nobody wanted to miss anything and the next few days were packed with excursions—a tour of the Poas Volcano grounds with its crater pouring out smoke and steam into the azure blue sky, a visit to the ebony seashore of Jaco Beach, and a tour of Sarchi and its world famous butterfly farm. By the end of the fourth day, both Thom and Amy were beat and chose to spend their remaining two days soaking up the sun, relaxing on the beach near their hotel. Ellen, on the other hand, still had the travelogues out, and as Thom and Amy were in the midst of scratching their mosquito bites from the trek up to Poas, she chirped up, "How about we go up to Monteverde?"

Long, low groans immediately and simultaneously emerged from the other two. "Hon, I'm tired, I must have a million bug bites and I don't know if I can handle going back into the jungle."

"Dad's right, Mom. Can't we just lie here in the sun? My legs ache."

"C'mon, you guys. You can sit in the sun at home. And besides, you're the ones who refused to put on bug spray before we left. This Monteverde place is supposed to be spectacular. The concierge told me there's some religious sect or something up there. We really should go."

"Ah, Ellen, I'd rather not. I really am beat."

Ellen looked down at Amy who was now peacefully dozing and she knew instinctively that she had lost the battle, something that almost never happens. "All right, you win," she announced. "If you two want to be couple of party poopers go right ahead." Then she pulled some cash out of her bag and announced that she was going to the market place, in search of souvenirs. Watching her walk away, Thom thought to himself, *Jeez, I hate when she does this.* Amy, with her eyes still shut gave a slight smile.

The next day was Friday and the Christophers were due to leave the following morning. In the early afternoon, on their trek from the mall area of town back to the hotel, after even more souvenir hunting, they stopped for lunch at a charming, but dark, little 'bistro' where they ordered *casado* along with some *plátanos*. Waiting for the arrival of their food, Thom decided to mark the occasion and have a picture of the family taken. He motioned to the waiter who was more than happy to oblige and the photo was snapped with Thom's new Nikon. A few minutes later, a large, pudgy man, with thinning greased-back gray-yellow hair and the cheeks and nose of a man who in the past obviously had had a long-term and rather intimate affair with alcohol, approached the table. In a low, almost inaudible voice, he addressed Thom, "Mister, could I speak with you?"

Thom looked at Ellen who raised her eyebrows ever so slightly and shrugged her shoulders, then turned and said, "Sure, I guess so. What's the problem?"

Motioning toward a side door leading outside, the man sheepishly asked, "Could we talk alone? Please?"

"All right," and the two made their way onto the verandah.

The man with the gray-yellow hair turned toward Thom and made the offer, "Sir, I'll give you fifty dollars for that roll of film in your camera."

Taken aback, Thom immediately straightened up and queried as if in disbelief, "Why?"

Obviously ashamed, the man looked down at the floor directly in front of him, shook his head, and mumbled, "Mister, this is embarrassing. If my wife ever saw that picture of me with my girlfriend down here, she'd take me for everything I have. I'd lose *everything*. I'd be ruined. You can understand that, can't you?"

Thom furtively glanced toward the restaurant window but was unable to immediately spot any possible girlfriend for this fellow. In a conciliatory voice, he answered, "Friend, I'm sorry but these are pictures of my family's vacation. I can't sell them."

"Look, I'll give you a hundred bucks for the film. C'mon, buddy, help me out."

The response was quick this time. "I'm sorry but I can't sell these pictures, even for a thousand dollars. I couldn't. But I will assure you, no one will ever see any of the pictures other than my family and a few of our friends back in the States. I'm really sorry but don't worry about them."

Bloodshot eyes peered for just a second into Thom's, and without a word, the man with gray-yellow hair turned and left the restaurant. Moments later, Thom related the story of the man, his girlfriend, and the film, and the three—Ellen shaking her head in mock disgust, and Amy chuckling just a bit—ordered dessert. At the end of the meal, Thom went to pay the check as his wife gathered up the miscellaneous bags she had filled with souvenirs from the various street merchants. Quite unexpectedly, Amy whispered to her mother, "Mom, why is that man watching us?"

Furrowing her brow, Ellen turned and scanned the crowd, seeing no one in particular looking in their direction. "What man? Who?"

Amy looked back into the crowd. "He's gone, Mom. But he was looking *right at us.*"

Ellen reached over, gently patted her daughter's hand, and in a quiet voice, attempted to reassure the teenager. "Amy, I didn't see anyone. You probably just imagined it. And even if there was someone, maybe he was just admiring such a beautiful young woman."

The young girl blushed slightly as Thom returned to the table and the family hauled up their plastic shopping bags and left for the hotel. As they entered the foyer, Amy turned, blanched, and stopped dead in her tracks. "Mom, he's there again."

"Where, Baby?"

"Over there, across the street."

Thom, bewildered, instinctively peered over the cars, the tourists, and the entourage of vendors along the boulevard. "What's this all about?"

When he was finally told the whole story of what Amy had "imagined" in the restaurant, he looked at her in an admonishing tone, but tinged with just a touch of humor, and light-heartedly remarked, "That was just your imagination. Or, then again, maybe the men down here appreciate beautiful young women."

Ellen laughed, "That's exactly what I told her."

They retrieved the keys to the rooms, went up to the third floor, and prepared to spend their one remaining afternoon on vacation soaking up the tropical sun of their own private beach. Before going out, Thom rewound the film in his camera, took out the used roll, inserted a new one, and took a few snapshots from the balcony as he made sure the new roll was threaded correctly. Carefully placing the Nikon into the top drawer of the bureau, he slipped the spent film roll into a prepaid Kodak mailer, and the Christophers left, Thom making sure the doors to his and Amy's rooms were locked. Heading down to the beach, he dropped the film mailer into a postal box to be developed and sent directly to his office at Texas State University in Conroe, Texas.

Two hours later, in the hot sun Thom, Ellen, and Amy, each cooled themselves by taking a quick dip in the Pacific, then dried off, picked up their paraphernalia, and made their way back to the hotel. Coming through the foyer, Ellen retrieved their keys, and this time, the three much more slowly climbed the steps to their rooms. As she was about to insert the key in the knob, Ellen stopped short. "Thom, you didn't lock the door."

He looked her, then at the open door, and stated very matter-of-factly, "I'm sure I did. I'd *never* leave it unlocked."

Ellen and Thom went inside, Amy in tow, and gave the surroundings a cursory look, and finding nothing obviously amiss, they all breathed a collective sigh of relief. In an instant, a pang hit Thom, *The camera!* He jumped across the bed to the bureau, jerked open the top drawer, and saw the Nikon sitting right where he had left it, amidst a few golf shirts and several pairs of Bermuda shorts. Thom Christopher breathed another sigh of relief and they all chalked up the open door either to Thom's absent-mindedness or some housekeeper's ineptitude.

About an hour later, Thom picked up the camera, walked over to the balcony, and took a snapshot of the dazzling, red, orange, and pink sunset, the clouds ribboned with dark, charcoal gray. When he cocked the Nikon to advance the film, he noticed something odd, the frame number indicator showed a "1." *I'm sure I took some pictures this afternoon. Certainly, I didn't open up the back when I slipped it into the drawer. Jeez, I really am starting to lose it.*

He never mentioned any of this to Ellen. She continued to be concerned about his still-healing body and the psychological effects of the trauma he had endured just a few short months before and Thom figured "Why needlessly worry her?"

*   *   *   *   *   *   *   *   *   *

That evening, while the Christophers ate dinner in a local café on Tamarindo's main beach road, in the darkroom of a small camera shop thirty miles away in San José, an older gentleman carefully placed a series of film negatives into an enlarger and printed one picture of each frame. Inspecting the prints as they came out of the developer and placing them into the stop bath, Philippe was amazed at the clarity of the pictures and his propensity to bring out the best in a print. When they had dried, he proudly gathered them up, went through the darkroom door into the showroom, and handed the packet to a pudgy man with greased-back gray-yellow hair and a face that was hideously streaked with broken, subdermal capillaries. The man quickly flipped through each print, looking for one in particular. Angrily, he turned toward the developer and spat out, "Where's the other one?"

"That's all there were. I swear it. There were only seven exposed frames on the roll."

"You're sure? If you're holdin' somethin' back, my boss ain't gonna like it. And I ain't gonna like it, either."

"I, I, I swear to you, there were no other exposed frames."

"All right. But you better be sure."

Apparently satisfied, the pudgy man proceeded to walk toward the front entrance of the shop. Reaching the threshold, in an almost casual manner, he turned, and looked back, smiling at the shopkeeper who remained standing in the middle of the room. Realizing what was happening, Philippe threw his arms out in self-protection, but was immediately and violently thrown backwards by the impact of three nine-millimeter bullets placed squarely in the center of his chest. The pudgy man calmly put the pistol back into its shoulder holster and entered the darkroom, dragging the body behind him. He made a meticulous search for any prints that might have been left behind, but found nothing—there were no more. When he finished, he reached into his suit jacket, pulled out a small incendiary device, set the timer, checked his watch, and left the shop. Twelve minutes later and five miles into the mountains, he noticed a flash of light in his rear view mirror followed by a slight concussion in the air. Although pleased with his performance in this part of the operation, he knew that his immediate superior would not be happy knowing that the picture may still exist. Still, he smiled to himself. He didn't have to kill Philippe but he enjoyed it—it was almost as good as sex, sometimes better, and it gave him the feeling of power and control over his own destiny.

CHAPTER 46

At one of Tamarindo's better restaurants, the Christophers toasted the evening with champagne, the waiter graciously turned a blind eye toward the glass Amy was drinking out of, and the three reminisced about their week in "Paradise." Thom was happy, and deep in his heart, he knew that his personal torment was over and that he had put the prison ordeal behind him.

A little anxious to get back to Houston, Thom seemed preoccupied about making sure they got to the airport on time to make the flight home. A shuttle left the hotel every hour, but to make their plane, they had to be aboard the 9:00 a.m. bus. Thus, during their stroll back to the hotel, he came up with his plan. As soon as they got back to the hotel, Thom and Ellen packed the bags, with the exception of their carry-ons, and delivered them to the concierge to be placed aboard the bus early in the morning. Thom even went down to the front desk, paid the remainder of the hotel bill, and "officially" checked out, although practically, they would leave early in the morning. When all was said and done, he called Ellen to come down, and the two spent the next few hours in the hotel bar, sipping margaritas and munching on plantaños.

*   *   *   *   *   *   *   *   *   *

While they enjoyed their drinks and the warm, romantic atmosphere of the bar, the man with gray-yellow hair was delivering a set of photographs to a large villa in the green mountains above San José.

"Here are the photos, Mr. V., I got everything that Philippe came up with."

The man, tall, slender, dark, and dressed in a white suit finished off by Gucci loafers, thumbed through the prints and tossed the entire folder on the coffee table. He glared across the table, "What the fuck is this, Max? You bring me a bunch of pictures of the ocean? Why the fuck do I want these?"

Max cowered. "Mr. V., those was the only pictures in the guy's camera. I even searched through the darkroom. There was nothin' else."

Venom spat from the man's mouth, "Look, you get Philippe over here. Now. I'll talk to him."

Max lowered his head and nearly silently said, "He's gone, Mr. V. I had to, he woulda talked."

"You idiot. Then where's the goddam' picture?"

"I swear, I don't know, it wasn't in the camera."

A piercing stare went straight to Max's very core. "You go down to that hotel and find that picture. Roust the whole place if you have to, but get that film. And then get rid of those people."

Max, always one to recognize an appropriate time to escape, quickly left the room and the villa and headed down the mountain. As he did so, he carefully patted his shoulder holster, making sure his nine-millimeter pistol was secure. He smiled once again to himself, things were working out.

*   *   *   *   *   *   *   *   *   *

Thom and Ellen finished off their last drinks, then got up from the table, leaving most of their remaining colones as a rather generous tip, and left the bar. Walking through the lobby, they noticed that the night concierge, who replaced the clerk they were used to dealing with, had arrived. Thom silently thanked God that he had dealt with the bags earlier.

Two hours later, the night clerk heard a loud banging on the hotel's glass front door. Not totally surprised by this intrusion, he calmly asked through the intercom, "Could I help you, sir?"

The response was urgent. "I must speak with Dr. Christopher. It's an emergency."

"Is this person a guest of the hotel?"

"Yeah! Now let me in—it's an emergency!"

The night clerk continued, his calm, if not bored, look at the man through the glass. "Could you please wait while I look in the register for this Dr. Christopher."

He reached under the counter, retrieved and opened a large album, and scanned the pages. "I'm sorry but this guest has checked out of the hotel earlier today."

Fuck! "Where the hell'd they go? This is urgent."

"I do not have that information but he is not at this hotel."

Max glared, looked past the man, into the semi-darkened lobby, turned, and walked back to his car where he punched the dial on the cell phone. "Mr. V., they ain't here."

"What?"

"They already checked out."

"Where the fuck are they?" There was a slight pause, after which Mr. V. continued very calmly, "You call the airlines, find out when they're leavin' the country, and then you get back to me. Understood?"

"Yessir."

The phone went dead and Max proceeded to make the various calls, explaining that he was Thom Christopher and wanted to confirm his reservations. On the third try, he struck pay dirt. The reservations were listed with Continental Flight 1508, leaving the island at 12:05 p.m. and arriving in Houston at 4:40 that afternoon.

*   *   *   *   *   *   *   *   *   *

Thom got out of bed at seven, got Ellen up, and called next door to Amy. With everybody dressed and ready to go, they took their carry-ons down to the lobby where they had their continental breakfasts and complimentary coffee. Finishing up her second cup, Ellen chirped up, "Dear, Amy and I are going to run down to that little market and get something for Richard and Jen. We'll only be a couple of minutes."

He furrowed his brow and forcefully stated, "No way, Babe. We already bought presents for the McClains, and we have to get on that bus."

"But we'll only be a few minutes. I promise."

"Ellen, if we miss that bus and then the plane, we'll be dead."

Cheerily, she responded, "Oh, just stay here and have an extra cup of coffee. We'll be back in plenty of time."

He had been married far too long to even conceive of the idea that he could win a discussion like this, so he relented, with his last words being, "8:50. Understood?"

Amy smiled brightly as Ellen quipped, "Understood," and the two women walked out the door and down the street.

Eight-fifty-five and Thom was on his fourth "extra" cup of coffee, pacing in front of the café. He peered down the street for his wife and child. At 9:05, his nerves jingling on yet more coffee, he watched as the shuttle bus, carrying all of his luggage, lumbered down the street on its way back to San José. Forty-five minutes later, the two women walked in, laden with bags of newly-purchased goods, and approached the piercing stare of the man of the family.

"Sorry, Hon, we just sort of lost track of time. Did the bus leave yet?"

Thom wanted to scream but quietly said, "Uh, yeah. I think so. Maybe forty-five minutes ago. Now we're stuck." Then his face hardened. "And I am not in a good mood."

"Oh, there'll be another shuttle later. We'll just take that one."

His lips pursed. "It won't get us to the airport on time."

"Then, let's get a cab. Surely that'll work."

He eased up just a bit. "All right, I guess we're screwed anyway. Might as well spend the rest of our retirement on a taxi."

Thom went to the phone and called the local cab company. Ten minutes later, the Christophers were on their way to the airport in an old beat-up Chevy that couldn't do over thirty. Ellen and Amy wisely kept quiet while Thom calmly let several expletives emerge from under his breath, not so loud that the driver could hear, but loud enough to be perceived by anyone who knew him. They got to the airport at 12:03, jumped out of the taxi, and raced for the gate. Thom flipped the tickets on the counter, pointed to the sign with the flight number, and told the agent they had to be on that plane. The man behind the counter merely shook his head apologetically. "I'm sorry, sir. That flight is just now taking off."

Thom glared at Ellen, snatched up the tickets, and because he knew they had to get back home, flipped his Mastercard toward the ticket agent and made reservations for the next morning.

"See, Thom, it's not so bad. We even get another day in Paradise."

As the Christophers wandered away from the desk, toward a large window looking onto the tarmac, Thom continued his near-silent swearing about non-refundable tickets and whose fault it was. Ellen, wisely, kept silent, knowing all of Thom's ire was directed right at her. Minutes later, tears welling up in Ellen's eyes, everything stopped with a piercing scream coming from the window. Both turned and saw Amy pointing at the sky where a plane, their plane, erupted into an immense ball of flame. They stood there, stunned, as the huge machine disintegrated into millions of tiny pieces of metal and burning plastic, all falling into the dense, green jungle. As the airplane parts, intermixed with its human carrion, fell, the hills became ablaze with burning jet fuel. Nobody would survive…one could almost feel the infestation of jungle life devouring any scorched evidence of humans that might remain. There would be nothing human left, alive or dead, to be found.

The Christophers stood there for what seemed to be hours when Thom finally spoke. "God Almighty."

Ellen and Amy were now in a state of almost complete shock and Thom led them to a nearby bench where, with tears in his eyes, he tried to comfort the two women. "Hon, it's all right. We're fine. Everything's going to be okay."

She choked through the sobs, "Thom, we should have died. We were supposed to have died. Oh, Thom."

He reached out, wrapped his arms around the two women of his life, and did his best to comfort them. A few minutes later, he realized that the news of the crash would almost immediately be broadcast throughout North America and pulled away. Thom raced to a bank of pay phones and made two collect calls. The first went to Ellen's parents, telling them that they were safe and not to worry, and the other to Richard and Jennifer McClain, who were supposed to pick them up at the airport in Houston, giving them the same message, that they had missed the doomed flight.

* * * * * * * * * *

The next morning at 8:30, in a small café in San José, Thom again sat, sipping his last cup of coffee. He looked up across the table. "Hon, do you want to do any last minute shopping?"

"What?"

"It can't hurt."

Ellen smiled, saying she was all shopped out, and the Christopher family walked out of the hotel and boarded the shuttle.

Two and one-half hours later, they were nestled into their seats, wait-ing for take-off, and four hours after that they landed at Houston Intercontinental Airport. Emerging from the customs area, Thom saw Richard and Jen McClain with Richard holding up a copy of that morn-ing's Houston Chronicle: PLANE ERUPTS, 183 KILLED. In smaller print under the headlines, Thom read, THREE HOUSTONIANS ABOARD DOOMED AIRLINER.

Jen grabbed and hugged both Ellen and Amy as Thom tore the paper out of Richard's hands and scanned the front page. He paled as he stood motionless and read his own obituary and those of his wife and child. Then he started to laugh and then tears welled up in his eyes. It was just too surreal.

That evening, Thom and Ellen watched the six o'clock news as an agent for the FAA announced that fragments of a bomb had been found at the crash site of Continental Airlines Flight 1508. Although no one had taken credit for the incident, the agent said that law enforcement officials throughout the hemisphere were currently working on several leads. The late-evening anchor for Channel 2 News then came on the air announcing the names of the three Houstonians who were aboard the flight. Thom and Ellen sat there, mesmerized, both as white as ghosts. Ellen eventually broke the silence by quipping, "I guess we should have bought the flight insurance."

Thom smiled and then went and called the Channel 2 Newsroom informing the reporter that the Christophers were very much alive.

CHAPTER 47

A week later, just after New Year's and after all the hullabaloo had died down, Thom got up early, and even though the university was not in session, showered and shaved, and drove to the campus. In his office, he puttered around for several minutes, getting his desk in order and updating some of the materials for the new semester. With all that done, he took a break and walked over to the post office to check the mail. He was in luck, all but one of his Kodak mailers had arrived.

Thom hurried back to the office and tore open the flap of the first mailer. He meticulously thumbed through the prints, subconsciously reliving each experience, then opened the second, and did the same until all the pictures had been viewed. The snap-shots were great, crisp and clear, and he was glad he had splurged and spent all that money on the Nikon.

The next morning, Thom followed much the same routine—getting his desk in order and then going to the mailroom. Aha, the last mailer! He carefully slipped it into his pocket and hurried back to the office where he viewed the last set of prints. The sunsets, with the purples, and oranges, and pinks, over the Pacific Ocean were stunning, the emerald green of the jungled mountains literally jumped out at you from the deep azure sky, and the photos of the deep green sea absolutely amazed him. When he reached the end of the roll, print number 24, he sat and admired how beautiful his wife and daughter were, sitting in the small, dark bistro, and how they looked like the perfect family. He truly was lucky.

Something about that last photograph nagged at him. He couldn't put his finger on it, but even after he had put all the prints into his brief-case and prepared to go home, he stopped and pulled out that last picture for another view. In an instant, it was as if somebody had put a plastic bag over his head, then wrapped a pair of mammoth arms around his chest in a bear hug, squeezing the life right out of him. He was dizzy, the visual world began to blacken, and he felt the room start to swirl around him. *It can't be. It just can't be.* Thom sat down, actually fell, into his desk chair and stared at the photograph and murmured, "Oh my God."

*   *   *   *   *   *   *   *   *   *

Minutes later, the spell Thom was under was broken by, "Damn, you look terrible. Costa Rica doesn't agree with you or is it knowing that your guardian angel again pulled you from the jaws of death that's get-ting to you?"

Thom looked up. His department head, Dr. Bryant, stood at the office door, smiling. Thom stared blankly at his friend for a few seconds, then apologized and excused himself, saying that he had to get home, there was an emergency. He pushed the picture into the briefcase, grabbed the satchel, and quickly walked to the car. It was not until he was halfway home that he realized he was still hyperventilating. He pulled over to the side of the road and willed himself to calm down—he knew he would die if he continued this way.

By the time he got home, he had calmed down but the excitement grew again upon seeing his wife sitting in the living room. "Ellen, you have to see this picture. Hurry."

"Thom, what's wrong? You look like you've seen a ghost."

"I have, Babe. I have."

Thom opened up the case and thrust the picture at his wife. "Look at it. Look at it closely."

Ellen examined the picture, then, looked at her husband with a smile, and said, "It's a great picture, I really like it. Doesn't Amy look beautiful?"

"No! Look at it closely. In the background."

She held the photo in the light and squinted a bit, then smiled. "Oh, you're right. He *is* there. What's the big deal?"

"What's the big deal?!!!"

Ellen stared at her half-deranged husband and stated very simply, "It's the man who wanted to buy your film. Let's see if we can find his girlfriend." Then she held the picture close to her face.

Thom grabbed the photo, inspected it, and finally realized that, in fact, the man with gray-yellow hair *was* in the picture. He thrust the print back in front of his wife and stabbed with his finger at the second man standing in the background of the photograph. "That's the guard!"

"Who?"

"That's the guard! At the Wynne Unit."

"Oh, Thom, you're not making any sense. The guard was killed."

"No, the second guard. That's him!"

For a second, Ellen thought about how to handle the situation, then, decided to be honest. "Thom, Honey, you've been through a lot. The thing at the prison, going back to work full-time, the airline crash, and everything else have just put too much stress on you too quickly. I think we should call the doctor and go in as a family to talk to her."

Thom stared at her, disbelieving his own wife's response, when Amy walked into the room. "Hey, Dad, are those more pictures of the trip?" Without waiting for a reply and with Thom still staring, mouth agape, at his wife, the young teen grabbed the photo out of Thom's hand and took a close look. Her first words were, "That's him!"

Simultaneously, both Thom and Ellen blurted out, "Who?!"

"The man who was following us. Who do you think? I told you it wasn't my imagination. And get this, he's talking to that guy who wanted to buy Dad's film."

Thom grabbed the photo and looked. It was true; the two were talking. Ellen, now pale as a ghost, whispered, "Thom, please call Richard. Please."

CHAPTER 48

Thom Christopher raced down Allen Parkway, made a left at Drake and another into the parking lot of what appeared to be an abandoned fire station, circa 1930s. He hopped out of the car, photograph in hand, hurried to the steel door at the front of the building, and pressed a button. The response over the speaker was immediate, "Please look into the camera and state your name."

"Thom Christopher. Here to see Lieutenant McClain."

With the familiar buzzing sound, Thom turned the door handle and let himself in to a small, cramped hallway. To his right, he recognized Sergeant Calabros, McClain's assistant, who was walking toward him. "This way, Doc, the Lieutenant's in his office."

Down the short corridor and into a small, cramped office, Thom found Richard sitting behind a desk piled high with stacks of paperwork. Behind him, bookshelves overflowed with what appeared to be hundreds upon hundreds of police training manuals. To his right was a twenty-one-inch color television set complete with two videocassette players.

"Well, I trust you didn't have *another* near-death experience coming down I-45."

Sweat poured down Thom's face, and without a word, he handed the photograph across the desk. McClain gave the print a cursory glance and said, "So?"

"Richard, the man in the background is the guard from the Wynne Unit."

The police officer looked again at the photograph. "Where'd you get this picture?"

The response was immediate. "In Costa Rica."

"Yeah, OK. So what's this about a guard?"

Thom rose, leaned across the desk and pointed to the man standing in the background of the picture. "That's him! That's the guard from the Wynne Unit. That's him!"

Richard pursed his lips. "Wait a minute...the guard was killed. You know that, and I know that. You're forgetting that I was there."

"That's not true. When we came out, everybody said the guard was dead. I thought he got killed, too. But he didn't." Thom shoved his finger at the picture. "He's right there."

"You're saying there was another survivor? That's bullshit. It didn't go down that way."

The situation was quickly getting out of hand. "Damn it—that's him!"

McClain quickly got up, and gently, as a friend, took Thom by the shoulders. "Sit down, take it easy. Let's talk this over."

Thom obeyed and Richard continued, "You know about post traumatic stress disorder?"

"I don't care—that's the guard."

"Think about it. The guard was killed. And regardless, you said the guard's face was bandaged the entire time you were in the unit. You *couldn't* have recognized him. That was months ago, for crying out loud."

Thom looked down and quietly said, "At the end."

"What?"

His voice grew. "At the end. They took the tape off. I saw him." Then, jabbing his finger at the photograph, he reiterated, "And that is him."

McClain's voice was now also loud. "You're imagining it. All the shit that's happened is just catching up with you. Or maybe that plane crash has you rattled. Man, you gotta talk to somebody."

Now, Thom lost it and screamed across the desk, "I'm not imagining it—it happened. He's really there. Believe me. And look at the other guy, the one talking to him."

Richard returned to his stoic mien. "Who's he?"

"The guy with the blonde hair. He tried to buy the film from my camera." Thom was still jabbing his finger at the photo. "And how come Amy saw the guard following us?"

The situation *was* out of control. "Fuck it—get a hold of yourself—this is nothing."

Thom was on the verge of tears. "Please, Richard, help me. I have to know."

At the point of exasperation, he finally relented and agreed to have the photograph circulated. He called in Calabros, had him make some photostatic enlargements of the picture, and then faxed a copy to a friend in the Criminal Investigation Division. To further placate his friend, he sent another to Ratley Mace at the local office of the FBI. That done, Richard looked at Thom. "There, if anything comes up, I'll know and then you'll know. Now, just go home."

Relieved, if not a bit embarrassed, Thom thanked the lieutenant, and headed toward the door.

*   *   *   *   *   *   *

By the next morning, McClain had put the whole episode of the previous afternoon out of his mind and arrived at work just before seven. He let himself into the building and walked down the narrow hallway to his office. To his surprise, the door was open. Upon entering, Richard spotted two men sitting in front of his desk.

"What the hell's going on? Who let you guys in…?" Richard's words were quickly cut off as he recognized Ratley Mace. "What're you doing here?

Mace was dressed in a dark gray business suit with a white shirt and black tie that seemed too taut for his thick neck. The other agent was dressed the same. "McClain, this is Murdoch from the Bureau."

Richard extended his hand and said, "Nice to meet you. Now, what're you guys doing here, and how'd you get in?"

Mace cut to the chase, "Where'd the picture come from?"

"What picture? What the hell are you talking about?"

"The one you faxed me. Where'd you get it?"

The realization hit Richard like a ton of bricks. He uttered a near silent, "Shit," then spoke slowly. "It *was* the guard, wasn't it?"

"I don't know anything about that. I just want to know where the picture came from?"

McClain was just a little guarded. "A friend of mine took it. Now, you tell me: Who is in the picture?"

Mace looked McClain squarely in the eyes. "The man is Sal Vizziani. Now, where'd it come from?"

"Thom Christopher took it. He and his family were in Costa Rica, a couple weeks ago…some little town."

Mace was incredulous. "What?! The same guy from the prison?"

"Yeah."

"*He* took this picture?"

"Yeah."

"McClain, Vizziani was in that unit about the time of the siege. We had a warrant for him, but by the time we went to pick him up, he was gone—just disappeared."

Suddenly, things clicked for McClain. "Mace, he was in on the whole thing. Christopher swears he was the guard during the siege."

"But they found the guard, dead in the lounge."

"That one had been dead for a couple days. There was a second guard, and it was your man."

"Oh, bull shit."

"He must've just walked out in all the commotion."

"But how? Where'd he go?"

A light again came on. "The fucking helicopter."

"What?"

"There were two med-evac helicopters, the first one left with no one on it. That's how that bastard pulled it off. He just flew away. I told you those assholes weren't smart enough to do it on their own. Someone on the outside was running the whole thing. They got that asshole outta there and now I want to know who did it."

Mace looked down, shrugged, and said, "We'll find out. We'll make the connection, leave it up to us."

"Mace, I want to know."

"You will, rest assured."

Moments later, secure in their government issue blue Taurus, Ratley looked at Murdoch. "We have him."

"Sal?"

"Not just Sal, the whole damn family. Remember the bomb fragments from that plane? It was linked to a drug cartel in Columbia. For years, the Bureau has figured that Garubba and the cartel were connected but we could never prove it. Vizziani's his brother-in-law. All we have to do is put a link between Sal and the bomb, and the whole Syndicate could fall. Let's get back to the office and get clearance from Washington." Mace sat back in the passenger seat and smiled smugly. "You know, this is the beginning of a great day."

CHAPTER 49

Across James Vernon's pristinely-kept desk, Phillip Kimble slid a large, brown folder marked "EYES ONLY." The Assistant Director broke the seal, removed the document, and read.

"Are there any other copies of this report?"

"No, sir. It came directly from Mace. He was instructed to keep this matter absolutely top secret."

"Good. Now you understand what has to be done?"

"Yes, sir."

Vernon's next words were stern, as though he were holding back a huge amount of anger. "You should have neutralized Vizziani at the time. God knows how you fucked it up, but you better not fail again."

Kimble stared at the floor directly in front of him. "Sir, we just had some bad luck down there. No one could have foreseen it."

Vernon, calmly but with an edge of sarcasm in his voice, responded, "Right. Now, how much does Mace know?"

Kimble shrugged. "Not much."

"What about this civilian, Christopher? And that cop, McClain? What do they know?"

"They're probably aware of the scam in the prison. As for our involvement, I suspect that they know nothing."

"But you don't really know." Vernon paused for a second as if trying to think what to do. He then looked across the desk and said, "Kimble, I want this taken care of—and don't leave any loose ends."

"I understand, sir."

*   *   *   *   *   *   *   *   *   *

When the agent left, James Vernon opened his top drawer, pulled out a black phone, and punched in a number. The response was almost immediate, "Federal Bureau of Investigation, Houston Office, may I help you?"

"This is Director Vernon in Washington. Put Agent Mace on the line, please."

"Yes, sir. Immediately, sir."

*   *   *   *   *   *   *   *   *

Thom and Ellen Christopher drank their morning coffee and read the Houston Chronicle while they watched the 7:30 a.m. news in the kitchen of their home in The Woodlands. The dogs, Beau and Daisy, sat at their feet, begging for scraps. Thom was still convinced that the person he saw in the photograph was the guard from the Wynne Unit and that he was somehow connected to the airplane disaster in Costa Rica. Knowing that Richard was already at work, his eyes quickly shifted from the television to the phone and back again. When it actually did ring, at about 7:45, he nearly jumped out of his skin.

"Hello."

"Thom, Richard."

"Hey! I was just about to call you. What's up?"

"Do you remember my telling you about the FBI agent, Mace?"

"Yeah. He was the guy who was hunting for that kidnapped woman and her baby."

"Well, he just left my office. The guy in the picture is some asshole named Vizziani. And get this, you were right; the prick was in prison when you were up there. Then, he just vanished."

Thom barely breathed the name, "Sal Vizziani."

"What?"

"He was the guard. Wasn't he?"

"Seems that way. From what I can figure, the plan was to get this guy out, no matter who got killed. Everybody was just a player."

"Samuels was right."

"Who?"

"Nothing, I was just thinking about something else."

"Well, Mace seemed pretty interested in the photo so he might be giving you a call. Just make yourself available."

"Sure, and hey, Richard, thanks."

"Look, Buddy, you were right."

Thom Christopher breathed the sigh, "God, I knew it."

"Yeah, congrats."

"So what do we do now?"

Richard was stunned, "What?"

"What are we gonna do about gettin' this guy?"

"The FBI is in on it now. *We* are not going to do anything. You and I are officially out of it."

Thom's heart rate went up and he could feel the head coming to his face. "He tried to murder my family—I'm sure of it. I'm not just going to sit around here and do nothing."

"You don't understand, it's up to the Feds now, and if you get in their way, you'll get nailed to the wall. So, in fact, you *are* going to sit around and do nothing. You got no choice."

Thom shook his head and mumbled, "Yeah, I guess you're right."

"Damn straight I'm right. Just let Mace do what he has to do. I think he's a pretty good guy. Now I gotta get back to work, so I'll talk to you later."

*   *   *   *   *   *   *   *   *   *

Early that afternoon, the phone on McClain's desk rang. "Lieutenant, Mace over at the FBI, I just got off the phone with Washington, and I wanted to let you know that we're taking care of this situation."

"You gonna go get him?"

There was a momentary hesitation. "This whole thing's pretty hot. We're working on a strategy right now, but everything should be resolved, and in a hurry."

McClain was pleased. "Good, let me know."

"Sure will. By the way, I have to get the picture and the negative from Christopher."

"That's kind of odd, isn't it?"

"All I know is that the boss, Vernon, said to get it."

*   *   *   *   *   *   *   *   *   *

At 6:30 that evening, Thom Christopher answered the door of his home in The Woodlands and was met by a man flashing a federal I.D. "Dr. Christopher, I'm Agent Mace with the FBI. Could I speak with you?"

"Sure, c'mon in."

Ratley Mace was led into the den where Thom immediately stated, "You were up at Huntsville. Richard McClain told me."

"Yeah, that's right. Glad you got out of there. Everything back to normal?"

"Pretty much. Anyway, what can I do for you?"

"I've been requested to pick up a photograph you showed to McClain along with the negative. Is that going to be a problem?"

There was no surprise at all. Thom responded, "No, I guess not." He walked over to the roll-top desk, retrieved the requested items and handed them to Mace. "Will I get them back?"

When the agent left, Thom walked out to the patio and casually remarked to his wife, "Thank God for double prints."

∗   ∗   ∗   ∗   ∗   ∗   ∗   ∗   ∗   ∗

Dutifully, Ratley Mace returned to his office, put the print and its negative into an envelope, and forwarded the packet by special courier to Washington, D.C.

CHAPTER 50

Once again, Philip Kimble stood in front of the desk facing Director Vernon. He had already anticipated the first question and had prepared himself. A hint of a smile crossed his face. "Sir, I think I have something you'll be pleased with."

There was not even the hint of a smile on Vernon's face. "Okay, tell me."

"Well, first of all, we get Mace, his partner, and the two civilians down to Costa Rica."

"Mace isn't a problem, but what about the others?"

"The story is that we need a positive I.D. on Vizziani for what happened in the prison so we can more quickly extradite him. Christopher's the only one who can do it."

"Will he go along with it?"

"Why not? If Mace's report is correct, Vizziani tried to kill this guy's entire family. Christopher's probably just itching to get back at this guy."

"What's the reason we give for the cop?"

"McClain and Christopher are close—drink together, family dinners, the whole nine yards. At Huntsville, McClain talked his way into running the show just to get his friend out. The way we handle it is that we tell him he's the stabilizing influence. It's gonna be stressful and Christopher will need someone to lean on. He'll go along with it."

"Maybe."

"We get them down there, locate Sal…."

Vernon interrupted, "Have you found him?"

"Not yet. But, I'm working on it."

"Get it done." Then, with a sigh, he continued, "All right, what happens next?"

"Christopher and McClain get into an altercation with Vizziani. Shots are fired. Problem's ended."

"You're confident?"

"Yes."

"What about Mace and his partner, Murdoch?"

"Once they get there, we recall them to Houston. Problem's ended."

"How?"

"Trust me, you don't want to know." Kimble paused for a few seconds, then continued. "I have to know about our contingency of agents. Who are we sending?"

"Just you. Use one or two local field agents but keep them away from Mace. Let's make sure this all goes down well—no traces, no evidence."

"Yes, sir. I'll have Mace call and get Christopher's and McClain's assistance. They trust him."

"No, I'll call," the Director said.

As Kimble left the room, Deputy Director Vernon took an envelope from the top right-hand drawer of his desk and opened it. He inspected the contents, a photograph and its accompanying negative, walked into his private bathroom, took a lighter out of his jacket pocket, and carefully lit the materials, dropping the ashes into a trash can.

✶   ✶   ✶   ✶   ✶   ✶   ✶   ✶   ✶

Thom Christopher was relieved that somebody finally believed him about the guard and that the greatest law enforcement entity in the world was hunting him down. Richard was right, it was now a matter for the FBI and Thom had to stay out of it. Still, he *was* part of it; had he not spotted Sal in the first place, nobody would even have known where he was. Whether it had been because of his own hostage situation, that he had tried to murder his family, or even watching Rambo and Indiana Jones movies—he wanted to be there, to be involved.

As he sat thinking about all the possibilities, the phone rang. "Thom, this is Richard."

"Hey, any news?"

"Actually, yes."

"Cool. What's up?"

"Well, it's kind of an odd deal. The FBI wants to make sure they have the right guy before they try to extradite him."

"Of course they have the right guy."

"They want us, you and me, to go down and ID Vizziani, apparently, it'll help in the extradition."

"You're kidding?"

"Hey, surprised the shit outta me, too. But, what the hell—a free trip."

"I'll have to ask Ellen. She's gonna be pissed."

"Thom, this is not exactly a request, it's from the FBI. It's more like, you be there."

Thom was so pumped that he found it hard to inhale. "When do we go? And how long?"

"Mace says tomorrow, leave from Ellington."

"The Air Force base?"

"Yeah. Private jet from the FBI, the whole deal. I'll pick you up at seven, tomorrow morning. Be ready."

CHAPTER 51

Thom's fears of telling Ellen were realized as a chilling frost pervaded the Christopher household that evening. Ellen reasoned that if Sal *had* been in custody in Texas before, the authorities certainly would have enough information on him, and thus, they don't need her husband. Thom countered with the fact that Costa Rica was a foreign country and who knew how their laws worked. Anyway, the thought of going down and nabbing Sal Vizziani so clouded his thoughts that nothing was going to get in his way. Besides, nothing in the past year made any sense, so why should this be any different. At one point, Ellen even suggested that she go along with them, but this was absolutely out of the question. The FBI hadn't invited her; she had no real first-hand knowledge of what Sal looked like; and if something did go wrong, Thom didn't want her anywhere near the place. She even threatened to just go on her own. When all was said and done, though, she knew he was going, and so did he.

That night, neither could sleep, the excitement too much for Thom, and the fear too much for Ellen. So they lay there silently, afraid to awaken the other even though each was wide awake. At six, Thom slipped out of bed, took a quick shower, went downstairs, and started the coffee. A half-hour later, he took a cup of tea up to Ellen and silently placed it on the nightstand. He leaned over, gave his wife a kiss on the cheek, and started out the door, knap-sack draping over his shoulder. Ellen, still awake, continued to seethe at what she considered incredible stubbornness—even stupidity—in the man she loved.

✻ ✻ ✻ ✻ ✻ ✻ ✻ ✻ ✻ ✻

By 7:30, Richard and Thom zipped down I-45, on their way to Ellington, then on to Costa Rica.

"How much grief did you get from Ellen?"

"You wouldn't have believed it."

"Yeah, I would, I was just smart enough not to tell my wife."

Thom was amazed. "You didn't tell Jen?"

"Nah. She'd a only bitched."

"Well, Ellen was even demanding that she come with me. When I told her that wasn't an option, she said she'd just go on her own. Can you believe that?"

"Hey, I'm not surprised. The woman showed up at the Wynne Unit when I specifically told her to stay home." This realization hit him, and he immediately picked up the phone.

"Mace. McClain here. We're on our way. Listen, I want you to do me a favor." McClain explained what he wanted from Ratley Mace who instantly agreed, saying that it seemed the best thing. The FBI man placed a call, and five minutes later, the plan was set in motion.

✻ ✻ ✻ ✻ ✻ ✻ ✻ ✻ ✻ ✻

With her husband gone, Ellen hopped out of bed, drank her tea, showered, and slipped into a pair of blue jeans and a light blue denim shirt. Next, she packed a small carry-on bag with some toiletries, a couple changes of clothing, and a pair of sneakers. She got Amy out of bed and safely off to a neighbor's house, then got into her car. She went down the Hardy Toll Road to the proper exit, then into the short-term parking lot. In the airport concourse, she went directly to the Continental counter. Check book in hand, she asked the agent for a direct flight to San José.

The middle-aged, gaunt-faced airline ticket agent, dressed in gray trousers and a blue blazer sporting the airline logo on the pocket, punched in a few symbols on the keyboard, and stared at the monitor. Without even looking up, he asked, "Passport?"

Ellen dug into the backpack and slid the small booklet across the counter where the agent inspected it. With a few numbers punched into the computer, he looked up. "Mrs. Christopher, I'm sorry but this passport isn't valid."

"What? That doesn't make any sense. I just used it last month. Look at the expiration date."

"Sorry, ma'am. Perhaps you should speak to Customs and Immigration."

Ellen was in a state of shock and then started to lose her temper. "No!" she yelled. "I want to speak to your supervisor. Get him in here right now."

The man behind the counter remained unperturbed. "I'm sorry, but I am the supervisor. There is nothing I can do. You'll have to speak with a representative of Customs and Immigration."

Ellen got directions, and stormed off, reaching the appropriate office in a matter of minutes. The large houseplant in the corner of the office seemed an incongruity: the room was your typical run-of-the-mill government office. Atop the gray metal desk sat a plastic "In/Out" box next to a government-issue computer terminal. Various files were neatly piled in the corner of the desk. The nameplate on the desk said, "Mrs. Corcoran," who sat, quietly filing her nails. Ellen tried to regain her composure. "Miss, the man from the airlines says my passport isn't any good. That can't be, I only used it a month ago."

Emery board still in hand, she glanced up. "Could I see your documents, please?"

The passport was slid across the desk, inspected, inspected again, then compared with data shown on another government terminal. She wrinkled her eyebrows as if questioning the screen and said, "Mrs. Christopher, I'm sorry, but I'll have to hold on to your passport—it's been flagged."

Ellen screamed, "What does that mean? By whom?"

"I'm sorry, that information isn't available."

She was livid. "Then give me my passport back. You can't keep it. Give it back to me."

Without warning, a uniformed security officer hustled in from a back room and perched himself next to Ellen's chair. "Is there a problem, Mrs. Corcoran?"

She looked across inquiringly at Ellen who by now had almost completely sunken into a chair, being dwarfed by the uniformed giant. Ellen shook her head, *no, there was no problem.*

With tears in her eyes, she politely asked, "Why was my passport flagged? It has to be a mistake."

She checked her computer screen again. "I'm sorry, I really am, but it only says here, 'National Security.' That's all the information I have."

Ellen then realized what had happened, *Damn that McClain, damn him to Hell!* She reached down, picked up her backpack, and without a word, left the room. By the time she reached the car, tears were running freely down her cheeks. She got behind the wheel, revved the engine, and roared out of the parking lot with thoughts of just driving to Costa Rica. Across most of Texas, then Mexico, Guatemala, Nicaragua, and all without a passport? No, that wouldn't work, and she reluctantly resigned herself to go home and sit by the phone. *He'll be home by tomorrow, anyway. All safe and sound.*

         *   *   *   *   *   *   *   *   *

While all this was going on, McClain, Christopher, and Agents Mace and Murdoch were flying at 22,000 feet over the Gulf of Mexico. Their gear, Thom's knap-sack and Richard's carry-on along with a briefcase, were stowed in under-seat compartments. McClain looked over at Mace, "So, you were pretty vague on the phone. Exactly what is the set-up for I.D.ing this guy?"

Without blinking, the agent said, "The entire op is compartmentalized. My orders are to get you down there. Then you'll be met by an in-country agent, probably go to the local jail, there'll be a line-up, and you guys pick out Sal."

"You used the term 'probably.'"

"I said it was compartmentalized. I don't know everything that's going on."

"Shouldn't this thing be really straight forward?"

"I can't talk about it. It's all 'need to know.' Came from the top and procedures are procedures. Sorry, but case closed."

The last statement broke off the conversation and all four men sat in their respective chairs, Richard looking out the window, Thom napping, Murdoch with a spy novel, and Mace jotting down notes on a legal pad. An hour or so later, McClain looked up at Ratley. "By the way, how long you guys had my phones tapped?"

With a look of absolute incredulity on his face, the agent blurted out, "What?! What are you talking about?"

"My phones are bugged. Home and work. How come?"

"Christ, McClain, we aren't in the business of spying on cops. You know that."

"Well, somebody is."

Wearily, the agent responded, "I'll check it out. Okay? Just give me a break."

McClain looked down and muttered, "Yeah, sure."

*   *   *   *   *   *   *   *   *

On the final approach into San José International Airport, Thom and Richard both gazed out the windows, each anticipating a quick end to this search for Sal. Murdoch never uttered a word and Mace did nothing but continue his apparent note-taking on the legal pad.

As they taxied toward the main building, Thom continued to stare out the window, once again mesmerized by the countryside. This time, though, it was not the beauty of the mountains that so fully held his attention; this time he stared in horror directly at the hillside where he had witnessed the deaths of one-hundred-eighty innocent victims—someone wanted him dead. The spell was finally broken by a meaty finger poking him in the arm. "Hey, Buddy, let's hit the road."

At the jet's portal, Mace was first carrying a small suitcase and a metal briefcase, then McClain with his duffel bag and briefcase, followed by Murdoch, and finally, Thom Christopher, the knap-sack slung over his shoulder. As they crossed the tarmac, the urge to flee back to the aircraft was almost unbearable. *Ellen had to be right. If they knew he was in jail in Texas, why do they need me here? Just turn around and get back on the damn plane. Just do it!* But he kept on, he had come this far, and he was going to see it through to the end.

They all entered a small hangar where Mace imperceptibly swore under his breath, "Damn." He then extended his hand to the man walking toward him and said in a rather guarded manner, "Kimble, I didn't realize that you were the contact man."

CHAPTER 52

In a beat-up sedan at the edge of the airport, he sat and watched the comings and goings across the tarmac with a pair of high-powered binoculars. The man followed the images into the hangar, flipped his Marlboro out the window, and picked up the cell phone on the seat beside him. "Talk to me, Max."

"They just arrived, right on time."

"How many?"

"Four got off the plane. That guy Christopher and three more. Two gotta be FBI."

"Good. The other one has to be McClain."

"Whaddya want me to do?"

"Just follow 'em. And keep in contact."

"You got it, Boss."

The phone in Max's hand went dead, and he continued his surveillance of the hangar.

* * * * * * * * * *

Inside the quonset-style hangar, Agent Kimble welcomed Thom and Richard thanking them both for coming down to make a positive identification. He then motioned Mace and Murdoch toward the door. Outside, Kimble handed over a sealed envelope that Ratley opened and scanned. "I don't understand—we're going back to Houston? What gives?"

"You got me but that's what the directives say. Hey, ask Vernon, all I'm doing if following orders. The man upstairs said I'm supposed to handle everything from here on out." While Mace reread the communiqué, Kimble cleared his throat, "The plane leaves in forty-five minutes. Just make sure you're on it."

Ratley Mace looked hard into Kimble's eyes, unable to discern anything but the cold hard look of a lifetime agent, and said, "I'll be there," then quickly added, "Listen, we haven't eaten since Houston. All right if I catch a bite in the airport lounge? I'll only be a few minutes."

"Sure. But keep an eye on the clock."

All three agents went back into the hangar where Mace signaled to Richard McClain who responded immediately. He told Murdoch to keep Thom, still ashen-faced, company until it was time to get back on the plane and suggested that he and Richard have a quick drink.

✶   ✶   ✶   ✶   ✶   ✶   ✶   ✶   ✶   ✶

In the dimly-lit bar at an out-of-the-way table, Ratley Mace did not mince words, "I don't like it."

Richard straightened up. "Don't like what? What are you talking about?"

"This op isn't right." He sipped a coke and looked squarely at McClain. "I did some checking before I left, asked around. Nobody seems to know anything about this, and I asked the right people—ones I can trust—they're clueless."

McClain took on a pensive mood as Ratley continued, "This kind of operation…." The agent glanced at his watch and told McClain he was going to be late for the jet back to Houston. He reached into his inside jacket pocket and withdrew an envelope. "Well, these are my notes. I wrote them on the plane down here. After I'm back in Houston, take a look at 'em. I'll do some checking as soon as I get to the office." He then pulled out his wallet and produced a business card, scribbling a number on the back. "If you have any problems, call me at this number, it's safe."

This interchange caused some uneasiness, even fear in McClain, a small amount of fear but fear just the same. He walked Mace through the terminal building and was about to leave when the agent looked out the door and stopped. "Crap. There goes the jet." He glanced at McClain and said, "Do me a favor and don't mention this. Kimble has the ear of one of the Directors. and if they know I missed the damned jet, I'll get all sorts of shit. I'll have to take a commercial flight back."

"Not a problem with me…. Look, I gotta get back to Christopher. I'll talk to you."

"Yeah, okay. Listen, McClain, things are probably all right down here, but it's just kinda weird. I can't explain right now, but if there's any trouble, call me."

With that, the two men parted company, Ratley Mace going toward a bank of airline desks and McClain leaving the concourse to meet up with his friend. As he got to the door, he heard Mace's voice, "McClain, watch your back."

Richard turned and continued his trek, lightly touching the envelope inside his shirt pocket.

*   *   *   *   *   *   *   *   *   *

Two hours later, Richard and Thom found themselves in a "gringo" hotel, reserved by the Bureau, in the middle of San José. Richard's uneasiness had waned, and he reasoned that any problems between

Mace and Kimble were just out of some unhealthy competition within the Bureau. He had actually put the entire episode out of his mind.

After settling in, Richard yelled over to Thom, "Hey, Buddy, let's go and get some dinner."

As they headed out the door, Thom asked, "Shouldn't we tell Kimble where we we're going? Maybe he'll need us to make the I.D."

"If he wants us, he'll find us. Besides, he ain't your mother, and I'm hungry and need a drink. Screw 'im."

✳   ✳   ✳   ✳   ✳   ✳   ✳   ✳   ✳   ✳

Several drinks later, McClain blearily looked up. "Incidentally, you call your wife?"

"Shit." He dutifully motioned to the waiter and had a phone brought to the table. A minute later, Ellen answered, "Thom!"

"Hon, we're down here, everything's okay."

"When are you coming back? Is this over yet?"

"Calm down. We'll be home, like, tomorrow. Oh, yeah, Richard says hello."

Simultaneously, McClain cringed and Ellen yelled into the phone, "Is that jerk there?"

"Sittin' right here. Wanna talk to him?" McClain quickly waved his hands to ward off any idea that he might speak, Thom got the message and said into the receiver, "Sorry, Babe, he's a little bit busy right now."

"You tell that jerk his wife thinks he's on a call-up. And, ask the S.O.B. why he cancelled my passport. I know he was behind the whole damned thing."

"Oh, uh, listen, I have to go now. Why don't you call Jen and tell him Richard's with me and that we'll probably be back tomorrow?"

"Probably? What does that mean?" Before the question could be answered, the line was disconnected. Thom replaced the receiver and looked at Richard who was peacefully sucking down another beer. "Ellen's calling Jen to give her the whole story."

"Ah, she'll get over it; she always does. By the way, how pissed is your wife at me?"

"Not at all. Somethin' about 'that jerk' and 'son-of-a-bitch.' She was pretty nice about it."

Finishing up their last beers, the two got up, paid the tab, and headed back to their room.

CHAPTER 53

Ratley Mace deplaned at Bush Intercontinental and made his way through customs, which was rather perfunctory given his Bureau I.D. card. Going through the doors into the main concourse, he glimpsed a television screen in the open-air bar to his left. Something about a private jet lost over the Caribbean, but Ratley was in too much of a hurry to pay any attention. He got to a bank of phones and called Cassie, his wife, Cassandra, and told her to meet him at the Spaghetti Warehouse for dinner. Mace then caught a shuttle into town and walked the extra block to the restaurant.

* * * * * * * * * *

At eleven o'clock that evening, McClain and Christopher saw the CNN report of a missing plane on the TV from their room in the hotel. It meant nothing until the reporter stated that the small jet had taken off from San José *en route* to Houston. McClain froze. Christopher sat and stared at the screen. *It's gotta be a coincidence.*

250

Without a word, the cop walked over to the dresser, opened the top drawer, and pulled out the folded legal sheets Ratley Mace had given him hours before. He opened the papers and held them at arm's length and felt a tightening in his chest and a chill in his spine.

"Hey, Buddy, how about we get outta here and get a coupla beers?"

The response was a quick, "Good," and the two headed out into the night, hunting for a friendly café and an even friendlier beer. On a side street, they found a quiet little place and Thom signaled the waiter, "Dos cervesas, Imperiales."

"Hey, I didn't know you spoke Spanish."

"I don't. 'Dos cervezas' is *about* the only thing I know. Means 'two beers,' I think. Dos mas means 'two more.'"

"Two very important words."

With the beers on the way, McClain's expression went from "good ol' boy" to "serious cop." "Ratley Mace doesn't trust this Kimble guy."

"So?"

"Well, Mace gave me this letter; it outlines how the operation should have gone down. Remember when they got that Kaczynski guy up there in Montana or Wyoming? They didn't need any civilians, they did their surveillance and went in and got the guy."

"Yeah, but this is different."

"There's more, they bugged my phone."

"Oh, bull shit. That's illegal. Besides, how would you even know?"

"There's a buzzing, sometimes a humming, on the line. And almost always there are nearly silent clicks."

Thom jolted upright. "That's what happened to my phone. Ellen's been bitchin' about it ever since we got back. Says the lines are crossed or something. Are you sure about this?"

"Yep. Assholes probably convinced some judge it was national security or some other bullshit. Who knows? Anyway, don't worry about it, let's just get back to business."

Why don't we just go down there tomorrow, wherever it is, I.D. Sal, and get outta here."

"That's the problem. Mace says there's no hard evidence that he's being held. As near as he can figure out, they don't even know where the hell he is."

Thom slumped in his chair. "Shit, Richard, what're we gonna do?" With a new wave of fear, he said, "Let's just leave—get a flight out tomorrow."

McClain thought thought about it, then sat back, smiled, and said, "Well, we could, or we could find the sonuvabitch, hand him over, and end this shit."

"You're serious."

"Sure, what the hell?"

Thom considered McClain's proposal for a second, thought about the prison, then about the safety of his wife and child, and with resolve in his voice, agreed. "Yeah, what the hell."

* * * * * * * * * *

At a table for two in the bar of the Spaghetti Warehouse, Cassie Mace looked at her husband, "Why aren't you eating? Did something go wrong at work?"

"Sorry, Babe. I can't talk about it."

"Well, whatever happened, don't worry about it. Try to relax. Here, have some more wine."

"You're probably right." He picked up the carafe of Merlot and poured both his wife and himself their drinks. Holding the wine goblet in the air, he toasted his young wife and both brought the drinks to their mouths. In an instant, Cassie Mace went white and then gasped as her glass shattered into a million shards on the restaurant floor. Ratley turned and looked up to see the image of his face and that of Murdoch on a television screen. They were identified as employees of Comptron,

Inc., saying they were apparently lost on an ill-fated flight from Costa Rica to the United States.

The couple sat and stared as the reporter speculated a connection between this flight and the airliner that had blown up in the mountains surrounding San José just a few weeks before. Moments later, when his composure returned, Ratley Mace turned to his wife and ordered, "Cassie, I want you to go home. Pull the blinds, don't answer the phone, and don't go near the door—don't talk to anybody."

Cassandra was visibly shaken. "Ratley, what's going on? What kind of trouble are you in?"

"Hon, please do what I say."

"Please, tell me."

But the agent was insistent, "I can't. Listen, I have to go to the office. I'll call you later tonight."

She was used to being the wife of a G-man, but this was different and her voice started to break. "Okay, I'll do it, but be careful."

In a reassuring tone, he told her, "Don't worry. I'm always careful." He opened his wallet, uttered an expletive, and asked, "You have any cash? I only have credit cards."

She went into her purse, pushed aside the paraphernalia all women seem to need to carry with them, and found a hidden compartment. She dropped a twenty on the table, and both silently left the restaurant. Outside, Ratley watched his wife drive away as he hailed a cab.

Mace checked his watch: *12:30 a.m. Good.*

Ratley Mace spent the next few hours on the computer in his office carefully looking for anything that might connect, even remotely, Sal Vizziani, Philip Kimble, the Bureau, and the Garubba family. At four, his phone rang. He picked it up and listened. "Hello, Mace? You there?" The voice was familiar. "McClain."

"You all right?"

"OK, now you watch your back."

"Keep in touch."

CHAPTER 54

In the beat-up sedan, Max punched in numbers on a cell phone and spoke, "Boss, the cop and the other guy are at that bar, Nino's."

"Anybody with 'em?"

"Nah, whaddya want me to do?"

"Just keep an eye on 'em. And don't do anything stupid."

When the phone receiver went dead, Max roughly shoved it back into its cradle, punched in the cigarette lighter, and waited to light up another Marlboro.

*　*　*　*　*　*　*　*　*　*

Thom Christopher glanced over at McClain. "So what's our first move?"

"First, we lose Kimble. Mace doesn't like him, and I trust Mace. Second, how much cash you have with you?"

"About two hundred bucks. Why?"

"Credit cards?"

"Yeah, but I don't use 'em. That's why I was teaching at the prison in the first place—to pay 'em off."

"We'll stick with cash for now, see how far we get. If we have to, we'll use the cards." Richard ordered two more beers and asked, "Where'd you say you took that picture?"

"Tamarindo. It's on the Pacific coast."

"How far?"

"Maybe three or four hours by car."

"All right, we get our shit outta that hotel and get lost until morning. Then we'll rent a car."

✶ ✶ ✶ ✶ ✶ ✶ ✶ ✶ ✶ ✶

The phone on John Vernon's desk rang. "Yes?"

"Sir, the birds have flown."

Vernon's blood pressure shot up, and he felt a sharp pain in the middle of his chest. "Where?"

"They've got to be in town. It's too late to get out into the provinces."

Vernon leaned back and tried to breathe slowly and evenly. "Make contact with our office down there, an agent named Connally. Have him pick up the trail. Say nothing, just have him locate them. And, you, you find Sal Vizziani."

"Yes, Sir."

✶ ✶ ✶ ✶ ✶ ✶ ✶ ✶ ✶ ✶

By one the next afternoon, McClain and Christopher were in the middle of downtown Tamarindo. Everything was as it had been just a month before—the street vendors, the tourists with their little name tags, and the men in their white chino pants trailing wives dressed in sun dresses.

Thom parked the rental car on a side street, and McClain got out and stretched. "Let's find some sort of hotel and get some rest."

"The Hotel El Milagro is just up the road a bit."

"Big? Touristy?"

"Yeah, it's a nice place."

"No way."

"Why?"

"Two reasons. Too expensive and if somebody's looking for us, that's where they'll look."

They made their way through some of the back streets and found what had to be one of the smallest, seediest hotels in the country. Over the door, the sign read: YOUTH HOSTEL. "This is the place."

They walked in and McClain cautioned Thom, "I'll take care of this." A portly Latin, dressed in baggy gray pants and a dirty white shirt emerged from a back room and announced, "¿Señors, en qué puedo servir les?"

Richard stood speechless, staring blankly, while Thom quickly interjected, "Señor, ¿habla usted inglish?"

Raising his hand in front of him with the tiniest distance between the thumb and index finger, the man answered, "Une pukito."

Thom breathed a sigh of relief. "Señor, we need a double room, two beds, and a hot bath."

"I am sorry, but we have only a single room with one bed. That is all."

McClain looked at Thom who looked back at Richard, and simultaneously, both men nodded. "I guess we'll take it."

On the way up the stairs, the cop turned toward Thom and told him point blank, "Look, Buddy, I ain't got a homophobic bone in my body, but if you come near me, I'll have to shoot you. Understand?"

Shaking his head, Thom only sighed.

*   *   *   *   *   *   *   *   *   *

Later that afternoon, in the cafe where the original picture of Sal Vizziani was taken, Richard showed the photo to the bartender and a few waiters. Nobody recognized anything. They made their way back out to the street, and as they did so, two pairs of eyes from opposite ends of the bar stealthily followed their every move.

Toward the dinner hour, they walked through downtown and chose a well-lit and crowded restaurant, one apparently catering to the non-locals. Max peered through the windshield of the beat-up Ford parked among several other cars as Thom and Richard went inside. A few seconds later, a second man, walking alone, went through the same entrance and pulled up a chair at the bar. Max thought to himself, *What a moron.*

Inside was the usual array of diners, mostly tourists in their sixties and seventies, sprinkled with a few honeymooners who were scattered throughout the crowd; there were neither children nor any apparent native Central American. Everybody wore the same flowered shirts, the women bedecked in light, pastel skirts, and the men wearing bright white chinos. A few new straw hats hung from the backs of chairs. Several guests sported tags that said, "HELLO, MY NAME IS _____," and were paying close attention to a man in his early twenties who apparently was their tour leader. The atmosphere was loud and jovial as everyone seemed to be looking forward to the next day's adventure in "Paradise."

Half-way through the meal, Thom spoke up. "Hey, I'd better phone Ellen. She's probably expecting me to call."

Shoveling a fork piled high with fried rice into his mouth, Richard shook his head and mumbled, "You nuts?"

"She'll want to know what's goin' on."

"And when you'll be back? Then what? You gonna tell her we're out chasing the asshole? That the guy would just as soon murder us all. *That* would certainly make her feel better."

Thom morosely looked at the floor. "Yeah, I guess you're right."

"And if you call, she'll only expect a call every night. You miss just once, and you're up a creek—she figures you're dead, and if you aren't, you're an asshole. Besides, easier to ask for forgiveness than ask for permission. Just eat your damn dinner."

Thom took the advice although he wasn't very happy about it.

About twenty minutes later, the sun settling down into the waters of the quiet Pacific, Richard looked at Thom. "Hey, I'm going to the can, but do something for me?"

"Don't worry, I'll take care of the check."

"Not that. Well, do that, too. But in about ten minutes, get up and stroll on out of this place."

A puzzled look came over Thom's face to which Richard replied, "Look, just do it. When you get outside, turn left. At the end of the block, walk around the corner toward the back. Got it?"

"Sure. But, why? And where are you gonna be?"

"Don't worry about me. I'll meet you back at the hotel. And remember, take your time."

Thom nodded agreement, and Richard got up. Ten minutes later, Thom signaled the waiter for the check, fumbled with some change for the tip, and made his way toward the front door. The dark pair of eyes at the bar darted from Thom to the door of the men's room and then back to Thom. The only thought behind those eyes was, *What the hell? Where's McClain?* Without waiting, the man jumped off his stool and rushed to the men's room, and swung the door open. *Nothing!* With one eye on Thom who was close to the exit, he pushed his way into the pandemonium of the kitchen—waiters carrying trays piled high with plates, dish washers speedily wiping and rinsing, a man in the corner tossing sprigs of parsley onto the dinner plates. Nobody took notice until the intruder grabbed a busboy and demanded, "*¿Hay una puerta que sale atras?*"

The young man, clad in a dirty white Eton jacket, responded, "*Sí, señor,*" and pointed toward the back wall.

"Damn it," was his only utterance as he raced back to the dining room only to find that Thom was gone. Rushing out the door and onto the street, he barely caught sight of Thom who was just about to the end of the block.

Thom's lone emergence from the restaurant at first puzzled Max, but when he saw the second man leave, he smiled and said out loud, "What a fool." He turned on the ignition, and slowly eased the car to the corner where he could get a better vantage point of his prey. Max pulled out another Marlboro, looked down momentarily, and pushed the lighter in. When he looked up again and peered down the street, his one thought was, *Shit!*

*   *   *   *   *   *   *   *   *   *

Field Agent Connally concentrated on the man several yards in front of him. He was trying to remain as unobtrusive as possible, relying on all of the training he had received at Quantico more than twenty years before. *Wham!* In a flash, his whole throat compressed to the point of fracture, his mind blanked, and he felt himself suspended above the ground. The voice was low, almost inaudible, "Who are you?"

The response was a choked, "Ackrrr," as he realized that the meaty arm around his throat was beginning to loosen its hold. Following a rush of adrenaline, he thought, *Can I take this guy? No, it's been too long. What's that smell?* With the last thought, Connally realized the faint odor he perceived was gun oil from the barrel of a .357 Magnum, firmly planted into his right temple. He heard the click of the hammer and again tried to get the words out. "F, ackrrr, B, ackrrr...."

"Look, asshole. Why are you following my friend up there? Whaddya want with him?"

"Please, ackrrr."

In one action, McClain both eased the grip around Connally's throat and thrust his face against the rough adobe wall that formed the exterior of the restaurant. The agent coughed forth, "I'm just going back to my hotel. I don't know what you're talking about."

The expletive was spat out. "Bull shit, you dirty little bastard! You got five seconds to answer or…." McClain's voice trailed off, leaving the man to wonder what the "or" actually was.

The voice was scratchy but managed to get out, "I'm FBI. I.D.'s in my jacket."

With no wasted motion, McClain jerked the man's frame around and pushed the back of his torso into the mottled adobe. With the gun pressed firmly against Connally's chest, Richard stuck his free hand into the suit jacket and removed the wallet. "Who's the head of the field office in Houston?"

"Mace. But he's dead."

"Yeah, I know. Why are you following us?"

"I was told to watch you guys, see that you didn't get hurt. That's all there is."

"Who told you?"

"Does it really matter?"

McClain cocked the gun and the response was instantaneous, "Kimble. He's concerned about you."

"He doesn't give a rat's ass about us. Now, where's Vizziani?"

"Who?"

The gun was pushed a little more deeply into the agent's flesh. "Where is he?"

"I swear, I don't know what you're talking about. I never heard of him."

Richard looked at the man and for a reason even he didn't understand, believed him. "Listen, I'm gonna let you go. I want you and whoever else you're running with to stay the fuck away from me and my friend." He then tucked his weapon back under his shirt and into the waist of his pants and gave the agent one more quick shove into the wall.

*   *   *   *   *   *   *   *   *   *

Thirty minutes later, Richard came in to find Thom nervously pacing the circumference of the hotel room.

"What happened? Where were you?"

"No big deal. I was just taking care of some business."

In the midst of brushing his teeth, McClain mumbled, "Did you call your wife?"

Thom ashamedly admitted, "Yeah."

"And was I right?"

"Yeah. And she called Jen. You're in deep shit."

"Well, when am I not?"

CHAPTER 55

The following morning was spent going from hotel to hotel, restaurant to restaurant, hoping that someone might be able to give them a lead on their fugitive. They had no luck whatsoever. Finally, Thom brought up the subject of going to the police and McClain reluctantly agreed. "Why not? Nothing else's working."

"They'll help, won't they?"

"Might just piss 'em off, but what the hell."

The Tamarindo police station was easily located in a fairly modern building in the center of town. Thom and Richard walked in and were met by a receptionist sitting inside the main entrance. Not a police officer, she was dressed casually with light-colored slacks and a pink pastel blouse. Thom first noticed that she had brilliant brown eyes that glittered in the morning sunlight. Richard noticed that she was incredible, mid-twenties, long, lustrous, ebony hair, and high cheekbones which only enhanced the beauty of her eyes. McClain announced that they wanted to speak to the chief of police. She rose, revealing a stunningly beautiful body, well-rounded breasts, and slender, shapely legs. She walked across the room to a side door, knocked once, and stuck her head in, saying something in rapid Spanish. A second later, she turned and motioned the two foreigners toward her. "You may enter, sirs. This is the chief's office. He will see you at this time."

They took their cue and walked into a crowded little office leaving the door just slightly ajar. The desk looked like McClain's, overflowing with papers that had to be dealt with sometime in the future and drawers half pulled out. The back wall was lined with some old photographs of former chiefs of police. To the right was a bulletin board displaying numerous pictures of men wanted throughout Central America. The mustachioed officer, dressed in a light, khaki shirt and pants, motioned to the two men to have a seat. "With what may I help you gentlemen?"

"We're from Houston, and we're hunting for a man; his name is Sal Vizziani." Richard showed him the picture and remarked that the man was last seen in a restaurant in town. Then, with a slight hesitation, he casually added, "We need to ask him some questions about a case in Texas. It's no big deal, but it's important that we talk with him." Then McClain showed him his badge.

The chief looked closely at the photo, then at the badge, and announced, "I do not know this man, and if he is in this country, I do not have information as to his whereabouts."

"You're sure?"

"That is correct. Now, if you will excuse me, I must get back to work."

* * * * * * * * * *

Outside on the sidewalk, Thom asked, "Do you think he was telling the truth?"

"Don't know. If Vizziani was just passing through, there'd be no reason to remember him. Regardless, looks like we're still screwed."

When they got back to the hotel, the day clerk handed McClain the room key taped to a sealed envelope. Richard looked at his name printed across the front then carefully slit the envelope flap and removed the letter. It read:

> Señor McClain,
>
>   Please meet me at the park on the north side of town
> at 10:00 o'clock this morning. I have information for
> you. Come alone.

There was no signature, and McClain was very uneasy about the possibility of an ambush, but he also automatically checked his watch. Twenty minutes. He handed the note to Thom who said, "What d'ya think? Is this our break?"

Richard sighed, "I don't know."

Thom realized an elation growing inside and blurted out, "Well then, let's get going."

"*We're* not going. I am."

"Wait a minute. We're in this together."

"Read the letter. Whoever wrote it is very specific about the time and that I come alone. You have to stay here. Besides, I'll probably not be too long." He reached into his shirt pocket, pulled the photo out, and handed it to Thom. "Also, take care of this. It's the only real proof we have that Sal Vizziani is alive."

Thom was dejected and curtly responded, "Sure, Boss. See you when you get back."

On the way out of the hotel, Richard stopped in the foyer to get directions, then slipped down the street. Occasionally, he would cast a glance to the right and to the left expecting to see some FBI agent tailing him. When he got to the park, he quickly scanned the surroundings, gripping the handle of his pistol, wary that this might indeed be a trap.

Then a woman's voice summoned him. "Señor McClain, we must go this way."

He turned and saw the girl from the police station, now even more beautiful than just an hour before. She took his hand as if they were lovers and led him around the fountain and along an old bridle path.

"Señor, my name is Carolina. I saw you at the police station. Please be as natural as possible. Don't look, but there is a man following you."

Richard breathed heavily. "Yeah, I figured that. It's just an FBI guy— more of a pain in the ass than anything else."

A puzzled expression crept over her face. "That cannot be."

"What?"

"I am sure this man works for the one you seek."

McClain stopped cold, took the woman's shoulders in his hands, and looked into her eyes. "You know Vizziani? You know where he is?"

"Yes. I know where he is."

"Then, where?"

"Señor, you must be careful. He is very dangerous."

"Where is he?!!"

"This man lives in a villa in the mountains just north of San José, but you must not go there. It is far too dangerous—the grounds are heavily protected."

"Listen, you tell me where he is. What's the name of this place?"

She paused, looked down at the ground, then back at McClain. "It is called Casa Blanca. If you ask in the city, they will tell you." She then looked more deeply into his eyes, almost pleading, "You must be careful. He has spies everywhere, and he knows you are searching for him. You must promise me to be very careful."

McClain looked back, almost quizzically. "Why are you telling me all this, anyway? What's in it for you?"

"Señor, I hate these men. They come to our country and ruin the land. They give us money, but they take our spirit. They don't care about us, they just wish to use us, and when they are done, they discard us just like garbage. I hate them all."

McClain looked at her and saw the tears welling up in her eyes. "That can't be all of it. What else is there? Why *are* you doing this?"

She grasped his arm even tighter and said in a low voice, "That man you look for took my sister and raped her." By now, the tears were flowing down her cheeks. "And then he threw her aside. He is evil."

She gently pulled back and McClain stared into her soft brown eyes not knowing what to do or what to say. Then, in a moment, she turned and disappeared among the gardens, a faint whisper of perfume being all that remained. McClain walked back toward the hotel, extra wary, glancing to the right and left, looking at the reflections in the windows of the shops he passed, considering that perhaps the woman was right, that he might be in great danger.

*   *   *   *   *   *   *   *   *   *

Back at the hotel, he bounded up the stairs and into the room. At the abruptness of McClain's entrance, Thom jumped. "What'd you find out? Did he know where Sal was?"

"It was that woman from the police station. She told me where he was. Now let's get packed and get outta here." Then, after a pause, he added, "And by the way, I think she's got the hots for me."

The response was a pathetic, "Yeah, right."

CHAPTER 56

The trip back to the capital took the better part of four hours, and McClain and Christopher arrived as the sun was still high over the hills. In a small hotel in one of the less seedy sections of the city, they unpacked, and asked the concierge for a map and directions to Casa Blanca.

"I am sorry, Señor, but that is a private residence. Individuals are not to be admitted."

Richard took the lead, "Oh, we don't want to be admitted. We just heard that it's beautiful from up there."

"Sí, that is true, but you cannot get to the top. There is only one road and that is private."

"All right, but you do have a map?"

"Sí, Señor." And the clerk produced a large, colorful map that detailed all of the major tourist attractions.

Back in their room, they circled where they were, pinpointed "Casa Blanca," and traced the quickest route between two points. It wouldn't be easy; the only road was no more than a dirt path and appeared to be almost impassable.

Thom was worried about the car. "You really think that piece of crap we rented can make it up there?"

"No. But the road'll probably be guarded anyway, so it doesn't matter. We'll go through the jungle. It's the closest way and the safest."

"You're nuts. Think about the bugs, the snakes, everything else."

"Think about Vizziani."

It only took a second and Thom said, "Let's go."

*   *   *   *   *   *   *   *   *   *

At the edge of town, they came to a fork in the road, the right branch led toward Monteverde, the left to Casa Blanca. McClain went right, and within a mile, he backed into a dense copse of trees, turned off the engine, and waited. Only moments later, Max's beat-up black sedan rambled past them.

"That asshole's been following us since Tamarindo. Let's give him a couple of minutes and see what he does."

McClain reached into the back seat, pulled out a small briefcase, and took out one huge revolver. He loaded six bullets into the chamber and attached a cylinder to the end of the barrel.

Wide-eyed, Thom asked, "Jesus, you gonna shoot the guy?"

"Just keep quiet."

Five minutes later, the beat-up sedan raced back down the road. As it passed, Thom heard a muffled "poof," exploding the front tire, sending the car careening into a ditch, and leaving the driver cursing a blue streak.

In an instant, the nose of Richard's silencer pushed against Max's temple. "Get outta the car, asshole."

Max didn't move but uttered an indignant, "What the hell?"

"Get out!"

Pinning his prey against the front door, McClain proceeded. "Who you workin' for?"

"I don't know what you're talkin' about."

"You got to the count of three. One, two," and Richard cocked the gun.

"Hey, don't do that. I was just followin' orders."

"Whose orders?!"

"It was just orders."

"THREE!"

Max screamed, "No!!! It was Mr. V.!!"

"Vizziani?"

"Yeah, yeah. Don't shoot—just put the gun down."

"How much does he know about us?"

"He knows you left Tamarindo."

"Where is he?"

The response was stammered. "Uh…Uh…," and Richard pushed the barrel of the gun into the side of Max's face.

Motioning toward the jungle, he grudgingly said, "He's up at the house."

"Who else's up there?"

"Nobody, he's all alone."

"If you're lyin', you sack of shit, you're dead. Understand?"

"I swear it. There's nobody else there."

"We'll be back."

Richard yelled over to Thom, who was still sitting in the car watching the whole sequence of events. "Hey, bring over the rope that's in the trunk and get the tape." They bound Max's feet and hands, duct taped his mouth, and tossed him into the back seat of the sedan. Richard leaned down, picked up the gangster's cell phone from the car seat and shoved it in his pocket. He then grabbed his satchel out of the car, emptied the contents of the briefcase into it, and turned and said, "Let's go."

*   *   *   *   *   *   *   *   *

Two hours of mucking through vegetation should have defeated McClain and Christopher. But the mosquitoes as big as birds, the scream of a howler monkey scaring the shit out of them, an occasional snake watching from the limb of a tree, and the constant fight to maintain their balance on the slippery slope, only made their resolve greater. They could see the lights of the house, now, and knew they were close. Finally, at the edge of the forest, Casa Blanca was in full view. It was more an old Southern plantation home with the wide veranda and arched supports than a jungle home. The large glass windows showed that all the lights in the house were on but there wasn't any movement to be seen. As they sat gazing, Thom heard a faint beeping. "What's that?"

"I don't know."

"There, hear it?"

Realizing the sound was coming from his pocket, Richard muttered, "Ah, shit, it's that asshole's phone."

"What're you gonna do?"

McClain shrugged. "Fuck, I guess I oughta answer it," and he reached down, pulled out the cellular, and pressed the "ON" button. "Yeah."

"Who's this? Max?"

"Max ain't here. He's a little indisposed right now."

"Then who the fuck is *this*?"

"McClain."

"Oh, shit."

"Hey, Sal, we're on the way."

✳   ✳   ✳   ✳   ✳   ✳   ✳   ✳   ✳   ✳

Seconds later, Christopher, still looking at the mansion, murmured, "Whaddya think?"

"Seems a little too peaceful."

"You think he's in there?"

"Don't know. All the lights are on, but I don't see shit. We had to have spooked him, and if he's there, he ain't movin'. Wait. Look—second floor, middle window—curtain just moved."

Thom squinted. "Is he up there?"

"Maybe. Just keep on watchin'."

Even before the words registered, there was a rapid chattering, and the vegetation surrounding them came alive in an explosion of activity. Richard yanked Thom to the ground.

"Fuck! That's a goddam' Mac-10."

Thom was breathless but managed an excited, "Where?! Where?!"

More shots erupted and Richard picked up a muzzle flash about fifty yards away. "Over there!" He grabbed for the satchel and pulled out two .357 Magnums. "Here, take this but be careful, it's ready to go."

McClain slinked across the ground dragging his friend by the shirt collar, to a small, protected knoll. He looked over the top as the vegetation around where they had been continued to explode. Richard's heart raced as he whispered, "Keep quiet, and do what I say. We're gonna jerk this bastard around." Then he gave his instructions.

Alone, McClain silently crawled across the length of the knoll and lay in wait as the next burst of fire erupted. Thom screamed, "Oh, God, I'm hit. Oh, fuck! Oh, God, please help me." And then there was silence.

It took a good five minutes before they heard the stealthy crunch of footsteps on the undergrowth. As the steps came closer and closer, they waited, and when the aggressor was literally on top of Thom, Richard leapt, screaming, "Vizzinai." Sal whirled around and the Houston cop pulled the trigger of his .357 three times, hitting the target once in the leg and again in the shoulder. The impact spun Sal, and he collapsed into the green vegetation, grasping at his left shin.

With only a quick glimpse of the gangster's face, blood oozing from his shoulder and leg, all of the rage and anger that had festered in Thom for the past months erupted into a huge fireball. He rose up and pounced, beating the prostrate man's face with the butt of the gun.

Richard, surprised as hell, reacted and ran over to pull him off. When he finally managed to subdue his friend, he realized that Thom Christopher had the barrel of the gun, hammer cocked, pointed directly at Sal's head. Richard screamed, "Don't do it."

"He tried to kill my family!"

Richard screamed again, "Put the gun down!"

"I'm gonna kill the dirty fuck!"

"Put it down. You do it, and you'll hate yourself forever."

The moment passed, the tears welled up, and Thom Christopher lowered his pistol. Then McClain turned to Sal. "Why, asshole?"

The response was a cocky, "Why what?"

McClain raised his gun to Sal's forehead and cocked the hammer. "Why?"

Sal's demeanor now turned to fear, and he began to plead, "Don't kill me. Please, don't shoot!"

"Why'd you try to kill my friend? Why'd you blow up the airplane?"

"I had to. If they find me, they'll kill me."

"What're you talkin' about? Who?"

"FBI."

"Bull shit."

"I swear to you, they'll kill me."

"Why'd you blow up Mace's plane?"

"What?!"

"Mace's plane—the FBI jet. You blew it up, you shit-ass."

"I don't know what you're talkin' about. I didn't have nothin' to do with that."

"Then who did?"

"I don't know, but they're gonna kill me, I swear it."

McClain was still incredulous. "Bull shit."

"No, man, I gave 'em the information, and they let it happen, anyway. Now, they want me dead."

"What the hell are you talkin' about?"

Now, Sal was close to tears. "That senator, the one that got assassinated, I warned the FBI, but they didn't believe me. I warned, 'em."

"Who? Who'd you warn?"

"Kimble. But he didn't believe me."

"Yeah, and I don't believe you, either, asshole." Again Richard cocked the gun.

Sal panicked. "Wait! I got proof. There's a video—in the house."

Richard thought for just a second. "Yeah? Where in the house?"

"In the parlor, the credenza. I swear it. It's marked. Number 7123."

"OK, how'd you know about us? Who tipped you off?"

By now, Sal apparently had completely lost it and lay there, sobbing, but still with his hand on his leg. "Kimble, it was all Kimble."

Richard turned to Thom, "If what he says is true, then Kimble's behind everything, but we gotta have proof—we gotta get the tape." He motioned toward the house and said, "Let's go"

Thom looked down at Sal. "What about him?"

"He ain't goin' anywhere. Let's you and me get the tape and then get the hell outta here."

They turned, leaving Sal still grasping at his left leg, and started the trek across the lawn, all the while with McClain feeling that something still wasn't quite right. Half-way up the path, he uttered a near-silent, "Shit," and man-handled Thom to the ground. As he did so, both heard a loud "crack" and Thom felt that same burning in his left shoulder that he had felt months earlier. In a split second, McClain spun and fired three shots into Vizziani's chest. The gun that moments before had been strapped to Sal's left ankle flew into the brush.

"You all right? Lemme see." Richard inspected the wound, and with a sigh of relief, pronounced it only a scratch.

Thom's voice trembled. "What happened? How'd you know?"

"I'm sorry. It was my fault. I just realized that I'd shot the bastard in the right leg, not the left." Then he looked away and sighed, "Fuck, I'm gettin' too old for this shit."

* * * * * * * *

Exactly where Sal had said, the video marked 7123 sat. They popped it into the VCR and hit the search button. Within seconds, they caught sight of Kimble's profile and watched as the convict outlined the entire plan to assassinate Senator Keith. Richard tossed the cassette into his bag, and they left the house without a word. In the back driveway, Sal's SUV sat. Richard quickly hot-wired it, and the two rambled down the path toward town. At the fork in the road, they made a hard left and went back toward where they had left Max. As they came around a corner, the headlights caught the images of two men, standing beside a car. They slammed to a stop, and a second of terror later, realized it was Philip Kimble, along with another agent. Richard cautioned Thom, "Don't say a word."

"Why not just take him?"

"Then how we gonna get home?"

"What if he tries to kill us?"

"Not with a witness. He ain't that stupid."

They got out of the truck as Kimble approached and said, "Hey, McClain, we've been hunting for you guys."

"Vizziani's dead. He tried to kill us."

The agent peered through steely eyes, his hand resting on the handle of his gun. "Did he say anything?"

"No, fucker tried to ambush us from the porch, so I shot his ass. He didn't even get close."

"He said nothing?"

"Not a word, and to tell you the truth, I'm glad all this shit is over. It's time to go home."

Kimble breathed a sigh of relief and said, "Yeah, let's get back to civilization. And good job, McClain."

               *   *   *   *   *   *   *   *   *

All the way into town and then to the airport, Thom was preoccupied, apparently mulling over the past several hours and how he had once again cheated death. When they arrived, all three, Kimble, McClain, and Christopher boarded a private FBI jet, leaving the "in-country" agent to drive back to town.

With both McClain and Kimble safely strapped in their seats, Thom jumped up. "I'm gonna throw up." He grabbed McClain, and pleaded, "You gotta help me. I'm gonna be sick."

The response was an irritable, "What the fuck," but he obliged his friend, unbuckled, and started toward the restroom.

Kimble chuckled at the whole set of events as he watched these two "amateurs" make their way to the back of the plane. Once there, though, instead of going to the "head," Thom jumped out an open rear hatch onto the tarmac.

"What the hell are you doin'?"

"Just get off." And then he winked.

Moments later, the twin engines roared to life and the aircraft glided down the runway. Thom Christopher and Richard McClain watched it all from behind a luggage tram.

"What's goin' on?"

"How many people does it take to keep a secret, I mean a real secret?"

"One, why?"

"There were three voices on that tape, Sal's, Kimble's, and somebody else's."

McClain breathed a long sigh. "Shit, you're right."

✻   ✻   ✻   ✻   ✻   ✻   ✻   ✻   ✻   ✻

They walked back to the terminal and made a call to the U.S. consulate's office for two temporary passports to get back to the States. Those being sent over, they went to the Continental Airlines counter, and purchased new tickets. During the next several hours, they wan-

dered around the airport, Thom called home with the flight information, and Richard phoned Ratley Mace. A little before noon, they
boarded the flight, and within a few hours, touched down in Houston.
Once on the ground, while going through Customs, an agent inspected
their papers, looked at the computer screen, and ordered them to a
small private office. McClain merely shook his head in disbelief. They
went in, and sitting behind the desk was Ratley Mace. To his left, were
Ellen and Jen, both with tears in their eyes.

"Hey, McClain, you got somethin' for me?"

Richard tossed the satchel containing the videocassette over to him
and only said, "Be careful with it."

"Don't worry, it's in good hands."

McClain then looked over at Thom, now in Ellen's arms, then back at
Mace. "There's another problem. Kimble's crooked."

Ratley looked at him with a touch of bewilderment. "You haven't
heard."

"Heard what?"

"The plane carrying Kimble back to the U.S. blew up over the
Caribbean, no survivors."

Richard blew another sigh and said, "No shit."

Epilogue

From behind a long, mahogany table, eight United States senators sat with their eyes glued on the large-screen television set. When the screen finally went blue, all swiveled their chairs to face the man and his attorney who were seated in front of and below them. With a look of absolute disgust, the Chair of the Senate Committee on Intelligence, leaned forward and contemptuously spat out the words, "Mr. Vernon, you are under oath to tell the truth, the whole truth, and nothing but the truth. You *will* explain your involvement in, and all knowledge of, the assassination of the late Senator Keith. You will also explain to this panel your involvement in the events that occurred in Texas one year ago, and the events that occurred in Costa Rica some eight months ago. Am I understood?"

James Vernon, looking paler and thinner than he had just weeks before, only managed a near-imperceptible nod.

About the Authors

The Wilsons live in Huntsville, Texas where D. C. Wilson is a professor of psychology at Sam Houston State University. He has taught university-level courses at several prison units that are managed by the Texas Department of Criminal Justice. As a consultant for the Houston Police Department, he teaches in-service programs on the psychology of gangs and prescription drug abuse to patrol officers at the Houston Police Academy. Nancy Rabuck Wilson has authored hundreds of educational video scripts for Educational Video Network. Dozens of these programs have won national and international awards for excellence. She is a columnist for the *Huntsville Item*.